MURDER ON NOB HILL

MURDER ON NOB HILL

SHIRLEY TALLMAN

St. Martin's Minotaur ✖ New York

M

www.minotaurbooks.com

Library of Congress Cataloging-in-Publication Data

Tallman, Shirley.
    Murder on Nob Hill / Shirley Tallman.—1st ed.
        p. cm
    ISBN 0-312-32855-9
    EAN 978-0312-32855-9
        1. Women lawyers—Fiction. 2. Serial murders—Fiction. 3. San Francisco
(Calif.)—Fiction. 4. Chinatown (San Francisco, Calif.)—Fiction. I. Title.

PS3620.A54M87 2004
813'.6—dc22

                                                                    2003070099

First Edition: June 2004

10 9 8 7 6 5 4 3 2 1

To Bob,
for proving that it's possible to be married to a writer
and keep your sanity—at least most of the time.

To Nancy Hersage and JoAnn Wendt.
Your love and faith are appreciated more than I can say.

And to HP,
for always being there for me, no matter what!

ACKNOWLEDGMENTS

Many thanks to the California State Bar Association for helping me locate and sift through mountains of legal documents, an especially daunting job considering the data that was lost in San Francisco's 1906 earthquake and fire.

Thanks also to the California Historical Society for maintaining a wonderful Web site, and for the personal assistance I received from members eager to help Sarah live comfortably (and accurately) in 1880 San Francisco.

My gratitude also to the Chinese Culture Center of San Francisco, and the generous people who helped guide me through the exotic marvels of pre-earthquake Chinatown.

Last but not least, very special thanks to the Women's Legal History Biography Project, run by Barbara Allen Babcock at Stanford University. You don't know me personally, Barbara, but your project and Web site helped me immeasurably in my research for this novel.

CHAPTER ONE

Despite claims to the contrary—some, I fear, voiced by members of my own family—I pride myself on being an honest woman. As a matter of principle, I hold dissimulation of any kind in contempt. That said, I probably should add that I also subscribe to the old adage "God helps those who help themselves," even if this sometimes entails being economical with the truth.

If this last statement seems contradictory, I apologize. What I'm trying to explain is how I found myself poised on the brink of the most extraordinary adventure of my, to date, twenty-seven years. Despite being essentially an ethical person, you see, I had told a lie. More to the point, I had deliberately misled a group of narrow-minded men into assuming something I knew to be untrue. Furthermore, I do not regret my actions. Faced with the same circumstances, I would not hesitate to resort to this ruse again.

In this year of our Lord 1880, those individuals who continue to hold that females should be denied educational opportunities beyond those required to secure a good marriage will undoubtedly blame my dear father for my "unwomanly moral turpitude" (their words, not mine). While I take full responsibility for my actions, I have to admit that this criticism is not without a grain of truth. Were it not for Papa—the Honorable Horace T. Woolson, Superior Court Judge for the County of San Francisco—I doubt I would have been standing on the corner of Clay and Kearny Streets, staring up at the law offices occupied by Shepard, Shepard, McNaughton and Hall.

The morning fog that had billowed in that morning through San Francisco's Golden Gate had begun to dissipate, taking with it the heavy, moisture-laden air that, even in late summer, can seep through one's clothing. While I'm not particularly affected by the cold, I did consider the emergence of the sun to be a good omen. Or perhaps I was looking for any sign, no matter how fanciful, to bolster my resolve. I realize I am considered by many—including the before-mentioned members of my family—to be willful and outspoken, unfeminine and certainly foolhardy in my determination to follow my own path in this world. What would these critics say, I thought with some irony, if they could see the unladylike beads of perspiration forming on my brow, or the cowardly pounding of my heart as I studied those unwelcoming windows?

But I was procrastinating, putting off the mission I had worked so long and so hard to achieve. Straightening my dress—I had chosen a two-piece pewter-gray suit with as little bustle as I could get away with since the reemergence of the overstuffed derrière—I checked the lapel watch pinned to my shirtwaist. Five minutes to the hour. Time to put my plan to the test!

Purposefully I crossed Kearny Street and entered the building. A directory in the lobby revealed that Shepard, Shepard, McNaughton and Hall held offices on the sixth floor, a level that I speedily, if somewhat jerkily, reached by means of one of Elisha Otis's new hydraulic elevators, or "rising rooms" as they were popularly called. The office I sought was guarded by a solid oak door upon which the firm's name had been discreetly embossed.

I entered a room furnished with half a dozen desks, behind which sat as many clerks. The one seated nearest the door rose and, adjusting his spectacles, inquired of my business.

"My name is Sarah Woolson," I said, with what I hoped was a confident smile. "I have an appointment to see Mr. Shepard."

I'm tall for a woman—a full five feet eight inches in my stocking feet—and I towered over the clerk, forcing him to look up at me at an angle. I have noticed that this makes some men uneasy.

"Miss Woolson? I don't seem to recall—" He checked an appointment book. "Ah, yes, I see we were expecting Mr. Samuel Woolson." He looked at me hopefully. "Your husband, perhaps?"

"Samuel is my brother," I said, forcing another smile. "I believe you were expecting S. L. Woolson. That is I."

The clerk's bony brow creased with uncertainty. "Oh, dear. Well, ah, yes. Perhaps I had better fetch Mr. Shepard."

"Thank you," I said, forbearing to remind him that was what I'd requested in the first place. The clerk scurried down a hallway, and as I waited for his return, I took stock of my surroundings.

The room was larger than I had originally thought; the wood paneling, as well as the way the clerks' desks were wedged in one upon another, made it appear dim and cramped. Against the back wall were four doors, the top half of each paned with glass. Inside these cubicles—for they were hardly bigger than large closets—sat what I presumed to be legal associates. At that moment one of them looked up and our eyes met. He seemed surprised, then annoyed, as if my chance glance had invaded his privacy. He glowered at me rudely, then with a scowl returned to his papers.

I won't attempt to deceive you. For a moment I forgot my manners and stared openly at the man. He was a remarkable-looking creature: long, clean-shaven, craggy face topped by a thatch of unruly red hair, skin burned to a golden bronze, tie askew beneath a slightly rumpled white shirt. Even seated, he was obviously very tall, and his shoulders were broad, as if he were no stranger to manual labor. I was surprised to find such a man inside an office at all, especially one of such limited dimensions.

As if sensing my eyes upon him, the man looked up at me again, this time with a glare so fierce I was taken aback. With a withering look of my own, I turned away in time to see the clerk returning, followed by a portly gentleman in his sixties, whom I recognized as Joseph Shepard, Sr., founder and senior partner of the firm. He had occasionally visited our home during my childhood, and I had always been fascinated by his thick shock of white hair and by the trumpeting sound he made at the back of his nose whenever he was annoyed, or when someone took exception to his views. It was obvious from the senior partner's distracted stare that he could not as easily place me.

"My clerk informs me there has been a misunderstanding, Miss Woolson." He placed his pince-nez atop a bulbous nose and subjected me to a squinting appraisal. "Mr. Samuel Woolson, whom my clerk informs me is your brother, has applied to our firm for the position of associate attorney. I assumed I would be meeting with him this morning."

"I regret the confusion, Mr. Shepard, but it was I who applied for the position. The qualifications listed are mine, as are the initials, S. L., which stand for Sarah Lorraine."

"They are also your brother's initials," he stated in annoyance. "It's common knowledge that Judge Woolson's youngest son has been preparing for a career in law. What were we to think when we received your letter?"

"I hoped you would think that S. L. Woolson was eminently qualified to be taken on as an associate attorney in your firm."

"But you're a woman!"

"As is Clara Shortridge Foltz," I replied, determined not to be intimidated. "And that good lady has been practicing California law for four years. In this very city."

"I meant, Miss Woolson, that such a situation is impossible in this firm. Everyone knows that the sphere of women, vitally important as that is, belongs in the home."

This feeble but popularly held argument never failed to raise my hackles. "I know that is where men have placed us and where they would prefer us to remain. However, I see no reason why misguided reasoning should interfere with rational behavior."

There was a shocked stillness in the room. Mr. Shepard's face suffused with blood, and for a moment I was afraid he might be suffering some sort of seizure. Then he started that dreadful sound at the back of his nose and I realized my words had brought on a fit of pique. Since there was little I could do to retract them now—even if I'd been so inclined—I decided to press on with my qualifications.

"As I stated in my letter, I passed my bar examinations last year and continue to read law with my father, Judge Horace Woolson, whom I believe you know and respect. At the risk of appearing immodest, I am confident I possess the intelligence and character necessary to practice law in your firm."

During most of this recitation, the senior partner had sputtered incoherently. "That is patently ridiculous!" he exclaimed when I had finished. "It is a well-founded fact that women lack the nerve or strength of body for such a rigorous profession."

Another statement so ludicrous I couldn't stop myself from blurting, "I find it strange that practicing law in a comfortable, well-heated office is considered too demanding an occupation for women, yet laboring from dawn's first light in crowded, drafty, ill-lit sweatshops is not."

Joseph Shepard seemed incapable of speech. Belatedly, he realized that everyone in the room was watching us. Out of the corner of my eye, I saw the red-haired man standing outside his cubicle, his mouth pulled into an ironic smile. I felt my face flush and turned away, aware that I would require all my wits to penetrate the formidable barrier of Mr. Shepard's prejudice.

"Miss Woolson," said the attorney, his several chins quivering with suppressed anger. "Out of deference to your father, I will ignore the underhanded means by which you gained entry into this office. However, the feminine hysterics you just displayed prove why women will never be able to practice law. I advise you to return home and—"

Whatever I was supposed to return home and do was lost as the door opened and a woman, perhaps a year or two younger than myself and fashionably attired in widow's black, stepped in. She had fair hair and a porcelain complexion, which contrasted starkly with her dark gown and hat. Normally, her azure eyes must have been her best feature. Today, they were red-rimmed and accentuated by dark circles, causing me to wonder whom she had lost to cause such pain.

Mr. Shepard's face instantly brightened and he hurried over to take the woman's hand. "Mrs. Hanaford," he gushed, "if you had sent word, I would have called upon you at your home."

"My business couldn't wait, Mr. Shepard," she said, her voice soft but determined. "Mr. Wylde seems incapable of grasping the severity of my situation."

"My dear," replied the solicitor in soothing tones, "Mr. Wylde is doing everything possible to expedite this unfortunate affair. As I've endeavored to explain, your late husband's will must be admitted to probate. These things take time."

"But I have expenses to meet," she protested.

"I understand," the lawyer told her, although it seemed clear from his patronizing tone that he understood very little. "I wish I could help you, my dear, but I'm afraid Mr. Wylde must approve any advances on the estate. In the meantime, I'm sure a few simple economies will see you through." He gave her hand a perfunctory pat, then pulled out his pocket watch. "Oh, dear. I'm sorry, but I'm afraid I have a pressing appointment."

The stricken look on the young widow's face was more than I could bear. After all, the desire to do whatever I could to ensure that the scales of justice weighed evenly for women as well as for men had been one of the reasons I'd chosen to become an attorney. True, I knew little about the case, but I felt compelled to make an effort to ease her misery. In light of subsequent events, I assure you this was my sole motive for approaching Mrs. Hanaford and introducing myself.

"My name is Sarah Woolson and I am also an attorney. Perhaps if I understood your problem I might be of some assistance."

The woman's expression went from surprise to guarded hope. "Oh, Miss Woolson, if you only could!"

Joseph Shepard registered shock at my temerity, but before he could erupt in another fit of pique, I boldly took Mrs. Hanaford's arm and led her toward the nearest office. It wasn't until we were inside that I realized it was the cubicle belonging to the red-haired giant. Sure enough, its outraged owner came charging after us as I attempted to close the door.

"What do you think you're doing?" the man demanded, his

voice flavored with a strong Scottish burr. Intense, blue-green eyes bored into mine. "This is my office."

"We require privacy," I said, as calmly as possible under the circumstances. Shepard had finally marshaled his indignation and was following like Old Ironsides in our wake. As I again tried to close the door, the man held it open with arms the size of small tree trunks. "Please, sir, let go! I must confer with my client."

"*Your* client?"

"Miss Woolson!" The senior partner had reached the door, but the oversized junior attorney blocked his way. "Come out of there at once!" he ordered from behind his subordinate.

I thought I saw a muscle twitch in the younger man's face, and unexpectedly the door slammed shut in my face. I hastily gathered my wits and threw the lock before we could be ejected.

Turning my back to the door—and studiously ignoring the senior partner's howls of rage—I gave Mrs. Hanaford what I hoped was a professional smile and motioned her into the room's only chair. She hesitated, then took the seat.

"I take it you are recently widowed," I began, "and that there is a delay in settling your late husband's estate."

The woman lowered her eyes, perhaps to collect her thoughts, perhaps to avoid looking at Joseph Shepard who was now railing at the owner of the pirated cubicle.

"My name is Annjenett Hanaford," she said in a voice hardly above a whisper. "My husband, Cornelius, died three weeks ago. He—" She looked up at me, her blue eyes huge. "He was murdered."

"Murdered!" In my surprise I forgot dignity and sank onto the corner of the desk, causing several books to tumble onto the floor. Neither of us took any notice. "How did it happen?"

"He was stabbed. In his study. I was there when it happened. Not in the room, of course, but upstairs in my boudoir."

"Have the police arrested anyone?"

A shadow crossed her lovely face. "Several items were stolen. They—the police seem certain it must have been an intruder. As yet, no one has been arrested."

I studied the woman. Something was troubling her, and I suspected it was more than the natural grief and shock one would expect after losing a spouse. She seemed frightened. But of what? Behind me, Shepard's pounding on the door became louder. Tempted as I was to probe further into the details, I decided to press on while there was still time.

"How long were you married, Mrs. Hanaford?"

"Seven years. I was nineteen when I—agreed to Mr. Hanaford's proposal."

"Did you bring any property or money into the marriage?"

She looked up, startled by my question. "Why, yes, I did. My father provided a generous dowry. Later, when my mother passed on, I received a substantial inheritance. Naturally, my husband managed these funds on my behalf."

"Naturally," I agreed dryly. This was neither the time nor the place to express my opinions concerning women's coverture, or civil death upon marriage, whereby the law merged the identity of wife and husband and severely limited her rights to inherit or own property. "The reason I ask is that the Married Women's Property Act entitles a wife to the separate property she brought to the marriage. I don't suppose you obtained your husband's antenuptial consent to retain control of your separate property?"

This notion was obviously foreign to her. Then she seemed to remember something. "Just before Cornelius commenced construction on our home, he had me sign something. As I recall, it listed my dowry, as well as my mother's bequest."

I felt a rush of excitement. To the best of my knowledge, the plan I contemplated was unprecedented in legal annals, at least those established on the West Coast. But I needed documentation.

"Do you have copies of these papers?" I asked intently.

"I don't know. My husband has a safe at home, of course, but I believe he kept most of his documents at his bank."

"Then that's an excellent place to begin." I rose from my perch on the desk in time to see Mr. Shepard insert a key in the lock. Our time alone was clearly at an end. "If it's agreeable, I will accompany you to your husband's bank to look for the papers."

She nodded hopefully as the door flew open and a red-faced Joseph Shepard burst in, sputtering charges of unethical behavior. Deciding that a rapid departure would not be amiss, I took Mrs. Hanaford's arm and swept past the senior partner.

The last face I saw before leaving the room was that of the muscular Scot. This time there was no mistaking the laughter in his eyes and I felt heat suffuse my face. The idea that this odious man found humor in the situation infuriated me far more than Joseph Shepard's tirade. Fixing him with the most disdainful look I could muster, I turned and pulled the heavy oak door shut behind us.

Since I had arrived that morning by horsecar, and Annjenett Hanaford's open-topped little Victoria was waiting on the square, we agreed the most sensible plan would be to travel to the bank in her carriage. After assisting us inside, the liveried coachman took his place in the elevated front seat and clicked the handsome bay into a steady stream of traffic.

It turned out that Hanaford was the founder of San Francisco

Savings and Trust, a three-story brick building on California Street. Inside, I followed the widow past half a dozen teller cages until she stopped in front of a glass partition and tapped on the window. She said a few words to the man seated there, and he instantly rose and hurried toward a door to the rear of the room.

"He's fetching the manager, Eban Potter," she explained. "Actually, Mr. Potter is an old friend and one of the kindest men I know. He and my husband went to school together. Fortunately, he's familiar with Cornelius's business affairs. I don't know what I would have done without him these past few weeks."

Just then a pencil-thin man in his late forties strode in our direction. He wore a conservative frock coat and dark trousers. His brown hair was receding and his face was pale, with a deep groove etched between his eyes, as if he carried the weight of the world on his narrow shoulders. The moment he saw my companion, however, his expression lightened and he smiled.

"Mrs. Hanaford, what an unexpected pleasure." His voice was high and as reed-thin as the man himself. From the way he took her hand, it was easy to see he held the young widow in fond regard.

"Mr. Potter—Eban—this is my attorney, Miss Sarah Woolson."

"Attorney?" Eban Potter was so taken aback by this announcement, he stared openly at me. "But I thought Mr. Wylde—"

"I'm assisting Mrs. Hanaford in a private matter," I broke in. "We're hoping to find some personal papers belonging to her late husband. We believe he may have kept them here at the bank."

Belatedly, the manager recalled his manners. "I apologize, Miss Woolson. I would like to help, of course, but I believe Mr. Hanaford kept few personal possessions in his office."

"Nevertheless, we would like to see for our—"

"Mrs. Hanaford?"

The widow and I turned to find a tall man approaching us. He was impeccably dressed in a navy blue, single-breasted frock coat and crisp gray trousers. His hair was very dark and worn longer than was the style. But it was his eyes that held me; wide set and nearly black, they stared straight into mine, giving the disconcerting impression they could read my most secret thoughts. From Mrs. Hanaford's flushed cheeks, I realized she was similarly affected by the man's penetrating gaze.

"Mr. Wylde, I didn't think—that is, I did not expect to find you here," she said, as he brushed the back of her hand with his lips.

"Nor did I expect to find you here, my dear," he said with no discernible trace of a welcoming smile.

His voice was well modulated and precise, as if he expected—no, *demanded*—that attention be paid to his every word. I must admit that my first impression of the attorney was not favorable. His manner was too arrogant, too much in control for my tastes. In a commanding, self-important way, he was not unattractive, although his features were too angular to be termed conventionally handsome. Here was a man, I decided, who might inspire confidence, but never ease.

"Miss Woolson," said Annjenett in a thin voice, "I would like to introduce Mr. Benjamin Wylde, executor of my husband's estate. Mr. Wylde, this is Miss Sarah Woolson—an attorney. Miss Woolson has kindly offered to represent my interests."

Other than a slight narrowing of his eyes, Wylde showed no reaction to what must have been a startling piece of news.

"My pleasure, Miss Woolson," he said, reaching out a hand.

I proffered my own hand and was annoyed at the presumptuous way his eyes raked slowly over my suit, all the way down to my boots.

"How do you do, Mr. Wylde," I said, making little effort to hide my disapproval of such rudeness.

For the first time, the hint of a smile played at the corners of that hard-etched mouth. I instantly regretted allowing my irritation to show. The sooner we attended to our business and took our leave of the bank, I decided, the better.

"I'm sure we're keeping Mr. Potter from his work," I told Annjenett. "Perhaps we should see to our errand."

"And what errand is that?" The attorney addressed this remark to me, and this time there was no mistaking the mocking tone.

I started to reply that it was none of his business, then thought better of it. Tempting as it was to put this arrogant man in his place, making an enemy of the executor of my client's estate might not be in her best interests.

"We're trying to locate some personal papers belonging to Mr. Hanaford," I told him, keeping my face, and my voice, civil.

The lawyer's eyes narrowed. "Miss Woolson, I'm sure you must be aware of Mrs. Hanaford's recent bereavement. It is both callous and insensitive to enlist her on this fool's errand. Her affairs are being competently handled."

"I don't doubt that for a moment, Mr. Wylde," I said, biting back another stinging retort. "However, as I said, our business is of a personal nature. There is no need to take up more of your valuable time." I heard his slight intake of breath as I turned back to the manager. "Mr. Potter, shall we proceed?"

I had placed Eban Potter in a difficult position. Clearly, he was in awe of the attorney, yet to object to our request would seem unreasonable and rude. At his hesitation, I sensed Annjenett wavering in her resolve and thought it best to press on.

"I assume that's the door leading to Mr. Hanaford's office?" Without waiting for a reply, I started toward the rear of the bank. Before the widow could follow, the attorney took hold of her hand.

I have since questioned whether the look I caught on Benjamin

Wylde's face at that moment was as malevolent as it seemed, especially since it was so quickly gone. Certainly his voice was calm enough as he told Annjenett, "I'm traveling to Sacramento this evening, but I will call on you upon my return." I don't think I imagined my client's relief when he released her hand and turned to me. "Miss Woolson, I trust you will find what you are seeking."

It was a tribute to the power of the man that we all stood rooted in our places while Benjamin Wylde made his way with long strides though the antechamber and out of the bank.

"Well, then," I said, breaking the spell. "Shall we proceed?"

In the end, we were disappointed. Mr. Hanaford kept no personal papers in his work safe. Annjenett looked crestfallen.

"The bank was a place to start," I told her optimistically. "Perhaps we'll meet with better success at your house."

Annjenett's home was located on Taylor and California Streets, atop Nob Hill. A block away on Mason stood the turreted monstrosity built by Mark Hopkins, one of the so-called Big Four associated with the Central Pacific Railroad. Next door was the equally ornate, barnlike mansion of Leland Stanford, former governor of California and one of Hopkins's railroad associates. Compared with these fortresses, Hanaford's house could almost be deemed tasteful.

Declining the widow's offer of refreshments, I asked to see her late husband's safe. His study, located to the right of the foyer, was a spacious, masculine room, decorated mostly in browns and deep greens. The heavy drapes were closed in mourning, but through the gloom I could detect a number of books and a large mahogany desk centered in front of a cloaked window. Annjenett paused at the doorway, looking uneasy.

"Cornelius—that is, my husband—was murdered in this room. Stabbed—as he sat at his desk." She indicated an imposing brown leather chair that backed against the drapes. "I've left everything as it was. The police, of course, spent some time examining the room."

"You heard nothing that night? No one at the door, perhaps? Or your husband crying out?"

"No, nothing. I retired to my room directly after dinner. I wasn't—feeling well."

It was only a slight hesitation, but it was enough to cause me to question this statement. The obvious anguish on her face, however, made me reluctant to pursue it further—at least for now.

"What time did you go upstairs?" I asked instead.

"About a quarter to nine." She faltered. "It was the last time I saw my husband alive."

"What about the servants? I'm sure they've been questioned?"

"Yes. So often that I live in fear they'll give notice. It has been a most unsettling experience."

"I can imagine." My sympathy was sincere, but I sensed her anxiety was caused by more than the difficulty of retaining domestic help. "You're sure your husband expected no visitors that night?"

"If he did, he didn't tell me. Beecher, our butler, denies letting anyone in." Her voice took on a hysterical note. "But someone did come in. They had to, didn't they?"

Unless Hanaford was killed by someone already inside the house, I thought. It was a disturbing idea, but one that couldn't be ignored. It also occurred to me that since the study was in such close proximity to the front door, Hanaford himself might have admitted a visitor without disturbing the rest of the household. Surely the police must have considered these possibilities. Keeping these thoughts to myself, I entered the study and pulled open the drapes so that I might better examine the murder scene.

"You said your husband's safe is in this room?"

She blinked against the sudden light, then crossed the room to a floor-to-ceiling bookcase. Reaching inside a panel, she tripped a hidden mechanism and a section of shelves slid open, revealing a concealed wall safe.

"Cornelius insisted I learn the combination, although I rarely used it, and always under his direction." With care she manipulated the knob and opened the door. "The police searched the safe, but I have no idea what they found."

I stepped forward and peered into the compartment, which was divided into five sections. The first cubicle contained deeds and other business papers, two more held letters, another a thin ledger, and the last a small stack of cash. Pushing up my sleeve, I reached inside and pulled out the currency that, I was happy to note, amounted to several hundred dollars.

"If nothing else, this should help to tide you over," I said, handing the money over to the widow.

Annjenett took the bills with delight. "I had no idea Cornelius kept cash in the safe. He led me to believe there was only his will and a few personal letters."

"Yes, well, let's see what else he kept in here," I said, placing the contents of the first compartment on the desk.

Annjenett watched while I read through deeds for various town properties, as well as one in Belmont where San Francisco society had recently begun to construct country homes. The last paper was a copy of Hanaford's will. Although pleased to see that he'd left the bulk of his considerable estate to his widow, I was disappointed not to find the document I sought. Placing the first set of papers back in their cubicle, I took out the second set and returned to the desk. It took only a moment to find what I was looking for. With a triumphant cry, I waved a paper at the widow.

"Here it is! Just as I hoped."

Annjenett flew to the desk. "What is it? What have you found?"

"A separate property list. I suspected that was what your husband was up to when he had you sign papers before starting construction on your home."

"But what does it mean?"

"Several years ago a civil code was passed enabling a wife to hold property and assets separate from her husband. These were to remain under her management and could not be taken by her husband's creditors. By listing your dowry and inheritance as separate properties, your husband protected them from being attached in the event he fell into debt. Of course he secretly retained control, as do a great many men who avail themselves of this code. In this case, however, the ploy works to our advantage."

I saw hope rise in Annjenett's blue eyes. "Miss Woolson," she asked intently. "How much money will be at my disposal?"

"I can't be sure until I've studied the papers, but I think it would be safe to hazard a guess of some ten thousand dollars."

"Oh, my!" She sank into a chair and looked alarmingly pale.

"Mrs. Hanaford, are you all right?" I began fanning her with the papers, regretting that it wasn't my practice to carry smelling salts in my reticule.

"Yes," she replied in a faint voice. "Actually, I'm very well now that you've happened into my life." She took a deep breath and smiled. "How do you suggest we proceed?"

"Tomorrow you may inform Mr. Shepard of our discovery and request that the properties and assets listed in this document be turned over to you forthwith."

Annjenett clapped her hands in delight. "Miss Woolson— Sarah—you've worked a miracle. How can I thank you?"

I felt my face flush at this praise and endeavored to keep my expression professional. Inside, however, I could hardly contain my excitement. Despite being summarily rejected by Shepard's firm, I had not only obtained my first client, but had actually been able to secure her financial independence. It was a heady feeling.

"It's a simple matter that could have been easily discovered had Mr. Wylde, or any of Mr. Shepard's attorneys, taken the time to investigate," I told her truthfully enough, as I closed the safe door and ensured that the lock was set. Annjenett triggered the hidden mechanism and the bookshelf swung smoothly closed.

"Yes, but they didn't." She looked at me, embarrassed. "I'm ashamed to admit that prior to meeting you, Sarah, I was prejudiced against women in the legal profession. Now I see that it presents decided advantages. Being a woman, you were instantly able to appreciate my predicament, something I have been quite unable to convey to either Mr. Shepard or Mr. Wylde. Please," she went on earnestly, "say that you'll go with me tomorrow."

"Nothing would give me more pleasure," I told her, delighted I would be there to see Joseph Shepard's face when he was presented with the separate property agreement. "Shall we say ten o'clock?"

"Yes. That will do nicely." She handed me the documents. "Here, take these with you. Study them until you are very certain of our position."

I agreed, but before I could leave she took both my hands in hers. "You'll allow my man to drive you home, Sarah. No, I insist. It is the least I can do."

"That's kind of you," I said, gratefully accepting her offer. "I look forward to seeing you tomorrow morning."

Annjenett Hanaford was still standing in the doorway as her coachman clicked the stately bay down Taylor Street toward Rincon Hill.

CHAPTER TWO

That evening everyone was home for dinner, even my brother Frederick and his wife, Henrietta, who had recently built their own house on Nob Hill, away from what they, and most of San Francisco, perceived to be the imminent demise of Rincon Hill. Once the most fashionable area of the city, it stood high above the Bay, half a mile from the nuisances of downtown traffic. Boasting royalty and the finest weather in town, Rincon Hill sat proudly upon its perch until some "big bugs" (one of Papa's pet terms) in city government decided pedestrian and carriage traffic around Market Street and the waterfront would be eased by bisecting it at Second Street.

Frederick urged Papa to relocate before word of the cut became public, but my father refused. Rincon Hill had been home for twenty-five years and, city stupidity notwithstanding, so it would remain. Four years after the first cut was made, Frederick and Henrietta moved out, preferring to borrow money to erect a home of modest but dedicated pretension on the fringe of the Nob Hill swells. As far as I was concerned, their presence in our house was not missed!

They had joined us this evening in order to put the finishing touches on the plans for a dinner party to be given on Saturday night, only two days hence, to mark Frederick's entrée into the political arena. He planned to start with the state senate, then work his way into the governor's mansion. Eventually—heaven help us—he hoped to take up a post in our nation's capital. I shuddered at the thought of Frederick in Congress. What the Confederacy had failed to wrest asunder by force, my brother's dull and extraordinarily narrow mind might well accomplish.

But I am getting ahead of myself. Allow me to acquaint you with my family. I am the youngest of four children and the only daughter of Horace and Elizabeth Woolson. Plagued by a surplus of lawyers in their hometown of Williamsport, Pennsylvania, my parents, two small sons in tow, left in the early fifties to make the long trek to San Francisco, where Papa was convinced there were fresh opportunities.

Indeed there were! My father's transplanted law practice flourished in this chaotic, prosperous town full of gold dust and the callow forty-niners bent on mining it. With such instant wealth, criminal defense, litigation and debt collection cases abounded. Horace T. Woolson's thriving practice soon catapulted him to public office, and eventually to the Superior Court of the County of San Francisco.

Frederick is the eldest of my three brothers and has—to my amazement—become a fairly successful attorney. Charles, three years Frederick's junior, is also married and has gained a reputation as a skilled, if impoverished, physician. My youngest brother, Samuel—my co-conspirator in the episode at Shepard's law firm—

is two years my senior. Samuel remains a bachelor and still lives at home, as does my brother Charles and his family.

There were eight of us, then, at dinner that evening. Charles and his wife, Celia, presented a handsome contrast, he with his dark complexion and Mama's thick ebony hair, she with her fair coloring and golden locks. After seven years of marriage and two lovely children, Thomas and Amanda, the looks they exchanged, the seemingly accidental touch of their hands, was almost—but not quite—enough to weaken my resolve to remain a spinster.

Frederick and his wife, Henrietta, presented a sadly different picture. Tall, heavy-set, looking older than his thirty-eight years, Frederick is, I am sorry to say, a humorless man. His appearance favors Papa, with the same nut-brown hair and dark eyes, as well as Papa's noticeable paunch. Henrietta is also tall, but where Frederick has turned portly, she has kept her thin, brittle figure. They make an impressive, if passionless, couple. I wonder sometimes how they ever managed to produce eight-year-old Freddie, a son of whom Ivan the Terrible would be proud. But that's another story.

That evening, I sat across from my brother Samuel, the self-proclaimed oddball of the family. In appearance, Samuel is a throwback to an obscure German branch of my father's family. Shorter than his brothers, he's blond and muscularly built. That is not to imply he's not handsome; any number of hopeful young ladies would happily attest to my brother's popularity. He is, in fact, counted among San Francisco's most eligible bachelors—a designation, I might add, that he's in no hurry to alter.

In temperament, Samuel is also considered odd. Trained in the law, he has persistently—or bullheadedly, as Papa describes it—delayed taking his California bar examinations. If Papa knew that Samuel was more interested in a journalistic career than in the legal profession—an obsession he's kept secret from everyone in the family but me—he might find even stronger words to describe his youngest son's behavior. If he also realized that Samuel has sold pieces to local newspapers (under the unlikely nom de plume Ian Fearless), I shudder to contemplate his reaction. Papa considers journalists to be social scavengers making their living at the expense of public awareness and debate. It would never occur to him that a Woolson would sully the family name by becoming a Robert O'Brien (Papa's nemesis on the *San Francisco Chronicle*), a Mark Twain, or even a Bret Harte (the latter two writers I personally admire).

Frederick and Henrietta's presence cast a pall on the usual lively tempo of our evening meals. Talk of Saturday night's dinner party dominated the conversation ad infinitum, and I began to despair that I would ever get a word in edgewise. Finally, while Ina, our Irish maid, served the main course of broiled turkey breast and steamed vegetables, a momentary lull in the conversation provided the opportunity I'd been awaiting.

"Papa, what do you know about Cornelius Hanaford?" I asked.

Seven pairs of eyes turned to regard me with interest.

"Hanaford?" Samuel said innocently. "Isn't he the banker who was murdered in his study several weeks ago?"

I had to suppress a laugh. Because of certain friendships he's cultivated within the ranks of the city police, Samuel was more aware of crime in our town than anyone else at the table.

Henrietta regarded me with the frosty disapproval she usually bestows upon me. "The discussion of murder is hardly an appropriate subject for the dining room. Even in this house." She darted a glance at Papa who, I noted with amusement, seemed to be enjoying the turn in the conversation.

"Quite right, my dear," Frederick agreed. "Really, Sarah, it's high time you learned to curb your tongue."

"Don't be pompous, Frederick," I retorted. "Any subject is preferable to your dreary party."

"Violent death is a dreadful subject at any time," Celia, ever the peacemaker, interjected. "But I confess to a degree of morbid curiosity. If you don't mind, Sarah, how did it happen?"

I spoke before either Frederick or Henrietta could voice another objection. "Actually, I know little about the case except that Mr. Hanaford was stabbed to death in his study sometime after dinner." I turned again to my father. "I hoped you might be able to tell me something about the man."

Papa regarded me from beneath bushy brows, showing, of late, rather more white than brown. "Hanaford made his money, actually a good deal of it, twenty years ago in the Nevada silver mines. He was a dry goods salesman in Sacramento before he was bitten by the gold bug and formed a partnership with several like-minded young men. Unlike most fools who dashed off to the mines with heads as empty as their pockets, Hanaford and his friends managed to do surprisingly well for themselves."

Papa was momentarily sidetracked by a platter of fried oysters. "To their credit," he went on at length, "all four men made the most of their newfound wealth. Hanaford established one of the city's largest banks. Rufus Mills, of course, became a successful industrialist, and I hardly need mention that Willard Broughton is serving his third term in the California Senate. The fourth partner, Benjamin Wylde, has made a name for himself as a trial attorney. All three will be at Frederick's soirée Saturday night, I believe."

"Mr. Wylde will be out of town," Henrietta put in. "However, Rufus Mills and Senator Broughton have promised to attend."

"As has Thomas Cooke, the hotelier," Mama added. "His daughter, Annjenett, is Mr. Hanaford's widow."

"Actually, I met Mrs. Hanaford this morning when I visited Mr. Shepard's law offices," I said, reaching for a roll. Once again seven pairs of eyes turned to stare at me.

"What possible reason could you have for consulting Joseph Shepard?" demanded Frederick, taking a sip of wine.

"Not that it's any of your business," I told him, "but I was inquiring about a position as associate attorney."

Frederick choked on his wine, inducing a fit of coughing.

I handed him a serviette. "You're dripping wine on Mama's tablecloth, Frederick."

"This is too much!" He turned a livid face to my father. "Now you see where your permissiveness has led."

Papa chuckled. "You might as well tell us the rest of it, my girl. How did you manage to get that old reprobate to see you?"

Realizing the subject could no longer be avoided, and taking care not to mention Samuel's role in the affair, I explained the confusion with our initials. Papa shot Samuel a suspicious look, but allowed me to tell my story without interruption.

"Oh, to have been a fly on Shepard's wall," Papa chuckled when I'd finished. "I'll wager you gave the poor man apoplexy."

"I admire your nerve, Sarah," Celia put in admiringly. "I think you'll make a splendid attorney."

"Don't encourage her, Celia." Frederick turned to Charles for support. "Surely you appreciate the gravity of the situation."

Charles took a moment to answer. My middle brother is the mildest of men, thoughtful and considerate to a fault. No one who calls upon him professionally is ever turned away, even when they're unable to pay for his medical services. Despite his kind heart, however, I knew his love for me and innate sense of fairness must be waging battle with his sense of propriety.

"I don't for a moment believe that women are incapable of grasping the finer points of the law—or of medicine, for that matter," he ventured. "But a woman would have to sacrifice a great deal to make a success of either profession. I don't want to see you hurt, Sarah, and I fear you'll face enormous opposition."

I regarded my brother fondly. "I appreciate your concern, Charles, but I relish hard work. And growing up with Frederick has given me no end of practice in dealing with bigots."

"I find Mr. Hanaford's death most unsettling," Mama put in before my eldest brother could explode. "You should speak to Edis, Horace," she went on, referring to the dour but devoted man who has served as our butler for as far back as I could remember.

Papa didn't appear unduly concerned. "I hardly think that's necessary, Elizabeth. We don't want to alarm the servants. Edis fusses like an old woman as it is. Pass the carrots, would you Charles?"

Mama did not look convinced. "Yes, but—"

"Trust me, my dear," Papa reassured her. "The police have the matter well in hand. Besides, Cornelius Hanaford's unfortunate death has nothing to do with us."

With these woefully unprophetic words, the conversation passed on to politics.

The opportunity to speak to Samuel did not present itself until the rest of the family had retired for the night. Slipping outside, I found my brother in the garden smoking a cigarette.

"It's about time," he told me softly. The night was chilly and I pulled my wool shawl closer about my shoulders as I sat beside him on a garden bench. Through the moonlight, I could detect the hint of a smile playing on his mouth as he asked, "So, are you to be Shepard's newest associate attorney?"

"Joseph Shepard is incapable of seeing beyond his nose. He recited a litany of reasons why a woman is unfit to practice law, ranging from physical frailty to mental impairment."

"So, now what?"

I was forced to confess I didn't know. "I'll probably try Avers and Brock. They're not as established or respected as Shepard's, but needs must. Or perhaps I'll open my own office."

This time there was no mistaking my brother's amusement. "And how will you lure clients, little sister? *Paying* clients, I mean. Or will you treat them all pro bono?"

"Sarcasm doesn't become you, Samuel," I told him shortly. "Besides, there are more important matters to discuss."

"Such as Cornelius Hanaford and his lovely young widow?"

I nodded and briefly described my meeting with Annjenett, as well as my plans for relieving her current financial problems. "I thought you might have discussed the case with George."

George Lewis was a boxing partner of Samuel's, as well as a member of the San Francisco Police Department. George's work on the force had provided my brother with material for several true crime stories which appeared, successfully I might add, in the city's newspapers. Due in no small part to Samuel's friendship with George Lewis, Ian Fearless was making a name for himself.

"He's talked of little else since it happened." He studied my face. "You do know how Hanaford was murdered, don't you?"

"Of course. He was stabbed."

"Yes, but do you know *where* he was stabbed?"

I looked at him blankly. "No. Why, does it matter?"

"It must have mattered to his murderer. Sarah, Hanaford was stabbed to death in the genitals."

I was momentarily struck dumb.

"Which means, of course," he went on, "that the murder was more likely a crime of passion than of chance or burglary."

"But what about the items that were stolen?"

"Another question the police would like answered."

I leaned back against the bench and thought of my talk with Annjenett. She'd said nothing to lead me to believe the murder was of a personal nature. Yet, as Samuel pointed out, the unusual manner of the attack was undoubtedly significant.

"The police have kept the more sensational aspects of the crime quiet," Samuel went on, breaking into my thoughts. "Lewis admits it has them baffled."

"I can imagine."

"Not surprisingly, the financial district is in an uproar. And there's a lot of political pressure to solve the crime quickly."

"Do the police have any suspects?"

"Hanaford's staff has been repeatedly interviewed. No one recalls anything out of the ordinary that evening."

"What about disgruntled bank clients? Or employees?"

"Nothing serious enough to result in homicide."

"Surely someone must have seen something!" I said, exasperated.

"If they did, they haven't come forward." He hesitated. "I suppose you've considered the more obvious implications of this case?"

I felt a shiver that had nothing to do with the night air. "The possibility is too obvious to ignore. Hanaford either let the murderer in himself, without the servants' knowledge. Or—"

"Or the murderer was already inside." Samuel crossed his legs. "Tell me about Mrs. Hanaford. I know, of course, that she was younger than her husband."

"Yes, considerably. It was an arranged marriage. And not, I gather, a particularly happy one." I added defensively, "That doesn't mean my client's a murderer."

Samuel darted me a look. "*Your* client!"

"At least until this business concerning Mrs. Hanaford's finances is settled."

"Well, that caps the climax," he said with a laugh. "Old Joe Shepard must have thrown a fit when you waltzed into his office and stole one of his prized clients."

"Joseph Shepard was less than useless. He brushed the poor woman off as if she were a piece of lint on his coat."

"And you rushed in like Florence Nightingale to save the day."

"I haven't saved it yet," I said dryly. "But if I fail, it won't be for lack of trying."

Samuel sat thoughtfully for several moments. "I think you'd better hope the police find a likely suspect soon, little sister. Otherwise your client may find more pressing matters to worry about than her finances."

I stared at my brother. His eyes, usually full of mischief, were deadly serious in the moonlight. "Surely it isn't that bad."

"Come on, Sarah. If there were no visitors, and no one broke in, what's left?"

"Not that," I insisted. I pride myself on my judgment of people, and I was convinced the young woman I had met that morning could not be a cold-blooded killer. "I'd stake my life on the fact that Annjenett Hanaford did not murder her husband."

My brother gave me a long look. "For your client's sake, I hope you're right."

In the distance, St. Mary's Cathedral chimed midnight. Samuel stretched and got to his feet.

"She's fortunate to have you, little sister," he said quietly, as I rose to join him. "The time may come when Annjenett Hanaford will need a friend."

My brother's words remained on my mind as I arrived at Portsmouth Square at ten o'clock the next morning. As I alighted from the horsecar, I was pleased to spy Annjenett Hanaford's Victoria across the street. The widow's hopeful face made it easy to dismiss Samuel's dire predictions, and I returned her bright smile. Before we entered the rising room, she took my arm.

"Sarah, do you really think we're going to succeed?"

Despite the fact that I'd asked myself that same question most of the night, I kept my voice optimistic. "I see no reason why we shouldn't. I've been over the documents at length and they're in order. According to the law, the money is rightfully yours."

"Then it really is true." Unexpectedly she threw her arms around me and kissed my cheek. "How can I ever thank you?"

For a moment I was too surprised to speak, then managed to sputter, "Yes, well, you can thank me when this business is successfully concluded."

"Oh, but you're bound to succeed, Sarah. I have every confidence that you can do anything you set your mind to."

Silently, I prayed I could live up to such lofty expectations! Then I asked Annjenett to pay me one dollar so that I might act as her legal representative.

She smiled as the sense of this plan became clear, then removed a silver dollar from her reticule. "I would be pleased to have you represent my affairs, Miss Woolson."

When we presented ourselves at Mr. Shepard's law offices, the ferretlike clerk I had encountered the previous day scurried off in a flurry of agitation. He'd scarcely left the room when I felt the small hairs on my neck begin to prickle.

Annjenett leaned closer. "There's a man staring at you, Sarah. I remember seeing him yesterday. He's—very noticeable."

Even before I turned, I knew it was the orange-haired associate attorney, ensconced in his cubicle of an office, eyes boring into my back in the rudest possible manner. I was annoyed to feel my pulse rate unaccountably increase. The man's audacity knew no bounds!

Furious, I returned his rude stare until, with a fierce frown, he bent his head to the jumble of papers and books spilled across his desk. For the life of me I couldn't understand why Joseph Shepard would employ such a man. If someone had been foolish enough to cast Paul Bunyan in the role of an attorney, he couldn't have appeared more incongruous than this churlish giant!

Joseph Shepard's arrival cut short my musings. With an ill concealed glare in my direction, he took Annjenett's hand.

"My dear Mrs. Hanaford. What a pleasure to see you again so soon. Although I'm sorry to inform you that, as yet, I haven't been able to reach Mr. Wylde."

"I'm not here to discuss Mr. Wylde," Annjenett informed him. "Miss Woolson wishes to call your attention to one or two items in my husband's estate."

Although I was prepared, it was nonetheless disconcerting when he produced that awful noise in the back of his nose.

"Not only can I think of no possible reason to discuss Mr. Hanaford's affairs with Miss Woolson," he informed us. "It would be unprofessional to even contemplate such a thing."

"Since Mrs. Hanaford has retained me to handle her affairs, I'm afraid you will have to contemplate it," I told him evenly.

I wouldn't have thought it possible for the man's face to become any more suffused with color, but I was mistaken. It was now positively purple, and the noises issuing from his mouth did not in any way resemble the English language. Since he seemed incapable of coherent speech, and we had once again become a spectacle for the entire office—including the irascible junior attorney—I was forced to take the matter in hand.

"Shall we adjourn to your office, Mr. Shepard? I would prefer to discuss my client's affairs in a more private forum."

"Your client. *Your* client—!"

In the back of the room, I observed the ill-mannered associate guffawing in his glassed den. Since I had no wish to afford him further amusement at my expense, I motioned Annjenett in what I thought must be the direction of the senior attorney's office. As I'd anticipated, Mr. Shepard had little choice but to follow. At the end of the hall, he unceremoniously motioned us into an over-furnished office of pretentious proportions.

"See here, Miss Woolson," he began, seating himself behind a heavy oak desk. "You go beyond the boundaries of legal propriety."

"I'm sorry you feel that way, Mr. Shepard," I replied calmly. I was determined—not only for my own pride, but because my client had expressed such a high regard for my abilities—that no matter what the provocation, I would conduct myself in a professional manner. "I seek only to settle Mrs. Hanaford's affairs as quickly and efficiently as possible."

"That is precisely what this firm has endeavored to do," the senior partner snapped. "May I remind you, madam, that we have represented Mr. Hanaford and his bank for close to twenty years?"

"Regretfully, Mr. Hanaford is no longer with us. His widow, on the other hand, faces a domestic crisis that can no longer be ignored. Yesterday, I became aware of certain documents that will enable her to attend to these responsibilities while awaiting the resolution of her husband's estate."

Shepard's small eyes gleamed. Clearly he thought he had me at last. My ignorance of the law had betrayed me. His jowls quivered as he hastened to point out the folly of my feminine naiveté.

"Such a discovery would be truly remarkable," he said in a voice dripping with sarcasm, "since I hold all documents related to the late Mr. Hanaford's estate. I can't imagine what you think you've found that can abridge the due process of the law."

Silently, I placed before him the papers I had uncovered in Mr. Hanaford's safe, then watched his expression change from smug dismissal to unmistakable shock. "Where did you find these?"

Briefly, I explained the events of the previous afternoon. "You may either transfer Mr. Hanaford's funds directly to her account at the bank," I looked to Annjenett to make certain this arrangement was acceptable, then at her nod added, "or we'll be happy to accept a note from you in that amount."

Shepard looked stunned. "You can't be serious."

"I assure you, sir, I never make light of the law."

"Then you have taken leave of your senses. That is a very great deal of money."

"It is indeed. Money which rightfully belongs to my client."

I watched the attorney fight down his fury. When he finally spoke, his voice was barely in control. "Miss Woolson, your behavior is not only impertinent, it is unethical. You've preyed on this poor widow's bereavement by making her believe that you—with no experience of the law—can accomplish what one of the oldest and most respected firms in San Francisco cannot. You, a—a woman moreover!"

I drew myself up until my eyes were level with the attorney's. He had touched upon a nerve that begged, nay, *demanded* a response.

"It is true that I lack experience of the law, Mr. Shepard. But who is to blame for that? How is any woman to receive practical experience when no man will hire her? But you are mistaken if you assume I lack knowledge. My father has more than done his duty toward his children. Now I propose to use that knowledge to rectify a grievous oversight."

"Really, madam, you go too far!"

"On the contrary, sir, I fear my breeding prevents me from going far enough." I gathered up the papers that would soon make Annjenett Hanaford a wealthy woman in her own right. "Today is Friday. We understand it may take a day or two to arrange for such a considerable amount of cash. We're willing, therefore, to give you until Wednesday of next week to complete the transaction. I trust that is satisfactory?"

"I assure you, Miss Woolson, there is nothing satisfactory about this business." He glared at me for a long moment, then turned to Annjenett. "My dear, I shudder to contemplate what your late husband would think of this. I daresay he would turn over in his grave if he knew you were contemplating leaving this firm. And for a— a woman who is foisting herself off as an attorney."

For the first time since entering the office, Annjenett spoke, and I was pleased to note her resolute expression. "I appreciate the help you have given me since my husband's death, Mr. Shepard, but I am determined that Miss Woolson shall continue as my personal attorney." She hesitated. "I can, however, think of a compromise. If you were to take Miss Woolson on as an associate, there'd be no need for me to leave this firm." She smiled, and it would have required a harder heart than Joseph Shepard's to resist such charm. "It would please me very much if you would agree."

"I, ah, that is—" The attorney stumbled to a stop and I watched a plethora of emotions cross his round face. In the end, I wasn't surprised when greed won the day.

"Such an arrangement will be fraught with difficulties," he told her unhappily, "particularly for Miss Woolson. I fear she'll find few friends among the staff. The hours are long and strenuous, the work difficult. Much of it, for that matter, will undoubtedly be beyond her comprehension.

As I began to protest this latest affront, he interrupted, saying, "I cannot imagine that any clients, other than yourself, will desire Miss Woolson's services." He paused, plainly waging one final internal battle, then continued, his voice edged with distaste. "However, for your sake we'll give it a try. At least for a week or two."

Annjenett gave him her most heartwarming smile. "That's most kind of you, Mr. Shepard. I'm sure you won't regret it."

Shepard grimaced. Even a client of Mrs. Hanaford's importance could not convince him of this unlikely possibility. Regarding me balefully, he rose and led us out of the office.

It took me but a moment to realize how loose this arrangement was to be. Judging by the speed with which we were being herded down the hall, I had the impression Joseph Shepard would be happy if his first female attorney were an unseen, as well as silent, associate. I immediately set out to rectify this miscalculation.

"I shall require an office," I declared, refusing to be led another inch until this matter was settled to my satisfaction.

Shepard turned and stared at me incredulously. "An office?"

"Unless you would prefer me to conduct my practice from the clerk's anteroom. Which I'm prepared to do, if necessary."

You might have thought I'd suggested opening a tea shop on the premises. After a half-stifled noise from his nasal region, he spun around and marched back down the hall, throwing open a door and motioning us inside. The room we entered was small and gloomy; the only light came from two small windows placed high on one wall. There was an old, very dusty desk and two straight-back chairs, one of them missing a leg. I guessed that, until recently, this space had been used as a storage room.

"You may work here in the unlikely event there is a need," he said crossly. "I do not expect Mrs. Hanaford's affairs will require your presence more than once or twice a month, if that."

This was another point I thought best to set straight. "On the contrary, I intend to carry my share of responsibility. I shall put in a full day's work, each and every day of the week."

When he appeared incapable of a reply, I decided this was as good a time as any to outline my goals. "I'm primarily interested in issues pertaining to women, although I'm prepared to handle other cases as the need arises. Of course, I'll have to do something about this room." Ignoring the man's incoherent sputters, I regarded the spartan chamber. "Several ideas spring to mind."

"May I ask, madam, why you should presume to have ideas about my office?" The irksome junior attorney stood in the doorway holding an armload of books. His fierce turquoise eyes darted from me to the senior partner. "More to the point, what are you doing here in the first place?"

"There's been a change of plans," Shepard told him shortly. Looking as if he might choke on the words, the senior partner explained that I would be joining the firm as an associate attorney. "On a trial basis," he hastened to add. "Miss Woolson will be— representing Mrs. Hanaford's interests."

The younger man emitted a half-strangled oath, then moved forward in such a rush that the books he carried tumbled onto the floor before he could reach the desk. "Good lord, man, have you taken leave of your senses?"

The senior partner was clearly at the end of his tether. If he could not take his wrath out on me for fear of losing one of his most valued clients, there was nothing to prevent him from venting his fury on a hapless junior attorney. "Whom I hire or do not hire is patently none of your concern, Mr. Campbell," he pronounced through clenched teeth.

"It is certainly my concern if this woman is to be placed in my office," the younger man argued. "I've waited more than two years to move out of that fishbowl. We had an agreement."

"You forget yourself, sir," Shepard snapped with growing fury.

I had grown weary of this juvenile squabbling. "I don't believe we've been introduced," I said to the red-haired associate. "I'm Sarah Woolson. And this is Mrs. Cornelius Hanaford. You are—?"

I'd caught the man off guard. "Robert Campbell," he replied. "But I have no intention of allowing some supercilious female to—"

"Your intentions are of no interest to me, Mr. Campbell. Despite your appalling manners, however, I believe in honoring a bargain. If you were promised this room, then you shall have it. I have no objections to using your cubicle until more suitable arrangements can be made."

"I require no favors from you, madam," said the ungrateful man, his Scottish burr becoming more marked by the minute. (Absently, I noted that his accent seemed to become more pronounced in direct ratio to the state of his perturbation.) "Trust a woman to intrude her meddlesome nose into affairs that in no way concern her."

"Trust a man to behave as if he were the only creature fit to inhabit the earth. I offer you justice and you thank me by behaving in the most overbearing, impertinent—"

"Enough!" Joseph Shepard glowered at both of us. "Miss Woolson will take this office. You, Campbell, will return to the room you've been using. Not one more word," he continued before the junior associate could protest. "The matter is settled."

His face dark, Campbell turned and stormed wordlessly from the room. Joseph Shepard mopped his brow with a handkerchief. "Rest assured I will report this business of Mrs. Hanaford's separate property to Mr. Wylde."

"You must do as you see fit, Mr. Shepard," I told him. "However, it will not alter the fact that we expect payment of Mrs. Hanaford's money by Wednesday of next week. I shall file the appropriate papers at the courthouse this afternoon."

I nodded to Annjenett and we started for the door. "I'll see you first thing Monday morning, Mr. Shepard. Good day."

Joseph Shepard was beyond speech. I caught a last look of him staring after us, openmouthed, as we marched through the antechamber and took our leave of the office.

You were splendid," Annjenett proclaimed as we reached her waiting carriage. "Please, let me give you a ride. You mentioned you were going to the courthouse?"

Before I could reply to this generous offer, a handsome gentleman, dressed in a stylish dark blue frock coat and jaunty necktie, approached us. Although I was certain I hadn't met the man before, he seemed oddly familiar.

"My dear Mrs. Hanaford," he said in a voice that was at once cultured and deeply resonant. He doffed his top hat. "I've been meaning to offer my condolences on your recent loss."

My companion seemed momentarily struck dumb, then belatedly remembered her manners. "Sarah, I'd like you to meet Mr. Peter Fowler, an old friend of the family. Mr. Fowler, this is Miss Sarah Woolson. Miss Woolson is an attorney."

"An attorney!" he said in surprise, and again I had the strange feeling I had met the man before. His distinctive voice, in particular, sounded very familiar. "How—interesting."

"More colorful adjectives than that have been used to describe my choice of professions, Mr. Fowler," I told him.

Turning my attention back to Annjenett, I was surprised to find her regarding him self-consciously, as if unsure what to do or say next. Her cheeks colored, and after an awkward moment, she made a move toward the carriage. Instantly, Mr. Fowler stepped forward and gallantly helped her into the seat.

"If there's anything I can do to help, Mrs. Hanaford," he said in that wonderfully rich baritone, "you have only to ask."

Annjenett flushed prettily. "Thank you, Mr. Fowler. It is generous of you to offer." With seeming effort, she pulled her eyes off the man and turned to me. "Sarah?"

With the driver's help, I took my seat in the carriage and we pulled out into traffic. Behind us, Peter Fowler stood as if glued to the spot, paying no heed to oncoming traffic. That fellow wears his heart on his sleeve, I thought. Even a fool would recognize the look in those handsome eyes. Whether Annjenett realized it or not, Peter Fowler was deeply in love with her.

From the way she sat rigidly upright beside me, however, not allowing herself a single glance back at the young man still staring at us in the street, it seemed clear to me that she did.

CHAPTER THREE

Frederick's guests Saturday evening had been chosen with an eye to their usefulness to his political career. City and state officials had been invited, as well as Papa's colleagues on the bench and every prominent attorney in town. Also included were bankers, industrialists, and the behind-the-scene politicians who wielded the real influence in state government.

Guests mingled to create a living kaleidoscope of colors. The women wore the latest fashions, many imported from Paris, and had arranged their hair into impossible styles punctuated by tiaras, bird feathers and every ridiculous manner of jeweled combs and pins. Beneath the gaslights, the rooms dazzled with a brilliant display of diamonds and precious stones.

Henrietta, I'm sad to say, resembled a confectioner's nightmare in a yellow-green satin gown that waged war with her pale skin and was decorated with an overabundance of faux gems and gold beading. Her intricate coiffure overpowered her thin face and seemed to be festooned with every outlandish ornament she'd been able to lay her hands on. She was obviously in her element, flitting about like an erratic hummingbird, an ingratiating smile pasted upon her lips as she bestowed and received false compliments.

I am sure it will come as no surprise when I say I have never been fond of these soirées, which have always struck me as pretentious and self-serving. An intimate gathering of friends, filled with stimulating and thoughtful discussion, is more to my liking. And since the sole purpose of that night's gala was to launch my eldest brother onto an unsuspecting public, I found it all the more ludicrous.

At Mama's insistence, I'd had a new dress made that was very à la mode, not at all my usual style. The gown was an alarming shade of violet, a color, Mama contended, that perfectly matched my eyes and suited my ivory complexion. On the matter of my hair, however, I drew the line. Nothing would induce me to decorate it with dead bird parts or gaudy baubles.

After Hazel, our ladies' maid, finally finished torturing me with the curling iron, I examined myself critically in the looking glass. Nearly thirty years on this earth have taught me to judge my looks objectively. I need no one to tell me that I am above the desirable height for a woman, that my thick hair is unruly and unfashionably black, my figure too slender, and my before-mentioned violet eyes too bold for the fairer sex. The reflection staring back at me, therefore, was a pleasant surprise. The dress Mama chose was not as disastrous as I had feared. True, the waist was impossibly narrow and the neckline too décolleté, displaying, despite my best efforts to tug the bodice higher, an alarming amount of cleavage. However, if I stood straight and took care not to bend, I judged the overall effect not entirely displeasing.

Supper was lavish enough to please even Henrietta, although I doubt she tasted more than one or two bites. Afterward, guests sat or circulated in small groups, the men discussing business or politics, the women concerned with family, fashion, or the latest social indiscretions.

Celia and Henrietta sat with a group of women that included Mary Ann Crocker, the railroad magnet's wife. Her husband Charles was a loud, blustering man, sometimes likened to a bellowing bull because of the way he had driven the Chinese brought in to lay track for the Central Pacific Railroad. Some people found him spit-on-the-floor crude and arrogant, but unlike some of his more portentous colleagues, I rather admired the man who had rolled up his sleeves and pushed the rails through miles of rock and sheer granite cliffs to Promontory, Utah.

Considering the presence of the Crockers a great coup, Henrietta had fawned over them all evening as if they were visiting royalty, which in a manner of speaking they were. Leland Stanford, Collis Huntington, and Charles Crocker—the surviving members of the Big Four who had amassed fortunes building the railroad—were a powerful economic and, consequently, political force in California. In order for Frederick to obtain a seat in the state legislature, he would have to win over the men behind the railroad.

The aspiring politician, I noticed, was holding court in another part of the room, parroting the current conservative line and promising to rescind business regulations imposed by Denis Kearney's Workingman's party during the last two elections. My brother Charles had been called out shortly after supper on a medical emergency and thus had escaped all the folderol, leading me to wonder if, after all, I had chosen the wrong profession.

Obeying Mama's orders to circulate among our guests, I spied Papa talking to Joseph Shepard. I couldn't hear what they were saying, but the elderly attorney seemed agitated, all the more so when Papa threw back his head and laughed. Shepard sputtered, and even from across the room I couldn't miss the annoying trumpeting sound in the back of his throat. At that moment, he saw me and his face darkened. Abruptly, he paid his respects to my father and strode heatedly from the room.

I joined Papa, who amused himself by repeating Shepard's litany of my sins. It was when Shepard had attempted to enlist my father's support in "curbing my unorthodox behavior" that Papa had burst into laughter, saying he would rather face a charging bull than stand in the way of anything I'd set my mind on. Papa's only regret, he told me with a hearty chuckle, was that he had missed the look on Shepard's face when I'd marched in like Sherman taking Atlanta and staked a claim to one of his offices.

"The poor man has absolutely no idea what to do with you, my dear," Papa said. "Truth to tell, he seems quite overwhelmed."

"He has no reason to be," I replied, failing to find humor in the situation. "I've requested no special treatment. On the contrary, I'm prepared, nay anxious, to accept my share of cases."

Papa's eyes twinkled. "That's precisely what has him worried."

He was still chortling as he walked off to join a colleague, leaving me at last free to pursue my plan. I spotted my quarry in the front sitting room, standing with a group of men by the hearth. The tall man occupying center stage was Willard Broughton, local Republican Senator and one of Cornelius Hanaford's mining partners. I was pleased to see that the man standing next to him was Rufus Mills, the industrialist and fourth partner who, along with Benjamin Wylde, had accompanied the late banker to Nevada City some twenty years earlier. I smiled as I walked over to the group, pleased I would be able to kill two birds with one stone.

"Good evening, Senator Broughton." I smiled at the distinguished man with the graying hair and neatly trimmed mustache, then turned to his much slighter companion. "Mr. Mills. I'm pleased you could come."

The two men were a study in contrasts. Broughton, in his late forties, was stylishly turned out. He was self-assured and possessed the easy conviviality of a born politician. Rufus Mills, on the other hand, was taciturn to the point of rudeness. I hadn't seen the man in several years, but I recalled him as outgoing and nattily attired. Tonight, his clothes were wrinkled and hung loosely on his narrow frame. His face was drawn and pale, and he sniffed and sneezed as if he were suffering from catarrh. His manner, too, seemed ill at ease, almost anxious. His gaze darted about from behind spectacles so thick his magnified eyes reminded me of a frightened deer. This was hardly the dynamic man who had single-handedly forged an industrial empire. What had happened, I wondered, to bring about such a drastic change?

"I was sorry to learn of Cornelius Hanaford's death," I said when I was able to maneuver the two men away from the others, determined to draw as much information from them as possible. "I believe he was once your partner?"

"That was a long time ago," the senator told me. "Of course his death came as a great shock."

Mills took out a crumpled handkerchief and wiped his brow. "Terrible, terrible," he said to no one in particular. His oversized eyes were currently focused on our parlor drapes.

"Were you acquainted with Mr. Hanaford?" the senator asked, his sober brown eyes regarding me with interest.

"Unfortunately, no. However, I have come to know his widow."

"It's very sad. She's such a lovely young woman."

"Yes, it's been difficult for her. I understand another of your former partners has been named executor of Mr. Hanaford's estate."

He nodded. "Indeed. Mr. Benjamin Wylde. A fine attorney, I assure you. Mrs. Hanaford is in capable hands."

"She is now," I agreed cryptically, then asked the senator if he had any idea who might have wanted to see the banker dead.

He seemed taken aback. "My dear young lady, you need look no further than the streets to find the killer. I assure you, Cornelius Hanaford did not have an enemy in the world."

"Come now, Senator," I gently chided. "Have you ever known a man of finance who didn't have adversaries?"

"Surely not the sort who would kill him," he protested.

"Perhaps not," I went on, ignoring his disapproving frown. "But if the servants didn't let the killer into the house, Mr. Hanaford must have opened the door himself. I hardly think he would have invited a stranger in at that hour of the night."

Senator Broughton's face suffused with color and I realized I had gone too far. Murder was not an appropriate subject for polite conversation, and certainly not at a social soirée. I was definitely not making a favorable impression.

"Are you suggesting," he asked darkly, "that Cornelius knew his assailant? That he ushered him into his study so the man could kill him?"

Out of the corner of my eye, I noticed that Rufus Mills had stopped fidgeting and was giving us his full attention. Again, his expression left me with the distinct impression that he was afraid.

"I'm merely stating the facts as they've been presented to me," I said, turning my attention back to the senator.

"That is the danger of listening to gossip," he said reproachfully. "It's usually silly and frequently dangerous. This is a matter for the police. That is what they are paid for and—"

"I must leave," Mr. Mills broke in. "My wife is unwell."

Broughton looked at his friend in surprise. "What are you talking about, Rufus? Martha spoke to Regina just yesterday and she seemed in excellent health."

"It was sudden. Quite sudden." Mills turned to me and nervously cleared his throat. "You'll inform your parents, Miss Woolson? And offer my apologies?"

"Yes, of course, Mr. Mills. But my mother is right over—"

He didn't so much as glance in my mother's direction. "I must go." He gave his friend a harried look, then spun on his heels and all but bolted for the door.

Broughton's expression was difficult to read. Behind his obvious bewilderment, he seemed both concerned and angry.

"You must forgive Mr. Mills, Miss Woolson," he said after an awkward moment. "He's devoted to his wife."

"So it seems." I wondered if his wife's poor health was the reason Mills had seemed so preoccupied. But that couldn't account for his surprising weight loss, or his slightly shabby appearance. Perhaps my initial reaction was correct and he, too, was ill.

Senator Broughton excused himself, saying he wished to have a word with his wife, who was seated in the group with Henrietta and Mrs. Crocker. I watched as he joined the women and said something that drew laughs, then looked meaningfully at his wife. She flushed, as if her husband had imparted some sort of private message, then quickly stood. Somewhat awkwardly she made her apologies to Mama and the other ladies, after which the Senator bowed, took his wife's arm and led her toward the door. As they crossed the room, I caught a glimpse of his face. It was no longer smiling. And Mrs. Broughton looked embarrassed and near tears.

"I saw you pumping the old boys for information," Samuel said, coming up behind me and causing me to jump. "Any luck?"

"No, but it was probably asking too much to suppose they'd tell me anything useful. Rufus Mills behaved strangely, though. He didn't look well, and he ran out of here as if the place were on fire. Oddly, Senator Broughton and his wife left on his heels."

"They'd probably had all they could take of Frederick and his mind-numbing party." He drew out his fob watch. "I wonder how long before I can decently slip out of here myself?"

"Don't you dare. Mama would never forgive you."

Spying Henrietta walking in our direction, my brother took my arm and drew me into the hall.

"I spoke to George," he said, referring to his friend on the police force. "Your client may be in more trouble than you know."

My pulse quickened. "Why? What did George say?"

"The police have discovered she has a lover. An actor by the name of Peter Fowler."

Of course! My mind went back to the scene outside Shepard's building the day before and I suddenly understood why Annjenett's friend had seemed so familiar. Just last year I had seen him perform a melodrama at the California Theater.

"You don't look surprised."

"I saw them together, Samuel. What you've just told me explains Annjenett's strange behavior." I had an awful thought. "What impact will this have on the murder investigation?"

"For one thing, it supplies a motive. And, of course, the widow is going to have to explain her relationship with Fowler."

"Poor Annjenett." Her behavior had been foolish, but surely not criminal. Of course she'd be ruined socially. A woman might be allowed a discreet affair—if it were circumspect and hidden from the public eye—but society would never accept a scandal involving murder and, even worse, an actor. There were some indiscretions even San Francisco could not forgive.

"After our talk the other night, I did a little poking around. Do you see that man over there?" Samuel indicated a stout, middle-aged man with ruddy cheeks and receding white hair. "That's Thomas Cooke, Annjenett's father."

Unobtrusively, I studied the man as my brother went on.

"Cooke was heavily indebted to Hanaford's bank. Then, after his daughter's marriage, his financial obligations were suddenly forgiven. I doubt it was by coincidence."

My eyes flew to my brother, thinking perhaps I had misheard. "Are you implying that Thomas Cooke all but sold his daughter into marriage? How could any father—"

I stopped, brought up short by a familiar face in the foyer, a face that towered at least half a head above the other guests. "What is *he* doing here?"

Samuel followed my gaze. "You know that fellow?"

"Unfortunately, yes."

Excusing myself, I started toward the door. Even if the man were not so tall, he would have stood out in the present company like an oak tree in a rose garden. He still wore his dark blue daytime frock coat and brown trousers—which, I noted, were sorely in need of pressing—along with a tan waistcoat and an unfortunate necktie that failed to match any other article of his clothing. His face was flushed, as if he had traveled in some haste, and his red hair flew about his head in more disorder than usual.

"Mr. Campbell," I said, reaching the foyer. "I didn't expect to see you here."

"I have a message for Mr. Shepard," he said, not bothering with civilities. "I was told he'd be here tonight."

"He left some time ago," I replied, then bristled when the arrogant man craned his neck, looking beyond me into the parlor. "Do you accuse me of lying, sir?" I felt my face flush at his rude behavior. "Do you think that for some nefarious reason we're hiding Mr. Shepard?"

"Don't be ridiculous. It's just that I've never seen such a display of ostentation beneath one roof."

I couldn't bring myself to admit that, for the most part, I agreed with this pronouncement. "You don't approve of Society?"

His eyes raked over the lavish gowns, the diamonds, rubies, and emeralds, the tiaras and ostrich feathers. "I see little to commend fatuous women whose sole purpose in life is to outspend, outdress and outglitter their neighbor."

"That's a generalization, Mr. Campbell," I said shortly. I thought of Mama and the hours she spent each week gathering clothing, food, and medicine for the poor. There was Mrs. Hearst's Settlement House in South Park, Mrs. Crocker's Boys' and Girls' Aid Society, not to mention the Old People's Home she had helped found. "There are members of Society who care deeply about the needs of the less fortunate. They give—"

He gave a snort of impatience. "I'm sure you know more about the vagaries of San Francisco Society than I do. However, since I didn't come here to debate social reform, I'll bid you good night." With a slight nod of his head, he turned toward the door.

"Wait," I called after him. Something in his expression made me uneasy. "Perhaps if I knew your message, I could help."

For a moment I thought he hadn't heard, but after one or two strides of those long legs he stopped and turned back. I don't know what made me think of Annjenett, but suddenly I was certain his errand concerned her.

"It's about Mrs. Hanaford, isn't it?" When he didn't answer, I said, "I'm her attorney. I demand to be told what has happened."

"You really are a meddlesome woman," he spat, but I could see his resolve was weakening. "All right," he went on grudgingly. "Earlier this evening Mrs. Hanaford was arrested and taken to the city jail. The police are still looking for her love—that is, a gentle-man of her acquaintance."

I could hardly credit this. "Annjenett, taken to jail? Why?"

He hesitated a moment, then blurted, "Mrs. Hanaford and a fel-low by the name of Peter Fowler have been charged with the mur-der of Cornelius Hanaford."

I was not allowed to visit Annjenett until Monday morning, a de-lay which seemed like an eternity. Through his friend George Lewis, Samuel learned that Peter Fowler had finally been arrested early the previous morning and that both he and Annjenett were being held without bail—not only because they were charged with a capital offense, but because the presumption of their guilt was too great to risk flight. Samuel insisted on accompanying me to the city jail, an unnecessary but welcome arrangement.

Our cab made its way through heavy morning fog to arrive at the jail shortly after nine. As it turned out, it was as well Samuel was with me, since Annjenett's jailers—rejecting the possibility that I might be her attorney—refused to allow me inside. It was only after my brother, without benefit of bar accreditation, insisted he was co-attorney that we were finally admitted.

It was unusual for the city jail to be called upon to house a woman of Annjenett's refinement, but the guard assured me that the widow had been allotted the best accommodations the institu-tion had to offer. Nonetheless, her bleak chamber shocked me. The cell was bitterly cold and barely large enough to hold three people. A narrow cot, covered by several coarse woolen blankets, took up the limited space. To one side was a cracked chamber pot and a porcelain bowl filled with water. There were no table or chairs. In fact there was no place for visitors to sit except upon the cot. A small, barred window, located high on one wall, provided the only source of light, and little of that on this dreary morning.

"Sarah, thank goodness you've come." Annjenett clutched my arm, her white face and red eyes making my heart ache in sympathy.

"How are you, my dear?" Anxious as I was to hear what had happened, I first had to ensure that she was being treated well by her jailers.

"Everyone is kind enough," she said with a weak smile. "They bring me extra food and blankets, but there's little they can do to change this . . ." She swept a thin hand around the cell.

Leaving Samuel to stand by the barred window, I took the young widow's hand and led her to sit on the cot. "I know this is difficult," I said, taking a seat beside her. "But if I'm to help, you must tell me everything."

Annjenett hesitated and looked toward Samuel, who, interested as he was in her narrative, instantly understood that she'd feel more comfortable if we were alone.

"I'll see what I can find out about Mrs. Hanaford's arrest," he said, knocking on the cell door to attract the guard.

I nodded my approval. "I'll meet you outside."

When he was gone, Annjenett said, "It was kind of you to come."

"Kindness has nothing to do with it. It should be clear to any fool that you're incapable of murder."

Her hands moved nervously in her lap. "You may change your mind when you've heard my story."

"I'll be the judge of that." In an effort to help her begin, I said, "I understand your father was in debt to Mr. Hanaford's bank, and that this debt was forgiven upon your marriage." I tried to keep my tone nonjudgmental, but some of my distaste must have shown.

"Please, Sarah, you mustn't judge Papa too harshly. He hated marrying me to a man we both disliked so intensely. But Papa has a penchant for gambling, and Cornelius preyed on that weakness by lending him ever-increasing amounts of money. When my father realized what he'd done, it was too late. He was forced to agree to Cornelius's terms or risk losing everything."

I shook my head at this cowardice and she rushed on, "At first it wasn't so bad. And I took hope from the fact that Cornelius treated me kindly. For the first year or two, I actually grew rather fond of him."

"Then what happened?" I prompted when she faltered.

"Cornelius—began to make certain demands of me. He—" Her pale cheeks flamed into color.

I patted her hand. "I have friends who are married. I think I know what you're trying to say."

"Excuse me, Sarah, but I'm not sure you do. For a long time I didn't either. I was too naive to understand that his—that my husband's appetites went beyond what is normally expected of a wife. I only knew that I found them coarse and humiliating. I tried to do what he asked, but it was never enough. Each time he came to my bed his demands grew more outrageous, more debasing. If I refused, he would sometimes strike me until I gave in."

"Dear god!" Tears streaked down Annjenett's face and I felt beastly. "Please, believe me, my dear. I would never make you go through this if it weren't so important."

"It's all right, Sarah, I understand." A smile touched her lips, but quickly faded. "Sometimes the beatings were so serious I was forced to stay in my room to hide the bruises from the servants. Then gradually, Cornelius came to my room less frequently. Over the past year he hardly came at all.

"At first it was a relief, but over time I began to grow lonely.

Then, about six months ago, friends asked me to accompany them to the theater. Cornelius was out for the evening and it seemed an innocent thing to do."

Her blue eyes met mine. "We went to the Baldwin Theater. They were doing *The Shoemaker's Holiday* and Peter Fowler played Simon Eyre. Oh, Sarah, he was wonderful! Afterward, he joined our party for a late supper and we were surprised to discover that we'd both grown up in San Francisco, actually within blocks of each other. We wondered if we might have even played together as children. Peter was so easy to talk to and he made me laugh. Heaven knows I hadn't laughed in a long time."

"So you began seeing each other?"

She nodded. "I'm not proud of my behavior, Sarah, but for the first time in my life I had fallen deeply in love."

"I'm not here to judge you, my dear. Only to clear you of these ludicrous charges." I looked her in the eye. "Now, I want you to tell me what happened the night your husband was killed. What *really* happened."

She looked at me miserably, then turned away. Suddenly, I understood. "He was there, wasn't he? Peter Fowler, I mean."

She nodded wretchedly. "Sarah, I swear he had nothing to do with my husband's death. Neither of us did."

"How did Mr. Fowler come to be in your home?"

"Cornelius had found out about us. The night before his death we had a dreadful row. When Peter saw marks on my face the next day, he insisted on confronting Cornelius. I tried to dissuade him, but he was adamant. After dinner I made a show of going upstairs, but in fact I waited on the landing. I answered the door at the first knock and managed to sneak Peter up to my boudoir. It was while I was trying to convince him that his presence would only make matters worse that—that Cornelius must have been murdered."

"Neither of you heard anything?"

She shook her head. "My boudoir is on the second floor, at the rear of the house. It wasn't until Peter stormed downstairs to have it out with Cornelius that we—we found him dead."

She began sobbing quietly while my thoughts raced. Only now did I fully comprehend the damaging case against Annjenett. I still believed her innocent, but I couldn't be certain of the actor. For all I knew she might, even now, be lying to protect him.

I hesitated, but the question had to be asked. "How much do you know about Mr. Fowler, Annjenett?"

She guessed my thoughts and her eyes flashed. "Only that he is the kindest, gentlest of men. Peter was prepared to fight Cornelius to protect me, but he would never have murdered him in cold blood."

I abandoned this line of questioning; Annjenett was obviously too smitten with the actor to give an unbiased opinion. Before I could think of another way to approach the subject, however, I heard the jailer's approaching footsteps. Hurriedly, I pulled a document out of my briefcase and handed it to her, along with pen and ink.

"If we're to secure your release," I told her, "we have to discover who really murdered your husband. This paper gives me authority to go through his effects. It also allows me to claim the money we've demanded of Mr. Shepard, which we'll need to pay your household expenses and, if necessary, use for your defense."

"Yes, of course," she agreed and quickly signed the paper. Her pale face showed a flicker of hope. "What do you expect to find in my husband's belongings?"

I was loath to admit I hadn't the faintest idea. She had little enough to sustain her through the coming days and nights, and far too much time to agonize over her situation. Temporizing, I said there was always the chance the police had overlooked something, and was pleased when she seemed to take heart in this possibility. A moment later the jailer threw the cell door open with a clang.

"There's a couple of gents waitin' to see the prisoner." He eyed me suspiciously. "One of 'em says he's the lady's lawyer."

It wasn't difficult to guess that Joseph Shepard, or one of his associates, was here to interview Annjenett. It was no less than I expected. I was only glad I had been able to speak to her first. I gave Annjenett a confident smile.

"Don't lose heart," I told her. "I'll come back to see you soon."

"Oh, Sarah, please do." Impulsively, she leaned forward and kissed me on the cheek. Taken aback, I smiled and mumbled something I hoped was reassuring, then turned and departed the cell.

Just as the jailer had announced, I found two men waiting in the jail's anteroom. One was a stranger, the other was the towering figure of Robert Campbell.

"You!" I said incredulously. "Don't tell me Joseph Shepard is allowing you to handle my client's defense."

"Your client, madam?" the second man said in surprise. "I was given to understand that I was to represent Mrs. Hanaford."

"Pay no attention to her, Paulson." Campbell's look was scornful. "The woman fancies herself an attorney and has somehow foisted herself upon Hanaford's widow."

Ignoring him, I extended my hand to the older man. "My name is Sarah Woolson, and Mr. Campbell's disclaimers to the contrary, I am a fully licensed attorney in the State of California. And you are?"

The man raised shaggy brows. He was of modest height, yet there was an air of authority about him that made him appear taller. His clothes were well cut and, despite his portly girth, he wore them with panache. His face was full and as he removed his top hat I could detect a good deal of silver in his brown hair. He regarded me speculatively, and for a moment I thought he might take Campbell's advice and ignore me altogether. Then, abruptly, he smiled and reached out a manicured hand to shake mine vigorously.

"Augustus Paulson," he said in a voice so superb it was easy to imagine it captivating a courtroom. "It's an honor to make your acquaintance, Miss Woolson. I've heard of Mrs. Clara Foltz, of course, but I've never before had the privilege of meeting a lawyer of the fairer sex. I admire your courage. It can't be easy penetrating such an established male bastion."

"There's no need to waste sympathy on this woman," Campbell broke in. "She has all the sensitivity of a charging rhino."

"Unfortunately, not everyone is blessed with your tact and refined social skills," I commented dryly, then turned to the elder attorney. I found myself liking Augustus Paulson and decided Annjenett could do a good deal worse then have this man represent her. It remained to be seen, however, how long he would continue to be sympathetic to female attorneys once he realized how closely I intended to work with him on the case. "I'm sure Mrs. Hanaford will be grateful for your help, Mr. Paulson."

"I gather you have already spoken to my—to *our* client."

I nodded, then glanced around with distaste at the peeling walls, the filthy floor, the chill that permeated every inch of the drafty hallway. "City jail is no place for a woman, Mr. Paulson. After you've met with Mrs. Hanaford, we must discuss a strategy for her defense and speedy discharge."

"*You* must discuss!" Campbell exploded. "Madam, will you kindly get it through your head that you're not part of Mrs. Hanaford's defense? If you really have her best interests at heart, you'll cease your confounded interference and allow your betters to get on with their business."

"By 'my betters,' I presume you mean yourself, Mr. Campbell? You who have had such extensive trial experience." My tone was scornful, having learned from my inquiries that the nearest the irritating man had come to a courtroom was as a research assistant.

"I meant Paulson, you obdurate woman," he shot back, his Scottish r's rolling at me like waves in a tsunami.

"Campbell, please," Paulson intervened, staring at the younger man until he clamped his mouth shut. "Miss Woolson, I apologize for my colleague's, er, exuberance. I'm afraid his concern over Mrs. Hanaford has caused him to forget his manners."

"On the contrary, I doubt Mr. Campbell has any manners to forget. His boorishness, however, is of no importance. What matters is getting Mrs. Hanaford out of this place."

"On that point, we are all agreed." Mr. Paulson consulted his fob watch. "I believe you've hit upon an excellent plan, Miss Woolson. After Mr. Campbell and I have spoken with Mrs. Hanaford, the three of us should meet to discuss how best to proceed with the case. Unfortunately, I have to be in court this afternoon. Would it be possible for you to come to my office at six o'clock this evening?"

Campbell started to grumble, but Paulson threw him another look and he fell reluctantly silent.

"That would be fine," I agreed, pointedly ignoring the Scot.

Mr. Paulson gave a polite nod, then turned and walked into the bowels of the jail. With a final glare, the irascible giant murmured something I couldn't quite catch and hurried after him.

Samuel was waiting for me outside the jail. Beside him was George Lewis. George is of medium height, with a round, amiable face and light brown hair that invariably spills in boyish locks onto his brow. Despite the unflattering uniform relegated to San Francisco's Finest, George wore his blue long coat and bowler hat with pride. It was reassuring to know that the appalling corruption that existed in our police department had not as yet filtered down through the entire rank and file.

One look at their faces told me that something was wrong. "What is it?" I asked without preamble. "What's happened?"

Samuel deferred to his friend, who regarded me unhappily.

"There's been another murder, Miss Sarah," he blurted. "Rufus Mills was found dead last night—in Chinatown. He was, er—" George turned red, stumbling to find the right words.

"There's no delicate way to say this, Sarah," my brother broke in. "Rufus Mills was stabbed to death in the genitals."

CHAPTER FOUR

We lunched at a nearby hotel, but I paid scant attention to either the food or my companions. While George and my brother discussed a story Samuel was researching for the *Police Gazette,* I mulled over Rufus Mills's death. According to George, the police surgeon speculated that Mills had been dead at least twenty-four hours before his body was discovered in one of Chinatown's back alleys. That meant he'd probably been killed not long after leaving Frederick's party Saturday night. Obviously his story about returning home to nurse a sick wife had been merely an excuse, since he'd gone to Chinatown instead. But why? I asked myself. What possible reason could he have had for venturing into an area considered so unsavory that even the police avoided it after dark?

"Sarah? You haven't heard a word I've said."

I came out of my thoughts to find both men staring at me. "I'm sorry, Samuel, what—?"

"I asked how your meeting went with Mrs. Hanaford?"

"She's understandably distressed and anxious to get out of that awful place," I replied, then looked at George. "Which, thankfully, shouldn't be long now. Horrible as it is, this second murder will at least guarantee her speedy release."

"Second murder?" George's intelligent brown eyes, normally cheerful and eager to please, were uncharacteristically serious. "I'm afraid I don't take your meaning."

"Surely it's clear enough, George," I told him. "Regardless of the alleged evidence against Annjenett for her husband's death, she can hardly be charged with killing Rufus Mills from her jail cell. His murder proves my client's innocence."

George cleared his throat. "I'm sorry, Miss Sarah, but we've found no evidence to indicate that the two deaths are connected."

For some reason, George always seems uncomfortable in my presence. Samuel insists it's because the man is enamored of me, a notion I find too absurd to credit. More likely, his uneasiness stems from my penchant for speaking my mind, a characteristic many men seem to find intimidating. Insecurity, however, is no excuse for pigheadedness.

"Then you haven't looked hard enough," I retorted. "It defies logic that Hanaford and Mills should be murdered within weeks of each other, and in an identical manner, and not be related."

George winced at my reference to how the two victims had met their unfortunate ends. "It's a coincidence, I assure you, Miss Sarah. I'd like to help your client, but I'm afraid the charges against her won't be dropped because of Mr. Mills's death. Unless you know something to link them?" He looked at me expectantly, as if hoping I might pull a rabbit out of my hat.

It galled me to admit that I had nothing substantive to offer beyond my own intuition. "A number of possibilities present themselves," I said, angry to detect a note of defensiveness in my voice.

"Cornelius Hanaford and Rufus Mills might have been associated in a way we're not yet aware. Perhaps they shared a common enemy who wished to see them dead. We also need to establish who gained from their deaths. Where were the two surviving partners that night? What was Rufus Mills doing in Chinatown, of all places? And so late at night. Was he alone or was he meeting someone? What time was he murdered? Were there any witnesses? Was the weapon recovered? Who found the——?"

Samuel had the poor grace to laugh. "Sarah, have pity on George."

I turned to our companion, who was staring at me as if he'd been hit by a runaway train. "You have given serious thought to these questions, haven't you, George?"

George opened and closed his mouth, but did not answer.

"I presume you haven't been assigned to the case or you wouldn't be wasting time dawdling over lunch," I went on. "But that shouldn't preclude you from offering sensible suggestions to those in charge. If the investigating detectives mean to turn a blind eye to the obvious similarities between the two cases, you'll need to speak up. A woman's life may depend on the three of us keeping our heads."

"Wait a minute," protested Samuel. "What do I have to do with this?"

"You have some influence with the local newspapers," I pointed out. "You can use their files to learn more about the four mining partners. I can't help thinking the answer to all this lies in the past. So that seems the most logical place to begin."

George continued to stare at me with his mouth open. If he weren't such a fine-looking young man, he would have reminded me of a large, floundering fish.

"Surely you aren't suggesting that Mr. Wylde or Senator Broughton has anything to do with these murders?"

"That's exactly what we need to find out. Really, George, you can't expect me to do all your thinking for you. You're a member of the police. They must teach you something about criminal investigation." The smile had returned to my brother's face. "I fail to see anything amusing about this tragic affair, Samuel," I told him hotly.

My brother regarded me over his coffee. "Your defense of Mrs. Hanaford is admirable, Sarah. But you can't order the police about as if it's your private corps of investigators. Besides, I heard at the jail that Augustus Paulson would be handling Mrs. Hanaford's defense. I think, little sister, you may be about to lose your first and only client."

"That remains to be seen." I wasn't pleased with his tone. "I had occasion to meet Mr. Paulson after my interview with Mrs. Hanaford. I have no reason to suppose he resents my collaboration."

Again Samuel laughed out loud. "Well, if he doesn't, Joseph Shepard certainly will."

George continued to look worried. "Samuel's right, Miss Sarah. I know you mean well, but the evidence against Mrs. Hanaford and Peter Fowler is compelling."

"We'll see about that." I'd had enough of cynics and naysayers for one morning. Pushing back my chair, I stood and rearranged my skirts. "If you'll excuse me, gentlemen, I have pressing business to attend to."

I turned and made my way through the restaurant without a backward glance at my startled companions.

I would be lying if I pretended I wasn't unsettled by the official reaction to Mills's death. Could the police really be so blind—

or pigheaded—that they failed to recognize the similarities between the two murders?

Consulting my lapel watch, I saw that my meeting with Paulson would not begin for another five hours, far too long to sit idly about twiddling my thumbs. Since no one else seemed inclined to ask the questions I'd posed to George, I decided I must do it myself. Annjenett's freedom—perhaps her very life—might depend on the answers!

Lacking a better place to commence my inquiries, I returned to Cornelius Hanaford's bank to speak to Eban Potter. He had known his employer since childhood, I reasoned, and Annjenett mentioned he had also been acquainted with Hanaford's mining partners. If the motives for the two crimes did lie in the past, I hoped the bank manager might at least be able to point me in the right direction.

I found Mr. Potter considerably shaken over Annjenett's arrest.

"Mr. Hanaford would turn in his grave if he could see his wife in such a place," he said, ushering me into a small but well-ordered office. He offered me a chair, then sat down behind an equally tidy desk. "What can the police be thinking?"

"They seem to feel they've discovered a reason why Mrs. Hanaford might wish to see her husband dead."

"You mean the actor?" Potter's tone clearly indicated his disdain for members of that profession. He shook his head. "I don't believe it for one moment."

Realizing that Potter's loyalty to the young widow made this line of inquiry unproductive, I changed tactics. "Can you think of any reason why Mr. Mills might go alone to Chinatown?"

He gave an involuntary shudder. "I can't imagine why anyone would venture into that dreadful place, especially after dark."

"I believe you were well acquainted with Mr. Hanaford," I said, trying yet another tack. "Do you know if he, too, made a practice of frequenting Chinatown?"

Potter looked stunned. "Really, Miss Woolson, I think you're wasting your time pursuing this line of inquiry. What possible business could Mr. Hanaford have had in that part of town?"

"The same might be said for Rufus Mills," I commented. "And it's necessary to cover every possibility." Again I shifted focus. "I know Mr. Hanaford and Mr. Mills were old friends, and in the past had been mining partners. Do you know if they continued to have business dealings? I thought perhaps Mr. Mills might have used the bank to finance some of his projects."

"Quite right, he did." The bank manager looked relieved to be on more certain ground. "Cornelius—Mr. Hanaford—provided most of Mr. Mills's financing which, considering his many successful enterprises, returned a nice profit to the bank."

"What about the other partners, Senator Broughton and Mr. Wylde? I understand you've known all four men since your school days."

"Mr. Hanaford and I grew up together. I met the others when he was attempting to finance a trip to Nevada. Rufus Mills, Benjamin Wylde and Willard Broughton had agreed to accompany him."

"I'm surprised you didn't go as well."

"Cornelius urged me to go, but it wasn't my sort of thing." He smiled. "I've never been particularly adventurous, I'm afraid. In any event, my wife was expecting our daughter, Louisa. Even if I'd been inclined, I couldn't have left her at such a time."

"No, of course not. You say Mr. Hanaford assumed responsibility for financing the venture?"

"Yes, Cornelius was always good at that sort of thing. People trusted him. He even convinced me to invest. And I had little enough put aside in those days."

"You must have been happy that you did, given their success."

"Cornelius more than repaid my original investment. And the money couldn't have come at a better time." He hesitated. "There were complications during childbirth and my wife never recovered her health. She passed away soon afterward."

"I'm sorry, Mr. Potter. I didn't realize—"

"Please, don't distress yourself, Miss Woolson," he broke in with a kind smile. "You couldn't have known."

When I rose to leave, the manager took hold of my hand. "If you see Mrs. Hanaford, please assure her that I don't for one moment believe the charges against her. Surely the police will realize their mistake and release her from that appalling place."

"I sincerely hope so," I agreed wholeheartedly.

Apologizing for taking up so much of his time, I thanked Eban Potter for his help and took my leave of the bank.

I arrived at Mr. Paulson's office promptly at six o'clock to find Robert Campbell already present.

He nodded his head with stiff courtesy. "Miss Woolson."

"Mr. Campbell," I returned with equal formality and accepted the chair Mr. Paulson offered.

"Mr. Wylde has expressed an interest in attending our meeting," the attorney informed us. "As an old friend of Mr. Hanaford, and executor of his estate, he's understandably concerned about Mrs. Hanaford. I trust this meets with your approval, Miss Woolson? And yours, Mr. Campbell?"

I bit back my true feelings on the subject of Benjamin Wylde. Since it was imperative that I continue to act in Annjenett's behalf, I couldn't afford to antagonize Mr. Paulson.

"Yes, of course," I replied, keeping my tone pleasant.

"It's fine with me," Campbell said, as if the matter were of no consequence to him one way or the other.

"Excellent." Mr. Paulson smiled. "While we wait for his arrival, I've taken the liberty of ordering tea."

We'd just been served refreshments when the office door opened and a clerk announced Benjamin Wylde. The man was much as I remembered from Hanaford's bank. He was impeccably dressed in a tailored frock coat and trousers; his longish black hair was neatly combed, his angular face defined by open speculation as he boldly took in the room and its inhabitants. His sharp eyes went to Robert Campbell, then to me, and it was infuriatingly clear that he found us a less than formidable addition to the defense team. My temper rose at the impertinence. He was present at this meeting as a personal favor, yet from the moment he entered the room he seemed to take it over. Catching Campbell's eye, I was pleased to note that he, too, seemed put off by Wylde's gall. At least we agreed on one thing, I thought.

"Before we begin," said Paulson, "I have disturbing news. When the police searched Mr. Fowler's room, they discovered the items taken from Mr. Hanaford's house the night of his murder."

This information struck me like a physical blow. "Have you spoken to Mrs. Hanaford about this?"

"Not yet," the lawyer answered soberly. "Please, allow me to be frank. There's little Mrs. Hanaford can say that is likely to diminish this blow to her case. She swears Fowler never left her sight the night of the murder. If this is true, the evidence found in his rooms is as damaging to her as it is to him."

Before I could object to this line of reasoning, Wylde said, "What defense do you have in mind?" He spoke directly to Paulson, rudely turning his back on both Campbell and myself.

"That's what we have gathered here to discuss," Paulson replied.

"Mrs. Hanaford will be arraigned next Wednesday morning. We shall have to be ready with her plea."

He looked at each of us in turn. "After giving the matter a great deal of consideration, it seems clear that there are three ways to handle the case. One, we can claim Mrs. Hanaford and Mr. Fowler acted in self-defense, which would be damn—" He glanced uncomfortably in my direction. "That is to say, it would be difficult to prove, especially given the, ah, nature of the victim's wounds. Two, we can contend that Fowler forced Mrs. Hanaford to act as his accomplice. Either way—"

"Either way you assume her guilt," I interrupted, appalled.

"I didn't say I liked our options, Miss Woolson," he told me unhappily. "I am merely stating the facts."

"Whatever the purported facts, the truth remains that Annjenett Hanaford did not murder her husband."

"Why? Because you think she's incapable of such an act?" Campbell snorted. "That's blind faith, Miss Woolson, not a viable defense one can use in a court of law."

Paulson broke in before I could justify my position.

"I appreciate your loyalty to Mrs. Hanaford, Miss Woolson. But Mr. Campbell is correct when he says we must structure a defense based on the evidence collected by the police. To do less would be grievously negligent."

"How damaging is this evidence—other than the discovery of the stolen items in Fowler's room?" asked Wylde.

Mr. Paulson put on his spectacles and opened a folder. "It seems that a neighbor saw Mr. Fowler enter the Hanaford house shortly after nine o'clock on the night of the murder."

I gasped, shocked by this belated revelation. "It's been nearly a month since Mr. Hanaford's death. Why has this neighbor waited so long to step forward?"

"Evidently the gentleman went abroad the morning after the murder and has only just returned," explained Paulson. "When the police revisited Mr. Hanaford's neighbors, he was able to relate for the first time what he'd observed." He gazed at us over his spectacles. "Besides the stolen articles, this is the most damaging disclosure to date. Unfortunately, however, there is more."

He looked uneasily in my direction, then cleared his throat. "Mrs. Hanaford and Mr. Fowler have been seen together on numerous occasions, it seems. Without Mr. Hanaford." He let the obvious implication hang in the air.

"How long had this been going on?" Campbell asked in the silence following this statement.

The lawyer consulted the file. "For at least six months. According to witnesses, they were circumspect. But this sort of thing can't be kept secret for long. In my opinion, it would be fruitless to deny that they were more than merely friends."

"An actor," Mr. Wylde said, his tone contemptuous.

"How could she expect to get away with it?" Campbell put in. "Her husband was certain to find out."

"That is undoubtedly what the prosecution will contend," Paulson said. "They'll claim that Mr. Hanaford discovered his wife's affair and that Fowler, aided by Mrs. Hanaford, was forced to murder him. After a discreet passage of time, they'd be free to marry and share in her inheritance."

Listening to these three men—the very attorneys whom Annjenett depended on to clear her name—calmly discussing her as if she'd already been tried and convicted made my blood boil. Despite Paulson's sympathy for the widow, he still stood with society in his judgment of her implied indiscretions, without any idea what loneliness and despair might have driven her to seek solace in another man's arms. What would they say if they knew of the beatings she'd suffered at her husband's hands, or the degrading acts she'd been made to perform? Or would that knowledge make any difference? Even if Annjenett had killed her husband in self-defense—something I would never believe—it would be a difficult case to defend. For this reason, I dared not tell these men what I knew about the physical and emotional mistreatment she had endured. To do so would provide the prosecution with an even more powerful motive: that she had helped plan and execute Hanaford's murder to free herself of a brutal husband.

"The police have also learned from the servants that the Hanafords frequently quarreled," Paulson went on, his expression grim. "One of their most rancorous fights was overheard by a maid the night before Mr. Hanaford was killed, an event the prosecution will surely use to disastrous advantage." He closed the file. "And, of course, Mrs. Hanaford is her husband's principal beneficiary. She stands to inherit a very large fortune."

"Unless she's convicted," put in Wylde.

"That is correct." Paulson agreed. "A murderess cannot profit from her crime."

Campbell stirred in his seat. "You mentioned three options for handling Mrs. Hanaford's case, Paulson. What's the third?"

Paulson again looked around the table. "After dismissing the first two alternatives as impossible to sustain in a court of law, I'm convinced there is only one feasible defense. We must plead Mrs. Hanaford not guilty by reason of insanity."

"No!" I protested, unable to hold my tongue another moment. "On no account must we do that. She's not insane. And police evidence notwithstanding, I'll never believe her guilty of murder."

"Calm yourself, woman," Campbell ordered, which only added to my aggravation.

"It's impossible to remain calm when my client's only hope

rests with men who believe her guilty. If you represent her protectors, God save the poor woman from her accusers!"

Benjamin Wylde glared at me darkly, but before he could speak, Mr. Paulson sighed and said, "Miss Woolson, however much you believe in Mrs. Hanaford's innocence, we owe it to our client to be practical. We cannot ignore the mountain of evidence that will be used against her by the prosecution."

"Nor can we idly stand by and do nothing to explain or disprove that evidence," I argued hotly. "Surely we can find a witness who saw someone else enter the house that night. Hanaford had to have had enemies. It's up to us to find them."

"This is absurd!" Wylde's voice rose. "I refuse to be lectured to by a woman who patently hasn't the first idea what—"

"Please, Mr. Wylde," interjected Paulson. "I understand Miss Woolson's concerns."

Wylde's face darkened, but he lapsed into resentful silence. Paulson turned to me, his mild brown eyes sympathetic.

"We're facing a difficult situation, my dear, and there are no simple answers. Once you've examined the facts, I'm sure you'll agree that there is only one defense possible if we're to save our client's life, no matter how abhorrent that plea may appear."

He opened a large tome to a marked page. "I propose to base our insanity case on the McNaghten Rules of 1843. We will have to prove that at the time the crime was committed, Mrs. Hanaford was laboring under a defect from reason and didn't know the nature and quality of the act she was committing. Or, if she did know, that she wasn't aware that what she was doing was wrong."

"That seems to be a sound plan," Wylde agreed.

"I don't anticipate any difficulty finding doctors who will attest to Mrs. Hanaford's troubled state of mind. The servants have spoken of the days she spent closed off in her room, as well as crying spells they witnessed and displays of nerves. Of course, the crime itself speaks to her fragile mental condition."

I started to protest, then decided it was useless. I was the only person in the room who believed Annjenett Hanaford innocent. Clearly, it would be up to me to prove that she was.

When the meeting was over, after the three men had agreed to base Annjenett's defense on temporary insanity, I politely refused Mr. Paulson's offer to share his carriage. Splurging on a hansom cab, I wearily requested that the driver take me home.

T hat evening I brought my father up to date as we sat in his study, enjoying freshly brewed coffee generously laced with brandy.

"All right, Sarah," he said at last. "If, as you believe, your client and Mr. Fowler are innocent, who do you suppose did kill Cornelius Hanaford?"

"I wish I knew." I ran a hand through my already disarranged hair, a habit I had acquired as a child and had been unable to break as an adult. "I believe that Hanaford not only knew his killer, but that he personally let him inside the house."

Papa nodded his agreement. "If Mrs. Hanaford and the servants are telling the truth, then that's the only possible conclusion."

"Which is why it's so vital to learn everything possible about Hanaford and Mills. Think back, Papa. Can you remember any scandals they might have been involved in? Or business dealings gone wrong?"

"Business dealings are always going wrong," he said with a wry smile. "Although I can think of none that might cost two men their lives—assuming, of course, that the murders are connected. As for scandals, well, that's another story."

I leaned forward. "What is it, Papa? What do you remember?"

"Nothing that's apt to help you, I'm afraid. Just some trouble Rufus Mills was in fifteen or twenty years ago. Too far in the past to have anything to do with his murder."

"Even so, I'd like to hear it."

My father made a tower with his fingers, something he often did when he was lost in thought. I knew enough to wait quietly until he was ready to go on.

"You have to understand, Sarah, Hanaford and his partners had reputations for being somewhat wild in their younger days," he said at length. "Of course, San Francisco was a rowdy town in the sixties, and what passed for law and order was disorganized at best. Even so, it made a big splash in the papers when a woman who had done housework for Mills's parents, insisted Rufus was the father of her son. The boy was around ten at the time, as I recall. The woman was sick and out of work. She demanded Mills give her money to care for the boy and get medical help for herself."

"What happened?"

"By all accounts he sent her packing. Said she was nothing but a gold digger and denied he was the father of her child. In desperation I suppose, she went to the newspapers with her story. Naturally, they fed on it like a pack of wolves. But in the end it was Mills's word against hers, and by then he was becoming a bigwig in the city. Regardless of what people privately thought, they aligned themselves on the side of money." He stared into the fire. "I heard the woman died not long after and that was the end of it."

"And the boy?"

Papa shrugged. "Probably took to the streets—like thousands of other poor waifs."

I shared my parents' sympathy for the city's homeless children, or street Arabs as they were called, who slept in doorways and lived from hand-to-mouth. We did what we could to help them, but it was never enough. It angered me to think that a man as wealthy as Rufus Mills would consign one more child to such a fate, especially one who might be his son. Still, I couldn't see how this incident, tragic as it was, could have a bearing on either murder.

Papa seemed to read my thoughts. "I warned you I didn't think it would be helpful. Other stories circulated about the four men from time to time—their drinking, gaming, carousing, that sort of thing. But, as I say, they were no worse than the hundreds of other young men who were bent on hell-raising in those days. I'm sorry, Sarah. I wish I could tell you something useful."

"I know." I tried to mask my disappointment. "It's just that matters are growing desperate. Paulson means well, but if he has his way, the best Annjenett can hope for is to be put in an insane asylum where she'll languish for the rest of her days."

"That's better than death on the gallows," Papa pointed out.

"Is it? I've read stories about self-styled mental asylums. Patients beaten and starved, kept in filthy conditions—treated worse than wild animals. A swift death might be more merciful."

"Then you must do what you can to save her." He patted my arm. "You have an advantage over Paulson and the others, my dear. You believe in your client's innocence. That passion may be all that stands between her and the scaffold. Or, as you have pointed out, perhaps an even worse fate."

It was almost midnight and I was sitting up in bed combing through legal volumes when I heard a soft knock on my door. A moment later, Samuel poked his head in.

"I saw your light," he explained.

I sat up straighter. "Come in. I was hoping to speak to you."

He entered quietly, closing the door behind him. "George told me about the stolen items they found in Fowler's rooms." He sat in the chair facing my bed. "That can't help your client's case."

"It was devastating news," I said, and went on to recount the meeting that afternoon, ending with Paulson's decision to plead insanity. "It makes me wonder what else Annjenett hasn't told me."

Samuel studied me seriously. "Sarah, be honest. Do you still think she's innocent?"

I didn't answer immediately. Just moments before, in the silence of my room, I'd asked myself the same question. Had my own arrogance—my need to be proven right about Annjenett—rendered me incapable of an unbiased opinion? After a great deal of what I hoped was candid introspection, I'd decided that it had not.

"I know it looks black, but I don't think I could be so mistaken in my judgment. Besides, she deserves to have at least one person believe in her." I closed the law book I had borrowed from Papa's library. "I could use some good news, Samuel. Tell me you discovered something useful about Hanaford and his partners."

"There's not a lot to report, I'm afraid." He crossed one neatly creased pant leg over the other. I smiled, wondering how my brother did it. Even after an evening out on the town, he looked as fresh and handsome as when he'd left the house. "The newspapers are full of stories about the four partners over the years, but I found nothing that's likely to help your client's case. After they returned from Nevada, Wylde went to Harvard, while Broughton attended Yale University. Hanaford and Mills used their newfound wealth to start businesses, and eventually made more money than their better-educated friends. Along the way, I'm sure they collected their share of enemies, but I came across no dealings so hostile they might lead to murder."

He paused, as if taking mental inventory. "Let's see. Ah, yes, here's an interesting piece of chimera. You knew Hanaford was a client of Shepard's firm. But did you know his three partners are also represented by your new employer?"

"No, I didn't," I said, sitting up straighter. Several possible ways to use this information instantly sprang to mind, all of them risky, one or two probably unethical. None, however, daunting enough to put me off trying.

"You've done very well, big brother," I told him earnestly. "I have no idea where any of this will lead, but it's a start."

My brother shifted in his seat but didn't get up.

"What is it?" I asked.

"I've given this a lot of thought, Sarah, and I think you might want to stop insisting that the two murders are connected."

"Why? I'm sure they are."

"I know. But it might do your client more harm than good if the police decide to agree with you."

Confusion must have registered on my face because he leaned forward and lowered his voice.

"I see this hasn't occurred to you. But just think, Sarah. We know Mrs. Hanaford had nothing to do with Mills's death be-cause she was arrested early the evening he was killed. Fowler, on the other hand, wasn't taken in by the police until several hours later."

I stared at my brother. "Are you suggesting Peter Fowler might have killed Rufus Mills?"

"I'm saying it's something you need to consider. Hanaford and Mills were powerful men; City Hall is under a great deal of pres-sure to solve their murders. If the police can't come up with a sus-pect for Mills's killing soon, they may decide it's in their best interests to connect the two crimes after all. It won't take them long to realize that Fowler had the opportunity to kill Mills as well as Hanaford. And he's already in custody. What a tidy way to wrap up both murders at the same time."

"Wait a minute!" I objected. "You just agreed that Annjenett couldn't have had anything to do with Mills's death."

"Not physically, perhaps, but she might be charged as an accessory. The authorities could argue that she helped plan both murders. When she was arrested before the second crime could be carried out, Fowler went ahead and committed the murder himself."

"But why? What motive could they have for killing Mills? Annjenett might have met Rufus through her husband, but it seems unlikely that Peter Fowler could have known him. They hardly traveled in the same social circles."

"I agree, Sarah. I'm merely pointing out the dangers in that line of reasoning. It might turn on you."

"Yes," I said slowly, still trying to absorb the idea that Annjenett might, however improbably, be accused of not just one murder, but two.

"What do you know about Fowler, by the way?" he asked.

"Frustratingly little. He's a competent actor and I'm sure Annjenett's deeply in love with him. Neither of which precludes the man from being a cold-blooded killer. We know from George that the police had to wait in Fowler's rooms until two in the morning the night Mills was murdered, which begs the question, where was he that night? More specifically, where was he at the time the crime was committed?"

"I can help with the earlier portion of the evening," Samuel offered. "For the past two months, Fowler's been appearing in *The Beaux Stratagem* at the California Theater. I saw the play myself last week, and with the intermissions it ran about three hours. The night Mills was killed, the evening performance started at eight o'clock. So we know where he was until at least eleven."

"The police seem to think Mills was killed sometime after midnight," I said thoughtfully. "The California Theater is on Bush Street—about half an hour's walk to Chinatown, wouldn't you say? Which means Fowler would have had ample time to make his way there and commit the murder."

"Depending, of course, on what he did after the show."

"Yes," I agreed, soberly. "That's what we have to find out. And as I said, we can't be certain Fowler even knew Rufus Mills. But if he can account for his whereabouts between the final curtain and the time he was arrested, it will be a moot point."

"And if he has no alibi?"

I pulled a face at Samuel. He was right, of course. I had to tread carefully.

"All right," I said briskly. "We'll start at the beginning and reassess our plan as we go along."

"This may not be as easy as you think."

"Nothing about this case is easy, Samuel," I groaned. "But we have to try. Everyone else has already given up—even the men Annjenett is counting on to defend her."

My brother looked worried. "I wonder if you realize what you're taking on, Sarah. The police have amassed a great deal of damaging evidence against Mrs. Hanaford. Convincing them that they're wrong isn't going to be easy. I know you don't want to hear this, but the truth is, it doesn't look good for your client."

I shivered and pulled my robe more closely about my shoulders. Suddenly I felt chilled and incredibly weary. I wanted nothing more than to sink beneath my covers and let sleep silence my mind as well as my fears.

"You're right, Samuel," I said with a sigh. "I don't like to hear it. On the other hand, I'm not as naive as you seem to think. I'm well aware that this is probably going to be an uphill battle."

"And no matter what I say you won't give up." He smiled ruefully. "But when have you ever given up—even as a little girl with three big brothers who ganged up on you?"

He leaned over and patted my hand. "Get some sleep, little sister. Something tells me you're going to need it."

CHAPTER FIVE

I was shocked by Annjenett's appearance as she was led into the courtroom for her arraignment. Her face was drained of color and the hands she held clenched in front of her plain woolen gown were visibly trembling. How many more days of this could she endure, I wondered? Because she was accused of a capital offence, I knew it was unlikely we would be able to get her released on bail. Still, I prayed for a miracle—anything, however unlikely, that would allow her to return home that very day.

On the other side of the room, Annjenett's father, Thomas Cooke, sat alone, face drawn, eyes fearful. He seemed oblivious to the curious onlookers crowding the courtroom, staring fixedly at the door where his daughter had suddenly appeared. The unpardonable act of marrying her off to settle a debt notwithstanding, I couldn't help but feel sorry for the man. He seemed to have aged ten years since I last saw him, and the love he bore his only child was clearly etched on his ravaged face.

Robert Campbell and I sat at the defense table with Augustus

Paulson. Despite a game attempt to tame his unruly hair—and dress in what was obviously a new morning coat and gray trousers—the volatile young attorney still looked as out of place in the courtroom as an elephant at a tea party. He'd given me a brief greeting, then steadfastly refrained from looking in my direction. Benjamin Wylde completed our defense team; he sat directly behind us in the area reserved for spectators.

As Annjenett's case was called, a guard ushered her to our table. After a brief, painful look at her father, she came to stand between Mr. Paulson and myself. Her icy fingers sought mine and held on for dear life as the judge read aloud the charge of murder in the first degree. When he asked for her plea, she was forced to repeat "Not guilty" twice before the court could hear her reply.

The entire affair was over almost before it began. The prosecution presented a strong case against granting bail and, despite Paulson's impassioned arguments, the judge concurred, banging his gavel to indicate the hearing was at an end. I barely had time to embrace Annjenett's thin shoulders and pledge my continued support before, head bowed and looking even more miserable than when she'd entered the courtroom, the young widow was given a brief moment to embrace her father, then led back into the wretched bowels of the city jail.

There was little time to talk with Paulson, either, as he was due to meet with other clients. His smiling assurance that all had gone as expected did little to hearten me. Nor did his opinion that, because of our planned insanity defense, the stolen articles found in Fowler's room would have little impact on our case. The day before, Annjenett had broken down and confessed it had been her idea for Peter to take the items so the crime might look like burglary, a strategy, I thought, that hardly sounded like the ravings of a mad woman.

It was just after ten o'clock when I caught a horsecar to Clay and Kearny Streets. Because of my preoccupation with Annjenett's case, this would be my first full day at the law firm, and there was much to be done before I could settle into my new office. Furthermore, I was anxious to carry out the mission I'd conceived after my late-night talk with Samuel.

I hadn't expected an enthusiastic greeting from my new colleagues, nor was I disappointed. Hubert Perkins, the nervous clerk who, as usual, lay in wait by the door, tried to intercept me, but I resolutely swept past him and down the hallway to the room that was to be my office.

I was delighted to find Joseph Shepard away for the morning. I was also relieved to note that Mr. Campbell had not yet returned from Annjenett's hearing.

Upon reaching my assigned storage closet—it would be pretentious to call it more than that—I examined the grubby interior with dismay. But not one to procrastinate, I rolled up my sleeves, pried open the room's two small windows with a broom handle, and began to scrub.

Two hours later, with the less than eager help of several clerks I had conscripted into service, the room was finally clean, though well short of hospitable. Taking stock, I decided that window curtains, some pictures on the barren walls, and perhaps a vase or two of flowers would at least make the place tolerable. I've long held the belief that tasteful, uncluttered surroundings are essential to foster a productive mind. In this case, I'd have to be satisfied with uncluttered. Good taste and this room were mutually exclusive.

As it turned out, my timing was perfect. Joseph Shepard had not yet returned to the office, and I was relieved to see that Campbell's cubicle was still unoccupied. Now that my corps of helpers had scurried off before I could find more work for them to do, no one exhibited the least interest in the newest and sole female employee of the firm.

Leaving my office, I made my way as unobtrusively as possible down the hall, stopping at each door until I found the one I was seeking. In a room hardly larger than my own were a number of old, very dusty file cabinets. Slipping inside, I closed the door and quickly set about my task.

I knew that what I was doing was unethical. I had no reason—no official reason, that is—for being in this room, much less tampering with its highly confidential contents. Unofficially, I was prepared to stifle my conscience and take whatever steps necessary to save my client.

The esteem in which the city of San Francisco held Joseph Shepard's firm was borne out by the vast number of files I was forced to sort through. Samuel's discovery that all four mining partners used the same law firm had given me the idea, of course. The knowledge that their personal files were housed under one roof made searching for the records too great a temptation to resist.

I started with Hanaford's file. I'd already read the copy of the will in his home safe, but the folder I now held was thick with other documents. Everything seemed disappointingly ordinary until, at the very bottom of the file, I came upon several papers listing the holdings of Hanaford's estate. The final entry brought me up short. It read: *Fifty thousand dollars in trust at First National Bank, 850 Clay Street, San Francisco.* Intrigued, I examined the firm's copy of Hanaford's will. I was right! There was no mention of a fifty thousand dollar trust—and this I found most peculiar—held at a bank other than his own!

I dug through more files until I found Rufus Mills's folder, which also contained his last will and testament. My heart skipped a beat. There, again entered last, was the same notation for fifty thousand dollars held in trust at First National Bank! My thoughts flew to the remaining partners. Was it possible they had similar funds?

It didn't take long to find Senator Broughton's file. It was just as I'd suspected! He, too, had fifty thousand dollars in an account at First National. I had just located Wylde's folder when a voice boomed, "What in damnation do you think you're doing?"

I was so startled I nearly dropped the file in my hand. Behind me in the open doorway, tousled red hair brushing the top of the wood frame, stood Robert Campbell, eyes glaring out accusingly from beneath fiercely knitted brows.

"Come in and close the door," I snapped, annoyed he had caught me unawares. "And for heaven's sake, lower your voice!"

His scowl deepened and, typically, the obstinate man refused to budge. "I asked what you're doing in here?" he repeated in what was, to my relief, a slightly lower decibel level. "Don't you know these files are confidential?"

"The only thing *I know*, Mr. Campbell, is that Annjenett Hanaford is languishing in city jail, while the very men who are supposed to be championing her cause blithely accept that she's guilty of first-degree murder."

"And what do you think you can accomplish?" he asked in a voice heavy with sarcasm.

"I can try to find out which of Mr. Hanaford's clients or acquaintances wished to see him dead, and who among them has no alibi for the night he was killed." I waved Hanaford's file. "I can also attempt to discover why the owner of one of the largest financial institutions in the city would keep a fortune in someone else's bank."

This brought the troublesome man up short. Without so much as a by-your-leave, he yanked the papers out of my hand and scanned them skeptically, stopping at the final, puzzling entry.

"There must be a reasonable explanation for this."

"Oh, really? Is there also a reasonable explanation why Rufus Mills, Senator Broughton, and—" I rifled through Wylde's file, then gave a little cry of triumph—"Benjamin Wylde should have matching deposits at the *same* bank?"

"I neither know, nor do I care. It certainly can't have anything to do with Mrs. Hanaford's case."

"We won't know that until I've had time to investigate. The logical place to start, of course, is with Cornelius Hanaford, since his account at a competing bank is—"

"Investigate! When will you get it through your head that Mrs. Hanaford's case is none of your confounded business? Furthermore—"

It was as well that I'd tuned him out, for as he blathered on, I heard footsteps in the hall, then the sound of Joseph Shepard's voice. I grabbed the file from Campbell's hand and threw it, along with the others, into the nearest file cabinet. I had just slammed the drawer shut and gone to stand by the startled attorney when the senior partner appeared, Perkins, the annoying clerk from the front office, at his heels. Shepard scowled.

"So you *are* here, Miss Woolson." His voice and his gaze were frosty. "May I ask what you're doing in this room?"

I sensed Campbell's quick intake of breath, but before he could speak, I gave the dour senior attorney my brightest smile.

"Mr. Campbell graciously offered to give me a tour of the office. This is an impressive collection of records."

"It is a *confidential* collection, Miss Woolson. No one is allowed in this room without permission from one of the partners." His glare went to the Scot. "You should know better, Campbell."

The younger man colored but I rushed in before he could reply.

"Please, it's entirely my fault. In my enthusiasm to see everything, I'm afraid I opened this door by mistake."

Shepard glared at my fuming accomplice but had little choice but to accept my apology. To do otherwise would make him seem churlish if the story reached my father. He forced a smile which, unfortunately, made him resemble a man with a toothache.

"See that it doesn't happen again," he told me sharply, then turned to the junior attorney. "I want to see you in my office, Campbell. Now!"

Before he could leave, I reminded the senior partner that the money from Annjenett's separate account was due that day. When he protested that Mrs. Hanaford's incarceration prevented him from carrying out this promise, I presented the note Annjenett had signed in her cell, assigning me power of attorney. His cheeks flamed and for a moment I feared we were in for one of his tiresome outbursts. Then he seemed to realize the futility of further argument and ungraciously gave in to my request.

When I left the office some half hour later, Mr. Shepard's bank draft for ten thousand dollars was safely tucked inside my reticule. I was understandably anxious to deposit it as quickly as possible and made directly for Hanaford's bank. There was, however, a second reason for my visit: I hoped for a word with Eban Potter. Perhaps he would know why his late employer had kept money at a rival bank. In this matter, however, I was disappointed.

"Are you certain of your information?" he asked, obviously taken aback. "I can't imagine why Mr. Hanaford would do such a thing."

"Nor can I," I admitted. "As you were old friends, I hoped he might have spoken of it to you."

" 'Friends' is perhaps too broad a term, Miss Woolson. While it's true we'd known one another for some time, we belonged to vastly different social circles and rarely met outside the bank. My employer was not in the habit of taking me into his confidence."

"I see," I said, finding it hard to hide my frustration.

After I thanked Eban Potter and took my leave of the bank, I decided to board a horsecar for Annjenett's Nob Hill home. I realized, of course, that the police had already searched the house—more than once, according to my client—but I wasn't necessarily looking for the same thing.

Fortunately, the widow's butler remembered me and readily admitted me to the mansion. Poor Beecher was distraught. Not only had his master been brutally murdered, but his mistress stood accused of the crime. He informed me that two of the maids had already given notice, and he wasn't sure how long he could persuade the other servants to remain. Although frantic with worry, his loyalty hadn't wavered.

"Mrs. Hanaford is the gentlest of women," he said fervently. "I will never believe she could harm anyone, especially given the way Mr. Hanaford was—" His face reddened.

"I agree, Beecher. In fact, that is why I'm here."

I threw open the door to Hanaford's study. The room was dark and had an unpleasant, musty odor. Beecher must have noticed the faint wrinkling of my nose.

"The maids refuse to enter the room," he explained by way of apology. "The situation with the servants being what it is, I decided it was best not to press the issue."

"Actually, I'm pleased the room has been left undisturbed. It may make it easier to find something the police missed."

His eyes lit with hope. "If only you could, Miss Woolson. Please, is there anything I can do? Perhaps some refreshments?"

I thanked the butler, saying that a cup of coffee would not be unwelcome. When he left, I threw open the heavy draperies to let in what remained of the afternoon sun. The layers of dust covering the furnishings confirmed that nothing had been touched since Hanaford's death.

I had just settled myself behind the mahogany desk when Beecher returned with a coffee tray and some small sandwiches. He seemed startled to see me calmly ensconced in the very chair where his master had been brutally murdered. Happily, I am not squeamish about such things. I thanked him for the refreshments and the man quietly withdrew, leaving me to my work.

Nibbling on one of the excellent sandwiches, I opened the first desk drawer. Hanaford had been methodical and neat, but the contents told me little about the man. What were his interests? His passions? His goals? His secrets? What fire had driven him to establish one of the city's largest banks? More importantly, who were his enemies?

When I'd finished examining the desk, I was no closer to answering these questions than when I'd begun. I sank back in the chair, frustrated.

I was wondering where to look next when I heard a loud knock on the front door and Beecher's muted footsteps as he passed through the foyer to answer. The booming voice demanding to be admitted was unmistakable. Robert Campbell! A moment later, there was a quick knock on the study door before it opened a crack.

"There's a—person to see you, Miss." Beecher announced, sounding distressed. "If you'd like, I could send him away."

Interesting as it might have been to watch the elderly, slightly built butler actually carry out this threat, the impatient attorney gave him no opportunity to try. Without waiting for a reply, he barged into the room like a charging bull.

"Thank you, Beecher," I told the startled butler. "Mr. Campbell is a colleague."

Somewhat dubiously, Beecher withdrew, but I noticed with amusement that he left the door slightly ajar behind him.

"What are you doing here?" I demanded of my brash visitor.

"I've come to prevent you from making a complete fool of yourself, and the law firm along with you," he replied in a rude voice.

"How did you know where to find me?"

"Once you'd gotten it into your head that Hanaford and his partners kept secret bank accounts, I knew you wouldn't leave it alone until you'd made laughingstocks of us all. Anyway, you all but announced where you planned to begin this wild goose chase."

Suddenly the real reason he was here occurred to me. "Joseph Shepard sent you to spy on me, didn't he?"

For a moment, I thought he was going to deny my accusation. Instead, he swore beneath his breath.

"You don't think I'd waste my time coming here on my own, do you? I have better things to do than play nursemaid to a supercilious female who thinks that by calling herself a lawyer she can set about saving the world."

"If that's all you have to say, Mr. Campbell, I suggest you get on with your pressing business and allow me to save the world in peace."

I lowered my head and once again pulled out the first desk drawer, this time running fingers along the top and sides. Nothing. I tried this with the second drawer, at the same time scanning the bottom of the first drawer to see if anything had been taped there. Again nothing.

"What in god's name are you looking for, woman?" Campbell asked, his r's rolling with Scottish indignity.

I ignored this latest burst of profanity. In fact, I was endeavoring to ignore the man altogether. When I didn't answer, he stalked around the desk to stand behind me.

"What the devil gives you the right to search this house in the first place?"

Really, enough was enough! "Not that it's any of your business, but Mrs. Hanaford has appointed me to handle her affairs while she's incarcerated. Now, I'd appreciate it if you would leave. You may inform Mr. Shepard that I neither require, nor do I appreciate, being spied upon."

With this dismissal, I pulled out the bottom drawer and ran my hand around the inside circumference. I felt it at once. Somehow during my initial inspection, it hadn't registered that this drawer was six to eight inches shallower than the others. With a cry of satisfaction, I scooted my chair back in order to pull the drawer out to its full extension. In doing so, I inadvertently ran the chair's casters over Campbell's foot, causing him to howl as if he'd been run over by a train.

"Oh, are you still here?" I asked without looking up.

"Of course I'm here, you aggravating woman!" he spat, rubbing his afflicted toes. I watched as he mentally measured the drawer's depth in relation to the side of the desk. "What have you found?"

I didn't bother to answer. The drawer seemed to be stuck. I yanked and pulled at it, but to no avail.

"Oh for the love of heaven! Here."

As easily as if we were made of feathers, he lifted aside the chair, with me in it, then hunkered down in front of the jammed drawer. He stuck his hand inside and deftly jiggled the compartment back and forth until he was able to extract a piece of paper wedged in the back. Once this was out, the drawer slid smoothly forward, allowing us to see the hidden compartment. How to get it open was another matter.

"I don't see a lock," I observed, bending over his shoulder.

"There must be a hidden mechanism." With surprisingly gentle fingers, he felt along the front and sides of the niche. He must have accidentally triggered the device because suddenly the front panel of the compartment sprang open.

"It's just a lot of papers," he said, sounding disappointed.

"What did you expect? Any real valuables would be kept in the safe."

I reached past him and lifted out a handful of documents. As I did so, I uncovered several magazines featuring lurid pictures of unclad women on the covers. Of course I had heard of such publications but I had never actually seen one. I must admit I was tempted to peruse one, just to see what all the fuss was about. Before I could act upon this impulse, however, Campbell's huge hand reached inside the drawer, scooped up the lot and tossed them, face down, on the floor behind the desk.

"What else is inside?" he asked shortly.

I was amused to see that his face had colored, and stifled a derisive remark. Commenting on his embarrassment would only invite howls of denial that I was in no mood to endure. Instead, I looked through the papers, finding nothing of interest until I came upon a small square of cardboard that I took to be a business card. Upon closer inspection, I realized the card contained no writing. Instead, it pictured four pick axes—such as those used by miners—grouped together, handles upright. Even stranger, the head of a devil had been drawn above the axes, a grinning, malevolent-looking Satan wearing, of all things, a black mask over its eyes.

Taking the card from my hand, Campbell studied it then handed it back. "It's obviously some kind of joke."

"Perhaps," I said thoughtfully.

A small black ledger lay at the bottom of the compartment. Thumbing through it, I realized it contained evidence that at least some of Cornelius Hanaford's business dealings had not been strictly on the up-and-up.

Campbell scanned the book, then tossed it aside in disgust.

"So now we know that Hanaford liked ribald magazines and that he altered his books. Neither of which suggests that anyone besides his wife and her paramour were responsible for his death."

I wasn't ready to give up so easily. As I went through the rest of the documents, I discovered, close to the bottom, a folded sheet of yellowing paper. Reading it, my breath caught in my throat.

"What is it?" Campbell demanded.

Silently, I handed him the paper, then watched as he read the single paragraph.

"It appears to be some kind of joint financial arrangement—a tontine," he said at last.

"Yes, that's just what it is," I said with excitement. "Hanaford and his partners each deposited twenty-five thousand dollars at the First National Bank soon after their return from Virginia City. According to this contract, the accumulated proceeds of the fund go to the last surviving member of the group. Don't you see? This explains the mysterious pages we found appended to each of the men's last will and testament—and why the currency wasn't kept in Hanaford's bank. The tontine money had to be kept in a neutral account. Over the past twenty years, the original investment has more than doubled."

I allowed my words to hang in the air, convinced that even he would recognize the significance of this discovery. Instead, the infuriating man just stared at me.

"Damn it all! I can see the wheels turning in that devious head of yours. You want me to believe that one of the most successful men in San Francisco would brutally murder two of his colleagues in order to be the final survivor in a tontine."

"The account now exceeds two hundred thousand dollars! Men have killed for far less than that."

"Not men like this!" His sea blue eyes blazed. "Think what you are suggesting. Of the two remaining partners, one is a respected attorney, the other a California State Senator. The idea that either of these men could be a murderer is utter balderdash!"

Realizing the futility of trying to reason with a man who wouldn't recognize a motive for murder if it bit him on the nose, I silently slipped the tontine agreement into my briefcase. Outside the study window, the sky had transformed into a vivid palette of red, orange and yellow as the sun sank over the Bay. It was time to leave.

"Where are you off to now?" he demanded, as I got to my feet.

"Why do you want to know? So you can report back to Shepard?"

"Blast it, woman, why must you be so mule-headed?"

"Why must you be so obtuse?"

In my irritation, I accidentally knocked over the papers I had placed on the desktop. Among them was the crumpled sheet my disagreeable companion had dislodged from the hidden compartment while prying it open. I picked it up and read it with interest.

Campbell was watching me warily. "Now what?"

"I'm not sure. It's a note arranging a meeting between Mr. Hanaford and someone called Li Ying. Hanaford is instructed to bring 'the payment' to the Little Red Cafe on Jackson Street." I looked up. "What do you suppose he means by 'the payment'?"

Campbell's arms flew into the air. "More intrigue! The next

thing I know, you'll claim Hanaford was murdered because he was a spy for the Afghanistan government. Are there no limits to what you'll concoct to support your outlandish theories?"

"Don't be ridiculous. I didn't manufacture this note. Nor did I invent the tontine drawn up by the four partners."

I wasted no time responding to his rude retort. Placing Li Ying's note inside my briefcase, I rang for Beecher and instructed him to lock Mr. Hanaford's study. I also promised him sufficient funds to cover household expenses until Mrs. Hanaford was home once again. This seemed to cheer the unhappy man considerably. Campbell mumbled something, but neither the butler nor I paid him the least notice.

Outside the mansion I hailed a hansom cab, leaving the ill-mannered lawyer to find his own way home in the gathering dusk.

That evening I was to accompany Charles and Celia to the theater, escorted by one of my brother's colleagues, Dr. William Ferris. Dr. Ferris and I had, on several previous occasions, formed a foursome with my brother and his wife. Like Charles, William Ferris is a dedicated healer, a talented surgeon with a brilliant future. Unfortunately, he is also a colossal bore. I have Celia to thank for the good doctor's attentions. She's a hopeless matchmaker; he is, I fear, but the latest in a series of gentlemen she has lured to my reluctant door.

On this occasion, however, I wasn't ungrateful for the invitation. Largely at my urging, we had settled upon seeing *The Beaux Stratagem* at the California Theater. It was, of course, the play in which Peter Fowler had been performing until the previous Saturday, the night of Rufus Mills's murder. I hadn't told the others my reasons for this choice, at least not yet. In truth I was looking forward to the production, as it was my favorite of George Farquhar's delightful comedies. Altogether, it seemed a fortuitous arrangement.

We arrived well before curtain time. The theater, which was built by W. C. Ralston, wasn't new. The year before, it had undergone renovations, including the installation of electric lights. Now, magnificent chandeliers glittered above our heads, still enough of a novelty to cause a stir among the theatergoers. I was intrigued by this new invention, but wasn't sure I liked the way this lighting threw everything into such a harsh glare. Perhaps I'm a romantic, but I rather favor the warm glow of candlelight, a preference that I suspect is shared by other women who have had an opportunity to experience both methods of illumination at first hand.

After settling into our seats, I studied my program. I was pleased to read that Michael Carstairs was playing Aimwell, a gentleman of broken fortune. A loose paper inserted into the program announced that an actor I didn't recognize would play Archer, Aimwell's co-lead, normally acted by Peter Fowler. No reason was given for this substitution.

"Look," Celia said, breaking into my thoughts. "There are Mr. and Mrs. Stanford."

She inclined her head toward a box to our right where Leland Stanford, the railroad mogul and former governor of California, and his wife Jane were taking their seats.

"Frederick will be disappointed he didn't come tonight," said Charles, also noting the Stanfords' arrival. "He's been trying for weeks to arrange a meeting with Mr. Stanford."

"He was devastated when they didn't make an appearance at his dinner party," Celia put in.

"I imagine he was," I said dryly. I knew my eldest brother was desperate to impress Stanford, who could be an invaluable stepping-stone to his entrance into politics. Secretly, I hoped the ex-governor had better sense than to allow Frederick inside that particular door.

But I had little time to speculate on Leland Stanford's political savvy, as my eye was caught by a man entering the box adjacent to the former governor.

"What is it?" Celia asked, sensing me stiffen.

"That man in the box next to the Stanfords'," I replied. "That's Benjamin Wylde, one of Mr. Hanaford's former partners."

"Ah, yes," Charles said, following our gaze. "The executor of Cornelius Hanaford's estate."

"I've been following the Hanaford case in the newspapers," Dr. Ferris said. "I've never met his widow, of course, but judging by her photograph in the *Evening Bulletin,* I find it difficult to believe she could have committed such a brutal murder."

"Actually, Sarah not only believes Mrs. Hanaford to be innocent," Celia offered with ill-concealed pride, "she's acting as the widow's attorney."

My escort's mouth fell open. "I beg your pardon?"

"Mrs. Hanaford has asked Sarah to represent her on some personal matters related to her late husband's estate," Charles explained, obviously wishing the subject hadn't been broached.

My escort regarded me in surprise. "I was aware of your interest in the law, Miss Woolson, but I never imagined it to be a serious avocation."

Undoubtedly alarmed by the doctor's expression of distaste, Celia tactfully broke in. "Excuse me, Sarah," she said, nodding toward Wylde's box. "Do you know the identity of Mr. Wylde's companion? She looks very young—and very beautiful."

Drawing up my opera glasses, I saw that Celia was right. The young woman sitting beside the dour attorney could not yet be twenty and was strikingly lovely. Her mass of honey-gold hair curled in soft, becoming ringlets about her oval face. She neither wore, nor required, any jewelry save for exquisite diamond-drop earrings that glittered beneath the dazzling electric chandelier. Despite her youth, the girl's features were well defined and of a classic line. But it was Wylde's expression I found most surprising. As they spoke over their programs, he looked at his companion with a tenderness so unlike his usual surliness that for a moment I feared I had mistaken his identity.

Celia broke into my thoughts. "Do you think she's his wife?"

"I don't think he's married," I said, continuing to study the girl.

"I don't remember seeing her before," Celia mused. "I doubt I could forget anyone so exquisite."

I had no time to reply as the house lights dimmed and the drop curtain—also new and depicting the majesty of Yosemite Park—rose. As it did, I forgot Benjamin Wylde and his mysterious companion and felt the familiar tingle of anticipation I always experience as a play is about to begin.

Tonight, I wasn't disappointed. Farquhar's writing, as usual, was crisp and witty, the acting first-rate. Living in the city, I appreciated the play's rural setting, but I was especially interested in the playwright's concern, subtly woven into the comic fabric of the play, with the social and moral problems of his day, issues that continue to plague us even now. As one character so aptly expresses, "There is no scandal like rags, nor any crime so shameful as poverty."

Once or twice I caught my escort glancing at me with an expression of curiosity and frank disapproval. I smiled to myself. Somehow I didn't think I would be forced to endure many more dreary evenings in the good doctor's company.

As we stood in the lounge during the first intermission, I knew the time had come to tell my brother the real reason I'd suggested we attend the California Theater. Dr. Ferris was at the bar ordering whiskeys for Charles and himself while Celia and I sipped cold lemonades. Taking advantage of his absence, I began, "Charles, you've treated Mr. Carstairs, haven't you?" I referred, of course, to the play's lead actor.

"For a fever, yes." He looked at me curiously. "Why?"

"I thought perhaps he might receive you, and your guests of course, backstage after the play?"

I caught Celia's eye and she quickly put in, "What a splendid idea. Do try, Charles."

"Try what?" Dr. Ferris asked, returning from the bar.

"We're going to go backstage after the play," Celia told him. "Isn't that exciting?"

Dr. Ferris seemed to consider this a somewhat dubious honor, but he had little choice but to go along with it. As we returned to our seats for Act Two, I whispered my thanks in Celia's ear.

"It's nothing," she said with a conspiratorial smile. "I can hardly wait to hear what you are up to."

The remainder of the play was as delightful as the first act, and the theater echoed with applause as our foursome made its way backstage. Michael Carstairs, it turned out, was delighted to greet my brother, who had treated him at a time when the actor was down on his luck and unable to adequately pay for Charles's services. The actor gave us an animated tour of the backstage area, introducing us to other cast members and explaining the use of various lights and mechanical contraptions.

"If I'm not mistaken, you appeared in a production of *Henry V* at the Tripoli Theater several years ago," I said as we ended the tour in Carstairs's dressing room. His Chinese manservant waited patiently at the dressing table, a jar of cold cream in hand to remove his master's makeup. After the actor took his seat, the man placed a cloth around his neck and adroitly set to work.

Carstairs looked pleased. "I'm surprised you remember. I had a very small role."

"It's not the size of the part that matters," I said, sincere in the compliment. "It's the quality of the performance—which, in this case, was very fine indeed."

The actor's reflection beamed back at me from the dressing table mirror. "Thank you, Miss Woolson. It's kind of you to say."

"If I remember correctly," I went on casually, "Peter Fowler also appeared in that production." My brother gave me a surprised look but held his tongue.

"Your memory is remarkable, Miss Woolson," said the actor.

"I was distressed to hear about Mr. Fowler's recent difficulties," Celia put in, ignoring Charles's censoring look.

Michael Carstairs's face darkened as his manservant removed the last traces of pancake makeup. "It's preposterous," he said. "The police have gotten hold of the little end of the horn if they think Peter could have killed that woman's husband."

"You weren't with Mr. Fowler, then, when he was arrested?" I asked the actor innocently, knowing full well that he wasn't.

"No. After the play, we held a party in honor of Miss Long's birthday—she's the actress who plays Dorinda in the production. Unfortunately, Peter had other plans and left directly after the final curtain. I read about his arrest in the papers the next morning. It was an awful shock, I can tell you."

"I wonder if the police have notified his family?" I said.

"You know, I don't think he has any family," Carstairs replied. "I seem to remember Peter mentioning that he's an orphan."

"That's unfortunate," Celia said with genuine regret. "At a time like this, a family would be a great comfort."

This seemed to prick the actor's conscience. "I've been meaning to visit Peter, but there never seems time." He looked shamefacedly at Celia. "That is a poor excuse, isn't it? You've made me realize my lack of Christian charity, Mrs. Woolson. Rest assured I will make time to visit Peter tomorrow."

Celia flushed. "Please, Mr. Carstairs, I didn't mean to imply—"

"Do you know where Mr. Fowler went after Saturday night's performance?" I cut in, eager to get the actor back on track.

I had caught Dr. Ferris darting a pointed look at my brother, obviously displeased by my bold behavior. While I cared little for his opinion, I knew his impatience would provoke my brother to leave. Out of the corner of my eye, I saw Carstairs's manservant start to lay out the actor's street clothes.

"I have no idea where he went after the show." The actor looked at me curiously. "Why? Does it matter?"

"I just wondered if you knew him to frequent Chinatown?"

There was no mistaking the actor's surprise. "Chinatown? What a strange notion. I have no idea."

"He never mentioned a man named Li Ying?" I pressed.

Behind me, I heard the Chinese manservant's soft intake of breath. When I turned to look at him, I caught a brief flash of what I can only describe as raw fear cross his previously stoic face. A moment later, he'd regained his composure and once again seemed disinterested in our conversation. Yet I was sure the mention of Li Ying's name had terrified the man.

"I've never heard the name," Carstairs said. "But my visits to San Francisco are brief. Aside from other actors, my circle of acquaintances is unfortunately limited."

Dr. Ferris's patience was clearly at an end. Charles apparently agreed. I could see by my brother's expression that I had overstepped even his generous boundaries of propriety.

"You'll have to excuse my sister, Mr. Carstairs," he said. "This is a poor way to repay your hospitality." His expression brooked no argument. "Sarah, it's time for us to go."

Dr. Ferris agreed with alacrity. "Yes, we've kept you too long as it is, Mr. Carstairs."

"Thank you for showing us what goes on behind the scenes," Celia told the actor with a dazzling smile.

"Not at all," Carstairs protested. "It's been my pleasure."

Realizing there was nothing further to be learned from the actor, even if I had the time to try, I added my own thanks and we departed the theater for a light supper before bringing the evening to a close.

CHAPTER SIX

I'm normally an early riser, but after a fitful night's sleep, I awoke later than usual the next morning. I hurried downstairs, just in time to catch Samuel as he was leaving the house.

"President Hayes arrives today," he said, then lowered his voice. "My editor wants me to write a piece about his visit. I'm sorry I can't stop to talk, but I'm already late."

I spied a brougham waiting in front of the house and made up my mind in an instant. "Wait, I'll go with you. Just let me fetch my hat and briefcase."

The cab made its way through morning traffic, already heavier than usual due to the arrival of the first United States' president to visit San Francisco. The city had been abuzz for weeks, arguing endlessly about how best to capitalize on such a historic occasion. In the end several events had been planned, preceded by a parade through the heart of the city by the Bay. Although it was not

Samuel's usual story, the honor of such an assignment demonstrated the newspaper's growing respect for him as a writer.

Outside the brougham, the sun had burned through the fog and the morning showed promise of becoming a splendid day. If nothing else, President Rutherford B. Hayes would see San Francisco in all its considerable glory.

I was too busy filling my brother in on the events of the previous day, however, to be concerned with the weather or even with visiting presidents. Succinctly, I told him about the partners' mysterious bank accounts, as well as their tontine agreement, then showed him the strange note I'd found jammed in the banker's desk.

"I thought you might have come across this Li Ying when you researched your Chinatown article last year."

He read the note with interest. "Anyone with more than a passing knowledge of Chinatown has heard of him. Li Ying is a very powerful tong lord."

"Tong lord?" I repeated. "You mean the leader of some kind of Chinese secret society?"

"In a way, yes. Originally, the tongs were set up as fraternal organizations to aid and protect newly arrived Chinese immigrants, as well as to set policies for the established Chinatown community. Unfortunately, over the years these groups have become increasingly competitive and violent. Li is generally considered the most powerful of all the tong lords. Some call him the God of the Golden Mountain."

"The Golden Mountain. Isn't that the name the Chinese use for San Francisco?"

"*Gum San Ta Fow*—Big City in the land of the Golden Hills."

I thought about this. I was aware of the recent burgeoning of crime in Chinatown. Thugs known as *bow how doy,* or hatchet men, banded together to create fighting tongs, utilizing blackmail, graft and murder to spread waves of terror throughout the district.

We were suddenly jostled as our driver swerved to avoid an open phaeton carrying three stylishly dressed ladies. I heard him swear something, then ease his horse back into an easy trot.

My brother looked amused. "What are you thinking, little sister? That a tong lord murdered Hanaford and Mills?"

"To be honest, Samuel, I don't know what to think. I'm just examining all the possibilities."

"No matter how improbable?"

"At this point, no lead is too unlikely to pursue. It would be helpful if I could speak to someone with an intimate knowledge of Chinatown, though. I don't suppose you know of such a person?"

He shot me a pointed look. "This is a dangerous business, Sarah. The *bow how doy* are ruthless. They wouldn't scruple to injure a white woman if they felt she threatened their power."

In light of subsequent events, I would have reason to regret not taking my brother's warning more to heart. At the time of our conversation, however, I felt confident that I'd heard enough about Chinatown, and the dark crimes rumored to be committed there, to comprehend the dangers involved. Foremost in my mind was the knowledge that a young woman's fate rested upon my ability to discover the truth. This was no time for weak resolve.

"But you do know someone who might be able to answer my questions?" I pressed on with well-meaning determination.

Samuel shook his head. "Against my better judgment, yes. A woman by the name of Margaret Culbertson runs a mission shelter on Sacramento Street. I've heard that she rescues young slave girls who've been illegally imported from China, sometimes from under the noses of their kidnappers. She gives them refuge at her mission house until they can either return to China or start a new life here. The stories of her exploits may be exaggerated, but even so, they're remarkable."

I was instantly struck by the valor and courage of such a woman. "She sounds like exactly the sort of person I'm looking for, Samuel. I'll pay her a visit this very morning."

He looked at me warily. "Promise you'll do nothing foolish."

"I'm after information. There's no need to be concerned."

He gave me a wry smile. "With you, Sarah, there's frequently reason for concern. I only wish I could go with you. If you could postpone your visit until tomorrow—"

"I'm sorry, Samuel, but this business can't wait. Whether or not Li Ying played a role in the two murders, I must follow every lead. And as quickly as possible."

With a final warning to be careful, my brother exited the brougham in front of city hall, whereupon I directed the driver to "China Street," as Sacramento Street was popularly known.

The ride took longer than usual due to heavy traffic, but we finally stopped in front of a nondescript red brick building perched on the side of one of the steepest hills on Sacramento Street. A sign above the door read: "Occidental Board Presbyterian Mission House." Farther up the hill loomed the mansions of Nob Hill, and I was struck by the contrast of such different worlds existing within a few blocks of one another.

As Samuel had already paid the driver, I got out of the cab and walked purposefully to the front door. It was opened by a very pretty Chinese girl in her late teens wearing traditional loose-fitting dark pants and a gray jacket. When I announced my desire to see Miss Culbertson, the girl smiled and invited me inside.

"Please, you sit," she said in broken English. "I get Mother."

She was gone before I could correct this mistake, for I was sure the girl had misunderstood me. A moment later, however, a tall, slender, middle-aged white woman appeared. Smiling at my confusion, this woman of obvious genteel refinement explained that she was known as "mother" to her rescued "daughters." She went on to tell me that the mission house had been founded some six years ago by the women of the Occidental Board, who were determined to provide a safe haven for the helpless victims of white slavery.

Miss Culbertson seated herself across from me in the pleasant, simply furnished chamber. The sun poured through an open window to illuminate several Chinese prints hanging on the walls. The highlight of the room, however, was an exquisite silk screen, delicately rendered in clear, brilliant colors.

Following my gaze, Miss Culbertson told me the screen had been a gift from a wealthy society matron whose treasured Chinese maid had been abducted in broad daylight from a city street not many blocks from her Nob Hill home. By a stroke of luck, Miss Culbertson had been able to locate the unfortunate girl and effect her rescue before she could be sold into white slavery.

At my look of disbelief, she explained that the men of Chinatown outnumbered the women by a ratio of more than thirty to one. Because of this disparity, there was a great demand for feminine companionship. Of the thousand or so Chinese women currently in San Francisco, at least half were "singsong girls," or residents of houses of ill fame located throughout the quarter. Many of these girls, some as young as eight or nine, had been kidnapped from their homeland or lured to San Francisco by deceitful promises of marriage or an education. After they were brought into the country—either by the use of false documentation or outright smuggling—they were sold into houses of prostitution. No Chinese woman, married or single, was safe, as evidenced by bold abductions carried out every day on the streets of Tangrenbu, or Port of the People of China.

Listening to this shocking narrative, I was overcome by a fury that such atrocities could go on in this day and age. When I demanded to know why the police had not put an end to this shameless situation, Miss Culbertson smiled at my naiveté.

"The police do not gladly enter Chinatown," she told me gently. "Nor do they involve themselves in its affairs unless it is absolutely necessary. Mayor Kalloch's administration is notorious for turning a blind eye or worse to the white slave trade. You'd be surprised by the number of public officials who share the profits from this despicable practice."

"But that's intolerable! There must be something we can do."

"I assure you, Miss Woolson, we're doing everything we can." She sighed, and I saw the weariness in her gray eyes and in the lines etched in her sensitive face. "It's not nearly as much as we might wish, but it is at least something."

I felt my face flush, belatedly realizing the criticism implied in my unfortunate choice of words. "Please forgive me. I didn't mean to devalue the vital work you accomplish."

"I know you didn't mean to offend. Most San Franciscans who hear about white slavery for the first time demand something be done. Unfortunately, the situation isn't that simple. Nor is its solution. Until the trade can be permanently stopped, we save as many poor souls as we can, one victim at a time." She smiled wearily. "Now, Miss Woolson, I assume you didn't call on me today for a lecture on corrupt politics. What may I do for you?"

Briefly I explained the reason for my visit. When I mentioned Li Ying's name, however, she frowned.

"You couldn't have chosen a more mysterious man to inquire

about, my dear. All I can tell you is that Li Ying is one of the most powerful and dangerous of all the tong lords."

"Surely something must be known about the man."

"Very little, I'm afraid. Now that I think about it, I've heard no rumors that he personally owns slave girls, although he may well be involved with one or more houses of ill repute."

I was struck by a sudden plan. Ignoring the possible dangers—or Samuel's reaction if he found out—I presented it to Miss Culbertson.

"Would it be possible for me to accompany you on a raid?"

She seemed taken aback. "My dear, are you sure you want to do such a thing? I always try to find at least one or two members of the police force brave enough to go with me, but even so, any raid is extremely risky. We're robbing the highbinders of valuable property, and they hate and resent us. They use whatever means at their disposal to stop us."

"Nevertheless, I should like to accompany you," I said, not allowing myself time for second thoughts.

"You must understand that I cannot guarantee your safety."

"I understand," I assured her. "And I promise to do nothing to jeopardize your mission. Please, will you take me?"

She studied me closely, her eyes so penetrating I had the uncomfortable feeling they could see right through me.

"I believe you possess the necessary nerve. And you don't appear frail or of a squeamish nature." She smiled. "All right then, Miss Woolson. As long as you're aware of the dangers, I'd be happy to have you accompany us on our next raid."

"Do you know when that will be?" I asked eagerly.

"I've received word of a young woman—a child actually—who is being held captive in Sullivan's Alley, one of the most treacherous bypasses of the quarter. I would prefer to help her tonight, but the situation is complicated. If all goes well, we will attempt to rescue her tomorrow night."

My pulse quickened as I realized my opportunity was to come so soon. "What time shall I be here?"

"If you haven't changed your mind, be at the mission by eleven-thirty. We'll leave promptly at midnight." She laughed. "You're quite remarkable, Miss Woolson. Most women of your gentle birth wouldn't even consider such an escapade."

"I assure you, Miss Culbertson," I said with heartfelt enthusiasm, "I relish the opportunity!"

We chatted for a few more moments, then I took my leave of this inspiring woman, promising to return the following night. In truth, the chance to visit Chinatown with an acknowledged expert was more than I had expected. Granted, it didn't guarantee I would learn anything more about the infamous Li Ying. But, I reasoned, any information I could glean about the district where Rufus Mills had met his death would be a step in the right direction.

Outside, there was a buzz of excitement as people hurried to line the streets in time for the parade. As I made my way through the crowd toward the California Line cable car, I debated where to go next. I would have to check on Peter Fowler, of course, but since I could think of no reason why he might want Rufus Mills dead, I decided to concentrate first on Hanaford's two remaining partners. Robert Campbell's arguments to the contrary, I remained convinced that two hundred thousand dollars was more than ample reason for wishing someone dead.

Of these two men, I least trusted—no, I must be honest, least cared for—Benjamin Wylde. Had anyone bothered to ask where he was the night of Hanaford's murder—or checked to see if he was actually in Sacramento when Rufus Mills met his death? What better disguise could a man don, I mused ruefully, than the mantle of money and success?

By the time I boarded the cable car, I had made up my mind to visit Benjamin Wylde's office on Montgomery Street. I settled back in my seat to enjoy the brief ride. Although some San Franciscans consider Andrew Hallidie's new inventions to be a public nuisance—some have gone so far as to refer to these vehicles as "Hallidie's Folly"—I must confess to a kind of fascination with the cable traction cars, notwithstanding their occasional threat to man and beast as they compete for space on the city's frequently narrow streets.

Not long after the contraptions were introduced seven years earlier, I determined to try them firsthand, and made the two-and-a-half-mile round trip from Clay and Kearny streets to Chestnut and Larkin. I found the experience stimulating, particularly the portion of the journey where we seemed to hang vertically suspended on the crest of Nob Hill. I had little patience, and even less sympathy, for the two silly women who made spectacles of themselves by swooning when we reached the most elevated portion of our journey. It is exactly this sort of behavior that perpetuates the unfortunate perception that women constitute the frailer sex!

As I walked the three blocks from the cable car to Wylde's office, I prepared the questions I wished to ask. I had no idea what I would do if Wylde himself were there, but that was no reason to put it off. I ran the risk of his presence whenever I made the visit.

I needn't have worried. When I requested an audience with Mr. Wylde, the clerk informed me that the attorney was not expected back in the office until that afternoon.

"Well, really," I said, subjecting the poor clerk to my best imitation of a distraught female. "This is the second time he's let me down. I was supposed to meet with him on the tenth of last month, but he was called out of town for the week."

The clerk looked surprised. "I fear you are mistaken, madam. Mr. Wylde was in the city trying a case during most of August."

I drew myself up in indignation. "I suppose the next thing you'll tell me is that he didn't spend last weekend in Sacramento."

"Certainly not." The clerk's expression left little doubt that he questioned my mental faculties. "Mr. Wylde hasn't left San Francisco in more than two months. If you have business with him, I'll be happy to make an appointment, Miss—"

"Nuisance," boomed a voice from behind me. "That's her name, sir. Miss Confound Nuisance."

The clerk stared at Robert Campbell—for that, of course, was the latest lunatic to enter the unfortunate man's domain.

"Excuse me, sir?" he asked in bewilderment.

I spun around. "I don't believe it! What are you doing here?"

"Looking for you, of course. When you weren't at Senator Broughton's office, I guessed you'd decided to harass Wylde first."

"You're the one guilty of harassment, Mr. Campbell!" I accused, furious that this person was hounding me like a common criminal. "I will thank you to cease doing so immediately."

Nodding to the clerk, I marched out of the office, allowing the heavy oak door to slam closed behind me for punctuation. I hadn't taken more than a dozen steps when I saw Benjamin Wylde's tall figure walking toward me from the stairwell. I looked quickly around, but there was no place to hide. Behind me, I heard Campbell's footsteps. I was caught squarely between two evils.

Just as the Scot caught up with me, Wylde looked up and saw us. His dark eyes narrowed.

"Miss Woolson. Mr. Campbell. What an unexpected surprise. Have you been to my office?"

I put on the brightest smile I could manage under the circumstances. "As a matter of fact, we have. I was curious to see how probate on Mr. Hanaford's will was progressing."

Common courtesy prevented Wylde from calling me a liar, but it wasn't difficult to see that was what he was thinking. Turning to Campbell, he raised one eyebrow.

"I'm surprised that should interest you, Campbell."

"I'm concerned with all aspects of Mrs. Hanaford's case," he said, looking uncomfortable with even this mild prevarication.

I made a show of consulting my timepiece. "Goodness, look what time it is. I'm afraid we're late getting back to the office."

Campbell seemed surprised, but before he could protest, I said our good-byes to an equally startled Benjamin Wylde and nudged my colleague toward the stairs.

"What was that all about?" he asked, when we were beyond the lawyer's hearing.

"It was necessary to get you out of there before you could make even greater fools out of us than we'd already managed. You're a dreadful liar, Mr. Campbell."

"Judging by the ease in which untruths flow from your mouth, I'm sure you consider that a fault, Miss Woolson. I, on the other hand, was raised to believe it a virtue."

"I'm happy for you," I said tartly, reaching the entrance to the building. Without a backward look, I stepped outside. "You may leave now," I threw over my shoulder.

He mumbled something I was just as happy not to catch, but continued after me. I started out at a brisk pace toward Market Street, amazed by how congested the streets had become in the short time I'd been inside Wylde's office. People brushed passed us, anxious not to miss the start of the presidential parade. Four giggling young girls went by wearing their Sunday best and carrying small American flags. A couple held tight to several small children as they hurried them through the throng. We passed two soldiers looking dashing and very young in their crisp uniforms. All about us, people ate fresh taffy and honey popcorn balls. The air was charged with a carnival-like atmosphere.

The sight and smell of so much food caused me to remember that I'd left the house that morning without breakfast. Spying a confectioner's shop on the other side of the street, I hastened to cross, determined to make amends to my complaining stomach.

"Where are we going?" Campbell called out, dodging a landau driven by a man I recognized as a physician acquaintance of Charles's. The man smiled and politely doffed his hat.

"I don't know where you're going," I replied pithily. "For my part, I plan to have something to eat."

Although he professed not to be hungry, my sullen companion did justice to an assortment of pastries and two dishes of ice cream. I contented myself with a single helping of each, followed by a cup of coffee. The shop was small and clean, with delicious smells emanating from the kitchen. Spread out on a counter was a delightful array of baked goods, artfully arranged to tempt the eye as well as the palate. All in all, the little shop presented a quiet refuge from the bustle of parade activity outside.

When he had finished his impromptu meal, Campbell ordered his own coffee, then sat back and regarded me with frank speculation.

"What did you expect to accomplish at Wylde's office?"

"I hoped to answer questions no one else has bothered to ask."

"They haven't been asked because the real murderers are in custody."

"That's an assumption I refuse to endorse."

"I suppose that means you plan to badger Senator Broughton as well."

"I'll speak to him, yes. If Hanaford and Mills were killed because of the tontine money, then one of the two survivors is in mortal danger."

"Blast it, woman! Why do you persist in this madness?"

"My 'madness,' Mr. Campbell, led me to learn from Wylde's clerk that he lied about his whereabouts the night Mills was murdered. Wylde told my brother he'd be unable to attend his dinner because he was traveling to Sacramento."

"Maybe the man simply didn't want to attend."

"He also told Mrs. Hanaford—in my presence, I might add—that he'd be out of the city that weekend. Why lie to her if his only intention was to avoid Frederick's party?"

"He must have his reasons. Perhaps he was protecting a client."

"Perhaps," I grudgingly admitted. "But I think something more sinister is going on. Then there's Li Ying's letter to Hanaford."

"I knew you'd find some way to drag the Chinese into this!"

"Aren't you the least bit curious about that note? What money was Li referring to? And what possible reason could a tong lord have for writing to a respected white banker?"

"Maybe he just wanted a loan."

"From what I've learned about the Chinese, they keep to themselves. And they have their own banks. They'd be unlikely to receive a loan from one of our banks in any case."

Unable to refute my logic, he grunted and drank his coffee.

"Besides, if Li were looking for a loan, he would hardly expect

Hanaford to hand deliver the money to Chinatown. And the tone of the letter is personal rather than professional. It suggests that Hanaford owed Li money. Don't you agree?"

"I find it highly unlikely. I still say you're manufacturing mysteries where none exist. But I can see you're determined to go on with this. Whom do you plan to pester next?"

Ignoring his tone, I considered my next move. "Senator Broughton is probably fawning over President Hayes with the rest of the city's politicians, so I can learn little from him today. I have some questions for Eban Potter, but I'm sure the bank is closed in honor of the occasion." I also knew, but refrained from saying aloud, that there was nothing I could do about Li Ying until the following night. My choices seemed to boil down to just one. "I think I'll spend the afternoon looking into Peter Fowler's past," I concluded.

Campbell's eyes narrowed. "So you admit there's reason to doubt his innocence."

"Not necessarily. But it would be foolish not to include him on the list."

He laughed aloud. "I don't believe that for one minute. You're the one, after all, who keeps insisting the two deaths are connected. Now it's occurred to you that while Mrs. Hanaford was in jail and can't have killed Mills, Fowler may have been carrying out a plan conceived by them both."

I looked at him in dismay. Ever since Samuel's warning, I'd been worried about this very thing. "If you believe that theory, why haven't you mentioned it to the police?"

"Whatever else you may think of me, I'm not stupid," he said shortly. "Nor would I knowingly compromise our client. But if the police decide to adopt your hypothesis, we're in trouble."

I didn't bother answering, and before I could object, Campbell paid our bill, saying he would expect recompense from Shepard. On that basis, I was content to let him perform the gentlemanly duty.

"Where do you propose to research Peter Fowler?" he asked when we'd left the confectioner's shop.

I was pleased to note that the crowd had noticeably thinned. Several blocks away we could hear the sound of marching bands and the shouts of the cheering crowd. Part of me regretted that I was missing the chance to see our nineteenth president. But, as I'd told Samuel, this business couldn't wait.

"I'll start at the Department of Records," I told him. "You may come along if you wish. But if you do, I'll expect you to shoulder your share of the work."

With that, I walked briskly to the nearest cable car stop. I didn't look back to see if my indomitable shadow would follow.

Fortunately, the Department of Records hadn't closed because of President Hayes's visit, and we spent the rest of the afternoon poring through a mountain of records. To Campbell's credit, he uncomplainingly assumed his share of the task. Still, in the end, our search turned out to be fruitless. Nowhere could we find any mention of Peter Fowler's birth. In fact, there was no mention of his name at all.

"How do we know he was born in San Francisco?" Campbell asked at length.

I lifted my head and was surprised to realize I'd developed a dull ache between my eyes. It's rare for me to experience a headache, and I attributed it to my lack of sleep the night before. That and the strain of reading so many entries, some of them written in such a cramped hand they were difficult to decipher.

"Mrs. Hanaford mentioned they'd lived in the same San Francisco neighborhood as children," I told him. "Before her father became a successful hotelier, of course."

"Maybe he's using a stage name." I could tell by his tone that he, too, was tired and unhappy to have nothing to show for the afternoon's labors.

"Yes, I've thought of that." Frustrated, I closed the book I'd been perusing. "There seems nothing for it but to pay Fowler a visit tomorrow."

"And you think he's going to smile and happily tell you all about himself."

"He will unless he wants to end his life on the gallows."

Campbell merely grunted. He presented a comical sight sitting across from me at the cluttered table. A smudge of dirt on his cheek gave him the look of a small boy who's been making mud pies. His tie was askew and the sleeves of his shirt were rolled up to his elbows, displaying the most impressive set of forearms I'd ever seen. Overall, he appeared thoroughly ruffled, both in appearance and in disposition. Not for the first time, I wondered what carrot our employer had extended to induce this incongruous man to agree to such a troublesome assignment.

"Why are you doing this, Robert?" I blurted, hardly noticing that in my curiosity to learn the truth I had addressed him by his Christian name. "Following me about like some overzealous nursemaid, I mean."

My abruptness seemed to catch him off guard. "I told you. Shepard wants you kept out of trouble."

"I'm not talking about Shepard. His motives are perfectly clear. I meant you. What are you getting out of this?"

"That is none of your concern." With a glare, he closed the book he'd been reading so sharply that a cloud of dust flew about his head causing him to sneeze.

"On the contrary, it is very much my concern," I retorted. "After all, I'm the one forced to suffer your company."

He swore beneath his breath. "Damn it all, woman, do you never give up? You're as tenacious as a terrier digging for a bone."

He ran a dirty hand through his rust-colored hair, causing one tuft to stand out in front like the golden horn of a unicorn. Then suddenly he stood, knocking over his chair in the process. He paid it no mind, but began pacing the room like a caged tiger. I watched him with interest. Here was a man, I thought, upon whom inactivity did not sit well. Not for the first time I wondered at his choice of careers. Surely he would have been more at home in the rugged outdoors of his native Scotland.

Abruptly, he ceased his pacing and looked down at me from across the table. His height was so great that my aching head throbbed from the need to peer up at him at such an angle.

"I see you'll give me no peace until you've bled me dry," he exclaimed. "All right, then, you shall have it. In return for keeping you out of mischief, Shepard has agreed to speak to Paulson on my behalf. I wish to act as his co-counsel in Mrs. Hanaford's upcoming trial."

I was momentarily struck dumb by the absurdity of this remark.

"But you have no trial experience. I'm not sure you even have experience in criminal law." I gave him a challenging stare. "Well, have you?"

"Blast it, woman, you know bloody well I don't. But I have the ability. I'm certain of it."

I started to retort this vainglorious statement, then stopped, taken aback by the fire in his eyes. To my astonishment, I realized that he had just revealed something extremely personal to me. This was his passion. His dream.

"That's why you left Scotland to practice law in San Francisco, isn't it?" I said. "To be a trial attorney."

He stood with his back to me, facing the window. Without turning, he nodded. Perhaps he felt he had already said too much. I judged the fiery lawyer to be an intensely private man.

"But how did you end up at Shepard's firm?" I persisted. "Why not stay in Edinburgh?" To my surprise, I really wanted to know.

Something of this sincerity must have shown in my voice, for he turned and walked back to the table. He stared hard at me for a moment, then righted the fallen chair and sat down.

"My father's also a lawyer. A prominent trial attorney. Too prominent," he added dryly. "When I couldn't escape the inevitable comparisons made between us, I decided to immigrate to the States. James McNaughton was one of my law professors at the University of Edinburgh. We kept in touch when he moved to America. When a position as associate attorney opened in Shepard's firm, James suggested my name."

"I see." So that was why this brute of a man had been willing to work in a closet-sized room and take orders from a man he clearly didn't respect. It seemed that my client was to be his long-awaited reward.

"You don't think I'm capable of handling Mrs. Hanaford's defense, do you?" he challenged.

I didn't immediately answer. There was no doubt he could be quarrelsome and annoyingly blunt. On the other hand, I could no longer deny he had a sharp mind and was more intuitive than I'd previously credited. If he believed in someone, he might be a formidable defender. The fact remained, however, that he had virtually no trial experience. Most disturbing, and potentially damaging to the widow's case, he wasn't convinced of her innocence.

"I honestly don't know your capabilities," I told him. "I do know, however, that my client desperately needs all the help she can get. If you're willing to keep an open mind, I see no reason why we can't work together in the best interests of her defense."

When he didn't answer, I began the tedious job of replacing the dusty tomes we'd pored over for the past few hours. Without a word, he began helping me until the task was completed.

"What's on the agenda for tomorrow?" he asked as we took our leave of the Department of Records.

I gave him a sharp look. "Are you asking as one of Mrs. Hanaford's attorneys, or as Joseph Shepard's secret agent?"

He had the good grace to smile. "A little of both, I suppose. I don't like playing the role of spy any better than you, Sarah. However, I do care that justice is served. Toward that end, I'm willing to help you search for the truth."

I returned his smile. "In that case, I accept your offer. I plan to visit Peter Fowler at the jail tomorrow morning. Shall we say nine o'clock?"

He tipped his hat. "Until nine, then."

I watched his retreating back until he was swallowed up by the crowd milling about in the wake of the parade, wondering all the while at the unexpected accord we had just struck. I wasn't at all sure what to make of it, but was forced to admit that when he was so inclined, Robert Campbell could be charming.

Then, no longer able to contain my fatigue, I hailed the first unoccupied hansom that passed my way and instructed the driver to take me home.

CHAPTER SEVEN

Peter Fowler seemed surprised but pleased when Robert and I entered his cell the following morning. He pressed for news of Annjenett, and after assuring him she was doing as well as possible under the circumstances, I asked about his own situation.

"I'm being treated well enough, I suppose," he answered. "It's the feeling of powerlessness that's the most maddening. Time has become my enemy. Each moment is a bitter reminder that my life is no longer my own, indeed that I may forfeit it for a crime I didn't commit. I've begun to suspect that even my attorney thinks I'm guilty." He looked at us through eyes that were bloodshot and sunken from lack of sleep. "A fine thing, isn't it, when your own attorney believes you to be a murderer?"

I glanced at Robert, who couldn't meet my gaze. Good, I thought, happy to see that the similarity in our own client's situation hadn't escaped him. Turning back to the actor, I asked if there was anyone we could notify on his behalf.

"My parents are both dead and I have no other family." His expression was rueful. "I never thought to hear myself say this, but in a way I'm glad they're gone. I don't think I could bear to have them see me like this."

I'd taken a seat on the room's only chair, a rickety affair that I doubted would hold either man's weight. Robert stood by the door, observing our conversation in unexpected silence.

"There are a few questions we'd like to ask you, Mr. Fowler," I began.

"Anything, Miss Woolson. I suppose you'd like to hear my version of what happened the night I went to Hanaford's house."

Without waiting for an answer, the actor took us through his actions the night Hanaford was murdered. I was pleased to note that his account tallied in most respects with Annjenett's. I was disappointed, however, when Fowler claimed not to have seen or heard anyone else enter the house after his arrival.

"It's difficult to hear the front door from Mrs. Hanaford's rooms," he explained, his face a mask of frustration and despair. "You don't know how profoundly I wish I had heard someone else come in that night. But the truth is, we heard absolutely nothing."

"Perhaps you were too absorbed in your assignation to notice," Robert put in.

Peter's face flushed. "I don't want to appear ungrateful, Mr. Campbell, but I can't allow you to malign Mrs. Hanaford like that. It's true I shouldn't have been in her room, but I assure you my motives were honorable. I was concerned about her safety and was determined to have it out with Hanaford once and for all."

"Thus provoking a scene that got out of hand," Robert retorted.

"No! By the time I convinced Annjenett—Mrs. Hanaford—that the only way to end her husband's brutality was to go down and confront him, he was already dead. Quite horribly so. I tried to keep her out of the room, but she pushed passed me. Seeing her husband like that was a terrible shock, as you can imagine. I'm afraid I was forced to put my hand over her mouth to keep her from crying out. Even in those first few moments, I realized the precariousness of our position. At all costs, we must not be found in the room with that body."

"So, you took some odds and ends to make it look like a robbery and fled, leaving the woman you profess to love to face the police on her own." Robert made no effort to hide his disgust.

"You make me sound like a cad," Fowler shot back. "It wasn't like that at all. How would it have looked if I'd been found there? We would have handed the police a ready-made motive for murder. Our only hope was to make it seem as if she'd been alone all evening. Fortunately, none of the servants saw me arrive."

"No, but a neighbor did," Robert pointed out.

"Yes," Peter said soberly. "Now my worst fears have been realized. They think we killed Hanaford so Annjenett would be free to marry me. And I'm stuck in this place, powerless to clear either one of us."

"It might help if you could account for your actions the night you were arrested," I told him.

Peter looked confused. "The night I was arrested? What can that have to do with Hanaford's death?"

"Last Saturday night, or early Sunday morning, a man by the name of Rufus Mills was murdered," I told him. "His body was discovered in one of Chinatown's back alleys."

Peter gave a nervous start and came halfway up from his cot. His face grew so pale I feared he was ill.

"I'm sorry," he said, sinking back down and belatedly attempting to make light of his reaction. "I don't know what came over me."

"The victim's name seems familiar to you," I observed. "I take it you knew Mr. Mills?"

The actor met my gaze, then looked silently at Robert.

"Come on, man, you might as well tell us the truth," Robert said. "Lying will only make matters worse."

With a despairing look, he dropped his head. "I didn't actually know Mr. Mills. Actually, I met him only once, when I was a young boy. He was—that is, he'd been a friend of my mother's."

"He must have been a bloody good friend to warrant that kind of reaction," said Campbell. "You should have seen your face, man."

"At one time I believe they knew each other quite well," the actor answered. "But that was a long time ago."

"I see." Of course I didn't see at all. At least not the part of the story Peter seemed unwilling to confide. Foolish man. How were we to help him if he insisted on playing these ridiculous games? "That was the night Mrs. Hanaford was arrested for her husband's murder. You, on the other hand, weren't taken in until several hours later. Where did you go that night after you left the theater?"

Peter's face showed honest bewilderment. If he was lying, I decided, he was a very good actor indeed.

"What possible difference does it make where I went?"

"Hanaford and Mills's deaths are nearly identical," Robert told him. "They were both stabbed to death in the—" He hesitated. "In the, er, same anatomical area."

"Our fear is that the police will eventually connect the two crimes," I broke in. "Especially since they've found no other likely suspects."

"But that makes no sense," Peter exclaimed. "Why in god's name would I kill a man I hardly knew?"

"That's what we're here to find out," Robert told him.

"If you can account for your actions that night, then Mills's death need no longer concern us," I pointed out.

Peter shook his head. "I—I'm not sure," he said vaguely. Sometimes I feel the need to unwind after a performance. That night I seem to recall going for a walk before returning to my room."

"For three hours?" Robert didn't bother to hide his skepticism. "The police waited at your boardinghouse until two in the morning, man. That was a very long walk."

Peter stared at Robert. Even he must realize how feeble this sounded. For all his acting skills, he was a poor liar.

"I was upset. About Ann—Mrs. Hanaford." Despite the cell's frosty temperature, the man's face was wet with perspiration. "The police wasted no time portraying our relationship as something sordid and cheap. I needed time to sort things out. I paid no attention to the time. I just kept walking."

For a moment, no one spoke, but Robert's expression left no doubt what he thought of the actor's story. "You'd better hope the police don't connect the two murders, Fowler. If they do, your story won't hold up for two minutes." He looked at me in exasperation. "We can learn nothing more from this man if he refuses to tell us the truth."

"One minute," I said, making one last attempt to get at the real story. "Did you meet anyone during the course of this walk? Someone who could corroborate your story?"

"No," he answered. "At least I don't think so. It was dark and very late. As I say, I was lost in my thoughts."

"Of all the fool nonsense—"

I rose to my feet, cutting off my colleague's diatribe. "Thank you for seeing us, Mr. Fowler. Mr. Campbell, would you call for the jailer?"

Robert glowered, but turned to bang on the door and call out for the guard. After a moment, a burly man appeared and without a word let us out of Peter Fowler's cell.

We'd barely taken a dozen steps before my companion erupted. "Of all the bald-faced liars, that man beats the Dutch! Make no mistake about it, Sarah, there's your murderer."

"Calm down," I said perfunctorily. "I agree he's lying. Whether or not he's the killer remains to be seen."

"Confound it, woman, he had guilt written all over his face."

"Something was written on his face," I admitted thoughtfully. "His reaction to the news of Mills's death was quite extraordinary. You're right, Robert. That young man is clearly hiding something."

When we reached the bedraggled anteroom, I informed my testy associate that I planned to visit Annjenett before we took our leave of the jail. I wasn't surprised when he insisted on accompanying me, but I was convinced she'd speak more freely if we were alone. I left him muttering something largely unrepeatable as I was led to Annjenett's cell.

"Sarah, it's so good of you to come," she exclaimed, rushing to take my hands. "The hours drag on interminably."

I could well imagine they did. Just the thought of being confined to such a place made my blood turn to ice.

"I've been to see your Mr. Fowler," I said, settling down beside her on the cot.

Her strained face brightened. "Oh, Sarah, how is he? I've heard nothing of him since I entered this wretched cell."

"He's holding up well enough," I told her, then paused. I had no wish to add to her worries, yet time was running out and the subject must be broached. "This may seem a strange question, but

have you any idea where Peter may have gone after his performance at the California Theater last Saturday night?"

Annjenett looked surprise. "Saturday night? You mean the
night I was arrested? Surely that's no mystery. Peter himself was arrested shortly after he left the theater."

"Actually, he wasn't apprehended until several hours later. We
need to establish where he went during the intervening time."

The small crease between her eyes deepened. "I'm sorry, Sarah,
but I don't understand why that should be important."

I sighed. It seemed I had no choice but to tell her the whole
story after all. "You've heard of Rufus Mills, the industrialist?"

She nodded.

"I'm afraid he was murdered that night—sometime after midnight."

The bewilderment I saw in her eyes had to be genuine. If, however unlikely, Peter Fowler turned out to be responsible for Mills's
murder, I was convinced Annjenett hadn't been involved.

"Years ago Mr. Mills was my husband's partner," she said, still
looking perplexed. "I'm shocked to hear he's been killed. But what
can it have to do with Peter?"

"Unfortunately, the circumstances of the two deaths are nearly
identical. As yet, no one has thought to connect the two murders,
but we must be prepared in the likely event that they do."

What little color was left in her face drained and I feared she
might faint. Then an angry flush appeared in each cheek.

"That would be monstrous!" she cried indignantly. "Peter did
not even know Mr. Mills."

"Can you be absolutely sure of that?" I laid my hand on her
arm. "Think, Annjenett. You may be Peter's best hope. Have you
any idea where he might have gone after the theater that night?"

She wrung her hands in distress. "I can't think of any errand that would keep him out that late. Unless—?" She seemed struck by a sudden idea.

"What is it?" I urged.

"It's probably nothing, but about a week ago when Peter and I were on our way to the theater, we stopped at a house in an unpleasant part of town. He said he was visiting a friend who was ill, an actor down on his luck. Because the house was so seedy, he insisted I wait in the carriage." She looked hopeful. "Perhaps that's where he went, to visit his sick friend."

I thought this explanation unlikely. If Peter had gone to visit an ailing friend after Saturday night's performance, why not simply say so, instead of inventing that preposterous story of walking the streets half the night?

"I'll look into it," I promised, hiding my skepticism. "I don't suppose you remember the address?"

"Actually, I do. The numbers were faded, but I had little else to do but study the house while I waited for Peter."

I jotted down the address, then chatted for several minutes of more pleasant things. When it was time to leave, I promised to do everything possible to prove Peter had nothing to do with Rufus Mills's death. I only prayed it was a promise I could keep.

Robert was pacing restlessly outside the cell block when I returned. "What have you been doing all this time?" he demanded.

"If you feel restless and claustrophobic after thirty minutes," I said, eyeing him reproachfully, "just imagine how that poor woman must feel locked inside that cell, day in and day out."

Although he guffawed and turned away, I could see that my

words had found their mark. Unable to find a suitable retort, he predictably changed the subject.

"We've wasted the entire morning on this fool's errand. I have to get to the office."

"Fine," I replied, as we exited the bleak, ever damp building. "When you report back to Mr. Shepard, please don't mention our visit with Peter Fowler. The fewer people who guess our suspicions, the better." I turned and started walking toward the corner, where I hoped to find an unoccupied cab.

"Wait!" With several long strides he caught up with me and took hold of my arm. "Where are you off to now?"

"That needn't concern you. I've taken up too much of your time already." I tried to pull free of his grasp, but his hands seemed made of steel. "Release my arm at once!"

He muttered something I didn't catch, then let go his hold, if not his determination to get his way.

"I don't see why you can't cease your infernal meddling for one day. This morning's interview with Fowler proves we needn't look any farther than that jail cell to find Hanaford's, and possibly Rufus Mills's, murderer. It's past time I attended to the stack of work piling up on my desk."

"Attend to it then, by all means," I replied tersely.

I turned my back to him, well pleased to set off on my own. Flagging down an approaching brougham, I gave the man the address Annjenett had provided then took my seat inside the carriage. We had barely started when the cab suddenly jerked to a stop and my watchdog clamored aboard, dropping into the seat next to mine.

"You must be very determined to earn Shepard's carrot to neglect all that important work piling up on your desk," I remarked, freeing the edge of my skirt, which had become entangled beneath his boot.

His only answer was a disdainful grunt. For the rest of the brief ride, he sullenly kept his head turned away from me and stared fixedly out the window.

The house I sought was located in the Barbary Coast district. I'd heard unsavory stories about the city's infamous waterfront, but since no self-respecting San Franciscan would venture onto those vice-ridden streets, I had no first-hand knowledge of the place. As our cab passed Powell Street, the neighborhood became increasingly rundown and dissolute. From the muttered comments of our driver, I knew he was as unhappy with our destination as my silent companion, whose grumbling increased with every street.

"Where are we going?" he demanded, curiosity at last getting the better of his ill temper.

"We're going to attempt to discover Peter Fowler's whereabouts the night of Rufus Mills's death."

"We already know where he was. In Chinatown—committing a—"

"It was your idea to tag along," I interrupted sharply. "The least you can do is make an effort to keep an open mind."

Robert's answer to this sensible suggestion was to turn away with a rude grunt and continue his vigil out the carriage window. The neighborhood was becoming more rundown by the block. We passed cheap hotels, pawn shops, saloons, dance halls and frame houses, the red lights outside their doors blatantly advertising their sordid trade. At this hour the streets were all but deserted, the inhabitants too weary, or too hung over, to be up and about.

"You can't mean to stop here!" exclaimed Robert as our cab halted in front of a dilapidated house close to the waterfront. The sign in front boldly featured a large rooster with a red light for a beak. "This is a broth—that is to say, it's a—"

"I know what it is," I broke in. To be honest, I found the neighborhood, and this house, as off-putting as my disgruntled companion. I checked the address Annjenett had given me. There was no mistake, at least on my part. I was, however, beginning to question the accuracy of my client's memory.

"Sarah, I demand you tell me why we've come to this place."

Briefly I related my conversation with Annjenett. His reaction didn't surprise me, since it so closely mirrored my own.

"She must be mistaken. Even an actor wouldn't stoop so low as to bring a respectable woman to a place like this."

My sentiments exactly, although I didn't say so. Distasteful as it was, we had little choice but to give the place a try.

Gathering my skirts, and my nerve, I stepped down from the carriage. Grumbling, Robert followed. We asked our nervous driver to wait, then walked to the front door where I rang the rusty bell. When there was no response, Robert pounded his fist on the splintering wood. This time I heard the sounds of approaching footsteps and in a moment the door was flung open by a tired-looking woman dressed in a faded robe, her hard, pinched face framed by a mop of unkempt gray hair. I suspected we had awakened her, since her pale eyes were puffy and rimmed with red. She stared myopically at us, making no effort to hide her annoyance.

"Whatcher want?" she barked. "We don't open till three."

I felt Robert stiffen beside me, but I gave the woman my brightest smile. "We're looking for a Mr. Peter Fowler. We were told he might be here."

"Well, you was told wrong," she snapped. "The old woman's

asleep. No need for him to be here when she ain't kickin' up a fuss, is there?"

She started to slam the door, but I pressed inside. I heard Robert step in behind me, but kept my eyes fixed on the woman.

"Would it be possible for us to see her?" I improvised. "The old woman, I mean. I'm sure it would mean a great deal to Mr. Fowler." This was a stab in the dark, but apparently the woman saw nothing unusual in my request.

"Just told ya she's sleepin', didn't I? If you think I'm gonna wake her up, yer crazier than you look."

Holding tightly to my smile, I ignored the insult. "There's no need to awaken her. If we could just take a peek."

Before she could answer, I heard shuffling footsteps in the hallway behind her. Through the dim light, I could make out an elderly, painfully thin woman, a shabby gray shawl draped over her nightdress. The old woman's face was ravaged by age and intemperance, but her wide-set eyes and finely chiseled bones attested to the fact that she'd once been a beauty. She hobbled closer to stare at us in obvious agitation.

"Is it Peter, Bertha? Has he come to get me?"

The woman at the door glared at us. "Now look what you've gone and done. I won't have any peace now for the rest of the day." Angrily, she snapped at the old lady, "Just a couple of busybodies, Mrs. Gooding. No need to go gettin' yerself upset."

Ignoring her, the old woman continued toward the door. Bertha, if that was her name, hastened to intercept her, taking Mrs. Gooding's arm and trying to pull her back down the hall. The old woman must have been stronger than she appeared, for despite Bertha's bullying efforts, she refused to budge.

"Why isn't my Peter here?" she demanded, beginning to cry. "Why doesn't he come to take me home?"

"For god's sake, quit yer whining," Bertha ordered, giving the old woman a shake. "Yer gonna wake the whole house."

"I need my medicine, Bertha," the old woman whimpered. "Please, can I have my bottle now?"

"Get back to bed and I'll bring it to ya. Just be quiet." Bertha shot us a sharp look. "You two, get yerselves out of here before she takes one of her turns and I have to send for her son. He's the only one can quiet her down when she gets like that."

With a final glare, Bertha led Mrs. Gooding away. Robert touched my arm and I allowed him to lead me outside. Neither of us spoke until we were back inside the carriage and the driver was urging his horse out of the Barbary Coast with jarring alacrity.

"Fowler told us he was an orphan," Robert said, breaking the silence that had fallen upon us since leaving the Red Rooster. "Yet another of his lies. I'm beginning to think the man is incapable of telling the truth."

"Why lie about such a thing?" I mused aloud. Then suddenly I remembered something Papa told me and it brought me up short. It was an improbable notion. Still, if it were true, it would explain a good deal. "Yes," I added more to myself than to Robert. "He'd be about the right age. I wonder—"

"You wonder what? Drat it, woman, stop manufacturing mysteries and tell me what's going on in that overwrought brain of yours."

But I wasn't ready to share what might, after all, turn out to be just wild speculation. "It's nothing," I said, making a show of rubbing my brow. "I'd hoped to return to the office, but I've developed a headache. I think I'll go home instead."

It was amusing to watch Robert try to hide his pleasure at this announcement. Of course I'd counted on his desire to be released from his nursemaid chores. Conscience clear, he'd be free to bury himself in his lair of an office, while I went about my business un-fettered. To my annoyance, he insisted on depositing me at my home on Rincon Hill before instructing the brougham to take him to Clay and Kearny Streets. Oh, well, I told myself, it was a small price to pay to be rid of him, and I was soon ensconced in a horse-car and on my way to the *Morning Call*. There, I hoped to either prove or disprove my theory.

Largely because of Papa's excellent recollection of the scandal, the job proved easier than I expected. And what a scandal it had been! At the time it happened, it had filled several front-page para-graphs every day for more than a week.

The year had been 1863. Rufus Mills, who'd returned from the silver mines a wealthy man, was making a name for himself in San Francisco industry. After establishing his first iron works factory, he had expanded into tool and machinery production, and finally into shipbuilding. His businesses and personal wealth grew exponen-tially. That year, he married Regina Olmsted, the heiress and only child of Herman Olmsted, the shipping magnate. The match not only doubled Mills's holdings, it solidified his standing in Society. Life had become very good indeed for a young man with little ed-ucation and even more limited prospects.

It must have been a shock when, shortly after his marriage, a woman appeared on Mills's doorstep claiming he was the father of her eleven-year-old son. Mills flatly denied the allegation and sent the woman and her boy packing. That seemed to be the end of the matter until a reporter got wind of the story. Hoping, no doubt, to shame Mills into acknowledging his paternity—and understand-ably angered by his cavalier treatment—the woman was induced to tell all. The affair quickly became the scandal of the year.

Aided by the newspaper, the woman took Mills to court. Un-fortunately, she could present no proof of her allegations and the trial was over in three short days. Despite the sympathy the news-paper stories generated for the woman, the judge ruled in Mills's favor. Eventually the furor, and the woman, faded from public memory, and in time took its place among San Francisco's scandalous tales of betrayal and misspent passion. The name of the woman who'd challenged one of the city's wealthiest and most powerful men was Jessie Gooding. Her young son was called Peter!

I sat for a long time staring at the articles. Any satisfaction I might have derived from confirming my theory was offset by the grim implications of the affair, not only for Peter, but for my client. Had Robert been right all along? Was it possible the actor had murdered not only Cornelius Hanaford, but also the man accused of being his father? Yet if he did kill Mills, what had he hoped to gain from his death? Surely not money, since the industrialist vehemently denied his paternity. Had Peter been so angered by Mills's shabby treatment of his mother seventeen years earlier that he had sought revenge? Is that why he had created a new name and identity? Had it all been a plan to get back at the man who had ruined his mother's life?

The whole business was maddening. The harder I worked to prove my client's innocence, the more reasons I found to support her guilt, or at least her association with the probable murderer. I wondered if Annjenett knew Peter believed he was Mills's son, then decided her reaction to the man's death had been too convincing to be faked. No, I was sure she was unaware of her paramour's connection to Mills. Unfortunately, my beliefs were inadmissible in court. I had to find proof. And soon!

I decided to take advantage of Robert's absence by running one last errand before returning home to prepare for that night's adventure. While it probably would have been foolhardy to visit the Barbary Coast alone, my next destination required no such precaution. It was, in fact, an interview best conducted on my own.

As I settled back in my seat for the brief ride to Nob Hill, I couldn't help but contrast the sordid district Robert and I had visited just hours earlier with the one I was entering now. Once again I was reminded of the wide chasm separating the "haves" from the "have nots" in the greatest city west of the Mississippi. Yet I must be honest. Social conscience aside, it was a relief not to have to hold my breath against the foul stench that permeated the waterfront, nor, despite Robert's presence, have to fear for my safety.

Rufus Mills's three-story, castellated house—located only two blocks from the Hanaford estate—resembled nothing so much as a towering mausoleum. It stood in stark silence on its hilltop perch, while afternoon fog from the Bay formed a swirling moat to mask its black-draped windows. A solemn footman wearing a black band on his arm answered my discreet knock. I presented my card, informing him in hushed tones that I had come to pay my condolences to Mrs. Mills. The footman politely led me into a sitting room and bade me wait while he inquired if his mistress was at home to visitors.

I passed the time examining family photographs and an array of bric-a-brac that seemed to cover every inch of flat surface. Heavy drapes blocked any light that might have found its way in from outside, and the fire blazing in the hearth merely added to the claustrophobic atmosphere. After a few minutes, I was far too warm for comfort and, without asking leave, threw open the sitting room door and relished the cool air that swept in from the hallway. It is my opinion that keeping rooms too hot is unhealthy; it weakens the constitution and makes one susceptible to illness. If I must be kept waiting half an hour, I thought self-righteously, I shouldn't be required to do so in an oven!

My indignation dissolved the moment the widow entered the room. Regina Mills was a small, plump, garrulous woman in her mid-forties, whom I knew from our work together for several charities. Today, dressed in a black faille mourning gown, unrelieved in its austerity except by a gold engraved mourning broach pinned to her bodice, she seemed a pale shadow of her former self. Her skin was pasty looking and drawn, and several strands of graying hair had broken free of the circle of black lace that crowned her head. Her brown eyes were puffy and red from crying and she appeared dazed, as if she hadn't yet absorbed the full extent of her loss.

Besides her obvious grief, however, I sensed another emotion not as easy to identify. Then, with a start, I realized it was shame. Of course, I thought, the shocking circumstances of her husband's death would, however unjustly, render his widow a social leper. Decent people didn't get themselves killed in Chinatown, Society would reason. There was undoubtedly as much speculation about what Mills was doing in such a place, as to who had wielded the knife that had ended his life. How many friends had visited to pay their respects, I wondered? Probably not many. The death of a spouse would be hard enough to bear, I thought, without being ostracized by one's supposed friends.

"Mrs. Mills," I said sincerely. "I'm so sorry for your loss."

"That's kind of you, Miss Woolson." With almost pathetic eagerness she bade me be seated. The normally gregarious woman must be aching for someone to whom she could pour out her confusion and grief. "My family is in New York," she went on. "It has made matters rather difficult. One feels quite alone."

As I asked if there was anything I could do to help, I felt a pang of guilt. It was unforgivable to pry, especially under the circumstances, but time didn't permit a more socially acceptable approach.

"This must be very hard for you," I began sympathetically, then lied, "I heard that it was a robbery gone wrong."

The widow seemed taken aback by my bluntness, and I feared I had crossed a line even a woman as lonely as Mrs. Mills could not accept. After several uncomfortable moments, however, a spot of color appeared in each of her pale cheeks.

"No, Miss Woolson, it was not robbery. This may shock you, but I almost wish it had been. Then, at least there would be an explanation why this terrible thing happened. I cannot imagine what Rufus was doing in such a dreadful place." She wrung her plump hands in distress, then suddenly looked at me. "Why, I remember now. Rufus was to be with your brother that night. Some political gathering, I believe. He said it would just be a group of men and unsuitable for a woman." The tears she'd been holding back with an effort began to flood her eyes, and she dabbed at them with a lace handkerchief. "If only I'd insisted on going with him, Rufus might still be alive."

I was surprised, not only that Mrs. Mills was speaking so freely, but also because of what her husband had told her. The night of Frederick's party, Mills had claimed his wife was unwell, had used this illness, in fact, as an excuse to leave early. Why had he lied? And why misrepresent the evening to his wife?

"I'm sure you knew nothing about it, my dear," she went on, sniffing back her tears. "It always amazes me how absorbed men become with politics. It all seems terribly confusing. I fear I wouldn't know what to do if I were called upon to vote. It's just as well such things are left to men."

I bit back the retort that sprang to my lips. I am sure there is no need to enlighten readers of this narrative concerning my views on women's suffrage. Arguing the case at this juncture, however, would not help me elicit the information I sought.

"Did Mr. Mills often attend such meetings?" I asked innocently.

She shook her head. "In the early years of our marriage, he was too preoccupied establishing his business to have time for that sort of thing. Of late, however—" She left the sentence unfinished.

"Yes?" I said, urging her on while stilling my conscience at this blatant invasion of her privacy.

She hesitated, and I read on her face the natural reluctance to discuss such a personal matter, especially with someone who could hardly be termed a close friend. I watched as loneliness warred with propriety. She gave me a wan smile. "You may think me fanciful, Miss Woolson, but, well, of late he seemed changed."

"Oh?" I gently prodded. "In a way to cause you concern?"

She blinked back fresh tears. "Over the past year I came to fear for my husband's health. He lost a great deal of weight, you see, and had difficulty sleeping. He suffered severely from catarrh. He tried all the usual remedies, of course, but none offered any sustained relief. Gradually, he became withdrawn and moody but would not tell me why."

"Was it to do with his business?" I asked, trying to direct the conversation to her late husband's partners. "Perhaps he said something to Senator Broughton, or Benjamin Wylde, the attorney?"

She considered this for a moment. "That's possible, I guess." She sighed. "But even if they did know what was troubling him, I don't suppose it matters now."

That remained to be seen, I thought, then said casually, "I had occasion to speak to Senator Broughton recently and was interested to learn that your husband and his mining partners signed a tontine agreement shortly after their return from Nevada."

She looked at me blankly. "A tontine? I'm afraid I don't—"

"It's a fund whereby each member puts in a specific sum," I explained. "The benefits go to the last surviving member. You might liken it to a kind of insurance policy."

Mrs. Mills was obviously taken aback by this notion. "I fear you're mistaken, my dear. I am aware of no such arrangement."

I allowed myself to look flustered. "Dear me, I do apologize, Mrs. Mills. I must have mistook Senator Broughton. It was not my intention to cause you distress—"

"Oh, but you haven't," she said, then looked embarrassed. "Financial matters are beyond my comprehension, I'm afraid. Fortunately, my attorney is dealing with Rufus's affairs." She picked fretfully at the folds of her skirt. "Hopefully, in time, we'll be able to explain how this terrible thing happened, how Rufus happened to be—where he was found. My husband was in poor health. Perhaps he suffered a seizure of some kind and became disoriented." Her eyes begged me to agree.

"You mustn't torture yourself, Mrs. Mills," I said soothingly. "It wouldn't do for you to become ill."

It was time to take my leave. "Are you sure there's nothing I can do for you, Mrs. Mills?" I asked, rising from my chair.

She got heavily to her feet, but managed a weak smile. "Your visit has been a great comfort, Miss Woolson. You must forgive me for going on about matters that cannot possibly interest you." Her voice trailed away and she looked at me self-consciously. I knew that already she regretted speaking so freely. Her admission hung in the air between us like an uninvited guest.

"Please, don't concern yourself." I took the hand she offered. It was cold as ice and trembling slightly, adding to my remorse that my questions had caused her further discomfort. I had to remind myself that I was trying to find her husband's murderer "I'll call upon you again, Mrs. Mills, if you'd like."

"Yes," she said gratefully. "I would like that very much."

I had a great deal to ponder as I found an unoccupied hansom cab and directed the driver to take me home. Settling into my seat,

I thought back to Rufus Mills's actions and lies the night he died. Why hadn't he wanted his wife to attend Frederick's dinner party? And what pressing business had enticed him to Chinatown?

I sat still as an idea formed in my mind. Then, on impulse, I knocked on the trap door of the carriage and informed the driver I had changed my mind. Instead of Rincon Hill, I instructed him to take me to another address, where I hoped to find some answers.

A n opportunity to speak privately to Samuel did not present itself until after the evening meal. Drawing him into the library, I related what I'd discovered about Peter Fowler's possible relationship with Rufus Mills, then asked, "Do you recall our conversation in the carriage yesterday morning? About the article you wrote on Chinatown last year?

"Yes. Why?"

"In it, you mentioned opium dens and other places where a white man could buy the drug."

He looked bewildered. "What does that have to do with—"

"Ever since Frederick's party, I've been troubled by Rufus Mills's sickly appearance that night."

"Come on, Sarah. The poor man was probably suffering nothing more ominous than the common cold."

"That's what I thought until I called on his widow this afternoon." Briefly, I described my visit with Mrs. Mills, including her concerns about her husband's health. "I know this is going to sound farfetched, but I think he might have gone to Chinatown that night looking for opium."

"Opium!" he exclaimed with a short laugh. "Good god, Sarah."

I leaned forward in my chair. "I paid a visit to Charles's surgery after I left Mrs. Mills. He agrees that, taken as a whole, Mills's symptoms over the past year are very similar to those of opium addiction."

"That may be, but I still think you're jumping to conclusions. And even if you're right—which I'm not ready to concede—it doesn't tell us why he was killed."

"No, but it would explain why he lied to his wife. And why he ventured into Chinatown so late at night. Surely that's one of the few reasons a white man would risk going there alone."

He looked thoughtful. "Have you mentioned these suspicions to anyone besides Charles?"

"No, and I don't plan to until I have proof." I regarded him hopefully. "I thought you might agree to ask some of your Chinatown contacts. Mills was well known. He might be remembered."

He looked skeptical. "Stories of white men lounging about smoking the drug in underground opium dens are highly exaggerated. For one thing, most Chinese don't want white men as customers. It makes them too conspicuous. The police may turn a blind eye to what the Chinese do among themselves, but it's a different story when Caucasians are involved. Besides, there are safer ways of indulging in the habit. Mills could simply send a servant to buy the stuff and smoke it in the privacy of his own home."

"Assuming his wife would permit it," I pointed out dryly. "And consider the risk. If it came out that Mills was an opium addict, he'd be ruined, socially as well as financially."

He was silent for a long moment, but I knew my theory, however improbable, had captured his journalistic curiosity.

"All right, I'll ask around the Chinese Quarter and see what I can come up with. But I can't promise anything."

"That's all I ask, Samuel." I leaned forward and gave him a grateful kiss on the cheek. "Just see what you can find."

CHAPTER EIGHT

That night, I was surprised to discover how hard it is to sneak out of one's own home. Indeed, as I watched my parents play what seemed an interminable game of chess, I began to despair that I'd ever be able to keep my eleven-thirty assignation with Miss Culbertson. I'd made my preparations earlier in the evening, but it would be impossible to leave the house until my father and mother retired for the night.

My nerves were seriously frayed when the infernal game finally came to an end, sometime after ten. The moment my parents' bedroom door was closed, I fled to my own room and changed into the most serviceable dress I owned, covering it with a dark gray woolen cape and hood. Then I forced myself to sit quietly, waiting until everyone in the house—including our butler, Edis—was in bed for the night. As the clock neared eleven, however, I could bear it no longer. Carrying a single candle, I crept down the stairs and gingerly drew back the bolt to the front door and quietly slipped outside.

The night was unseasonably cold, but there was a full moon, and thankfully the streets were clear of the earlier fog that would have hindered my efforts to find a cab. Even so, it was necessary to walk several blocks before I located an unoccupied hansom and climbed gratefully inside. I was prepared for the driver's shock, first to have as his fare an unaccompanied female so late at night, and second to be given an address on the fringe of Chinatown. Still, it required even more persuasion than I'd anticipated to convince the obstinate man that I understood where I was going and, moreover, that I was anxious to arrive there as speedily as possible. It was only when I offered the driver a generous reward for his efforts that he finally, if unhappily, clicked his horse and we were off.

Miss Culbertson, aided by a lovely young Chinese woman, was completing her final preparations for the night's raid when I arrived at the red brick house on Sacramento Street. Both women wore dark clothing, although in the Chinese woman's case it was the customary loose-fitting cotton shirt and pants.

"I wasn't sure you'd come, Miss Woolson," Miss Culbertson admitted with a smile. "Most women would have found good reason to change their minds about such an undertaking."

"On the contrary," I said, "I'm more determined than ever to see the night through. I trust your arrangements have gone well?"

The woman frowned. "Not entirely, I'm afraid. Unfortunately, I could find no policeman available, or willing, to come with us. I considered postponing the rescue, but the situation is too dire. The girl will almost certainly be sold into slavery before dawn. We must act immediately if we're to save her."

She motioned to a short, wiry Chinese man standing out of range of the gaslights. He stepped forward and I observed his wizened face, shaved forehead and ears, and long black pigtail, or queue, trailing down his back from beneath a skull-like cap. The man, also wearing a dark-colored cotton tunic and trousers, seemed nervous, a fact I did not find reassuring.

"Hi Gim will be with us on tonight's raid," Miss Culbertson continued. "It's not as much security as I would wish, but as I say, the circumstances are desperate." She turned to the young woman. "This is Gum Toy. She'll act as our interpreter." Then her dark gray eyes fixed on me, taking in my plain, dark-colored woolen dress and cloak. "You've dressed sensibly, Miss Woolson. Before the night is over, I think you'll be glad that you did."

Our little party of four drove by carriage to Dupont Street, where we entered the streets of Tangrenbu, a dense ten-block area so alien I marveled that such a place could exist in the middle of San Francisco. The streets were narrow, the wooden structures to either side piled so tightly, one upon the other, that I was reminded of a child's house of cards. Through the moonlight I could make out signs whose graceful characters identified restaurants, barbershops, laundries, vegetable, fruit and fish markets. By night the pungent smells of the Chinese Quarter seemed all the more intoxicating, and it was possible to imagine I had been transported to an exotic land across the sea.

We turned onto lower Jackson Street, and our carriage passed a Chinese theater that was still open. Inside, I could hear the voices of noisy patrons seeking relief and entertainment after their long day's work. Next to the theater was a brilliantly painted pagoda advertising a Chinese temple. In contrast to its noisy neighbor, it sat in eerie silence, patterning the moonlit street with exotically shaped shadows.

As we made our way farther up Jackson, the character of the street changed. We began to pass narrow houses—actually more like shanties—with scantily clad Chinese girls standing in open doorways, or provocatively posed in gas-lit windows. I was shocked by the tender age of some of these girls; they were little more than children!

"It's heartbreaking," Miss Culbertson said, guessing my thoughts. "Most of these girls are slaves in a very real sense of the word." Her voice grew hard and I sensed her anger and frustration. "They're treated as chattel, kept virtual prisoners inside those filthy walls. Then, when they're of no more use, their owners sell them, or put them out on the street to die."

I stared helplessly at the pitiful young women, filled with shame that I had naively looked forward to tonight's mission as an adventure. There were so many of them! The utter futility of freeing so many poor souls suddenly overwhelmed me. How did Miss Culbertson do it? She must face this frustration every day, yet she seemed not the least deterred. I marveled that night after night she risked her life to save one wretched victim at a time.

My thoughts were still on the singsong girls when our hackman—clearly no novice to these raids—stopped at the end of Sullivan's Alley. Miss Culbertson instructed the man to wait, then informed me we'd go by foot from there. In low tones she explained that the alley was too narrow for a vehicle to pass through, but that we'd need it for a quick escape once we had found the girl.

Despite the late hour, men still mingled in the alley and our little group kept to the shadows. The dirt lane was so narrow that the overhang from shops located to either side nearly met overhead to form a canopy, blocking out much of the moonlight. Most of the shops were closed, and I was surprised to see that many had rows of sliding iron doors in front.

"Those bars are to keep out the police," Miss Culbertson whispered, stopping inside a darkened doorway. "At the first sign of trouble, they're pulled closed."

"Are the police often required here?" I asked softly.

"The Chinese prefer to take care of their own problems, but occasionally the constabulary find it necessary to intervene. Beneath these stores an underground culture of gambling, prostitution and opium dens flourishes, controlled by rival tongs." She indicated a store across the alley marked by several colorful lanterns. "My informant said we'd find the girl in a room above that toy shop."

I followed her gaze and detected a faint light flickering inside an upstairs window.

Miss Culbertson plucked at my sleeve. "Come, it's time. Our best chance is to catch them by surprise."

We waited until a group of laughing men passed by, then moved to the darkened shop. I was shocked when Hi Gim pulled an axe from beneath his tunic and at Miss Culbertson's signal, struck a blow to the door. After several more strikes, the wood finally gave way and we made our way inside.

"They'll have heard Gim's axe," she said, hurrying through the cluttered shop to a narrow stairway. "Up there!"

She took the steps so quickly I was hard pressed to keep up, and marveled that a woman her age could move with so much energy. At the first landing we heard the sound of a muffled scream. Miss Culbertson ran toward a closed door, but it was locked.

"Fi dee!" she cried to Hi Gim. "Hurry!"

Hi Gim again produced his axe and soon the door lay in pieces at our feet. We rushed into the room only to find it empty.

"They've taken her out through the back," Miss Culbertson cried, running through another door that stood slightly ajar.

We followed to find ourselves in a small storage room. Using a candle, Miss Culbertson rapidly took in the room, then looked up at the ceiling.

"The skylight," she said, pointing to the rectangular opening above our heads. "They must have taken her up to the roof."

Hi Gim found a ladder and Miss Culbertson nimbly ascended the rungs and pushed her way onto the roof. Hi Gim went next, followed by Gum Toy. Swallowing my reservations, I gathered up my skirts and scrambled through the opening to see the others jump to the roof of an adjoining building. Through the moonlight, I saw that the block of buildings were built so close to one another it was possible to move in this manner from one rooftop to the next. Taking a deep breath I leapt after my companions, landing more or less intact near another skylight. I was in time to see Hi Gim lower Miss Culbertson through the opening by her arms.

"Mother, look for steps," Gum Toy explained.

Sure enough, a moment later a ladder protruded from the skylight, and Hi Gim started his descent to the room below, followed by Gum Toy and myself. Miss Culbertson, who had relit her candle, motioned toward a door.

"I heard footsteps running down the stairs," she told us.

As the last one to descend the narrow stairway—well behind the only candle—I was forced to proceed in near darkness. Reaching what I assumed to be the final step, I discovered to my chagrin that there were still several more to go. Caught off balance, my boots tangled in my skirts and I fell, landing heavily against a wood panel at the foot of the stairs. In my attempt to get up, I leaned against the panel, and to my shock it gave way beneath my hand, propelling me down yet another flight of stairs that seemed to have been carved out of the ground. I tumbled for several feet before I was able to bring my fall to a painful stop. Almost immediately, a flickering light appeared above me.

"Miss Woolson, are you all right?" Miss Culbertson's voice was raised in alarm as she reached her candle through the opening, straining to see me.

"I—I think so," I replied, gingerly moving my arms and legs. "I'm not sure what happened."

"You stumbled—quite literally, it appears—upon a trap door."

Despite her concern for my well-being, our leader couldn't hide her excitement as she descended the stairs. "We're in your debt, Miss Woolson. This stairway is very likely where they took the girl. But you took a very nasty fall. I fear you've injured yourself."

"I don't think so," I answered, embarrassed by my clumsiness. "At least nothing more serious than a few bumps and bruises." I got somewhat unsteadily to my feet, fearful that my ineptness would sabotage our mission. "Please, let's proceed."

Miss Culbertson held the candle up and studied me closely. Then she nodded, and I could see that my determination met with her approval. "I knew you were made of sturdy stuff, Miss Woolson. Very well, then. Let us see where this staircase leads."

This time I took my place directly behind the older woman—and the candle she was holding—and was thus able to make my way safely down the remaining stairs. I was vaguely aware of a stab of pain when I put weight on my left ankle, but I was too caught up in the urgency of the moment to give it more than passing notice. When we reached the foot of the steps, I was disappointed to find our way blocked by what seemed to be a solid wall of stone.

Without a word, Miss Culbertson held up the candle and ran her hand over the rough surface. After a few moments, she stopped and addressed the three of us in a soft voice. "I'm going to blow out the candle. Please, stay close behind me." I watched as she pressed what must have been a hidden mechanism in the wall, then

I heard a section of the rock wall begin to slide open as she quickly extinguished the candle.

I was instantly assaulted by an odor so putrid it was all I could do not to gag, and I was disoriented by dozens of fireflies dancing about and making strange hissing and gurgling sounds. As my eyes adjusted to the gloom, I realized these insects were actually glass lamps set next to shelflike bunks built against the walls. Chinese men, curled up in fetal position, occupied these beds. The peculiar noises I had heard seemed to come from a black substance resembling India rubber that the supine men held at the end of wire pokers over the lamps' flames. Judging by the long pipes they were smoking, I guessed the significance of the room even before Miss Culbertson whispered, "It's an opium den, a sepulcher filled with the living dead."

Boldly, she approached a row of bunks and peered into the bottom cot. I watched as the bunk's occupant opened his eyes to behold what to him must have seemed a drug-induced nightmare—a female Fahn Quai (white person) had somehow invaded this most inaccessible of sanctums. The man blinked, then turned over and resumed smoking his pipe. As Miss Culbertson passed on to the next bunk, Hi Gim and Gum Toy set off on their own search.

Earlier in this narrative, I proclaimed my contempt for dissimulation. I will not, therefore, attempt to portray my actions in a light more favorable than they actually were. The humbling truth is that I stood for some moments fighting my disinclination to approach the forlorn creatures who lay about me like so many corpses. The smell of the cooking opium, and the disgusting sound of its juices gurgling about in the addicts' pipes, made my stomach churn in revulsion. I wanted nothing more than to turn and run from this miserable den of vice and despair.

Then I thought of the piteous young slave girls we'd passed in the quarter and took myself in hand. It is at just such moments of adversity that we're able to perceive ourselves—souls stripped bare of all pretense and self-delusion—for who we truly are. After all my bold words, the time had come to prove my mettle. Swallowing my queasiness, I marched across the room, resolved to do whatever I could to help the hapless victims of such merciless villainy.

Once again, fate stepped in to play its own, inexorable role in the night's drama. I had taken but a few steps when I felt, rather than saw, something brush against my lower limbs. Heart beating wildly, I froze, trying to convince myself the creature was nothing more than a cat. Then the beast passed from beneath my skirts and I realized with a horrifying chill that it was a huge gray rat—a creature, who now sat brazenly staring up at me as if challenging my right to invade its domain.

I'm ashamed to admit that I screamed. Loud enough, I'm afraid, to wake the dead—which, in a manner of speaking, I did. All about me, men stirred, shouting angry, unintelligible words that I knew were directed at me.

Before I could slink away in disgrace, a movement in the corner of the room caught my attention. As I watched, a pair of terrified eyes peered up at me from behind the back of a man lying, face to the wall, in a bottom cot. Instantly, the girl's head was pushed down, but it was too late. I knew what I had seen.

"Over here!" I shouted on the run, triumphantly pointing at the bunk where I had spied the child. "I've found her."

The man in the cot catapulted to his feet. Holding the girl beneath one arm, he shoved me aside with the other. The blow thrust me onto a wooden crate, upon which rested an opium lamp and other drug paraphernalia. The lot crashed beneath my weight; earthenware bowls shattered and the nut oil in the lamp spilled out across the dirt floor where it instantly caught fire. I watched in horror as the flame snaked its way toward the nearest cot.

Scrambling to all fours, I half walked, half crawled from the impending conflagration. Some of the more alert men had grabbed blankets and were trying to beat out the flames. Amazingly, a few smokers still lay in their bunks, too drugged to comprehend, or care, what was happening. I saw my three companions struggling with the highbinder who held the girl firmly in his grasp. Almost effortlessly he threw them aside, and I realized that he was going to make good his escape, taking the child with him.

Not pausing to think, I grabbed a heavy metal urn and bolted forward. With a loud cry, I crashed it as hard as I could over the hatchet man's head, then watched with a mixture of horror and satisfaction as he crumpled to the floor. There he lay, eyes closed, groaning softly, the young girl whimpering beside him. Without hesitation, Miss Culbertson sprang forward and lifted the child into her arms.

"Hurry," she cried. "Before he regains his senses."

She turned to flee, but after a few steps it was obvious the girl was too cumbersome for the older woman to carry. Hi Gim mumbled something in Chinese, then took the child from his mistress. As he did, I saw that his eyes were wide with terror, and for the first time I understood how much courage it must have taken for him to oppose a force as dangerous as the tongs.

"We go quickly!" he pleaded, as the hatchet man beneath our feet stirred and opened his eyes.

Although concurring wholeheartedly with this course of action, I wasn't sure how it was to be implemented. The fire appeared to be out, but the room was now so filled with smoke we could barely see each other, much less locate the passageway that had led us into this wretched cesspool of humanity.

Once again Miss Culbertson took charge, leading us—presumably by instinct, for it certainly could not have been by sight—through a tangle of shouting, drug-dazed Chinese, toward the stairs that would lead us above ground to safety.

Or so we hoped. After making our way up the stairway, we stumbled through the unfamiliar clutter of the shop above the opium den only to discover that the building's heavy iron bars had been pulled closed and locked across the front door.

"To the roof!" Miss Culbertson yelled.

Matching action to her words, she pushed Hi Gim, who was still holding the girl, toward a flight of stairs similar to the ones we'd ascended in the Sullivan Alley toy shop. Gum Toy and I followed upon their heels.

The fine hairs at the nape of my neck rose as we ran. I was terrifyingly aware that our last hope of escape could be cut off at any moment by the furious *bow how doy* who'd taken chase behind us. If we were caught, what would they do to us? I wondered crazily as, skirts held above my knees, I ran behind Gum Toy like a hare pursued by a pack of ravenous wolves. I needed no one to tell me that if we fell into their hands, we could expect no mercy, nor any assistance from the familiar world we'd left behind.

Hi Gim was pushing the little girl onto the roof when, breathless, I joined my companions in the attic room containing the skylight. Even as she urged Gum Toy up the ladder, Miss Culbertson ordered me to block the door behind us. I looked for something to jam the entryway, but could find only some wooden boxes and a few dirty rags. Working feverishly, I propped the crates beneath the doorknob, then stuffed rags under the door. It wouldn't hold for long, but I prayed it might buy us enough time to escape.

Miss Culbertson motioned me up the ladder next and I scuttled up the rungs with an agility born of desperation. Below me, I heard the door crash open as Miss Culbertson scrambled up the ladder behind me and banged the skylight shut. Rushing to the others, we executed the jump back to the roof of the first building we had entered.

Instead of descending the original skylight, however, Miss Culbertson led us with practiced familiarity onto another roof, then yet another, moving as if she were on level ground instead of flying from building to building like a circus performer. Behind us, the hatchet men pursued us relentlessly. Suddenly, one grabbed my foot as I hesitated a moment too long before leaping across a precipice that was dauntingly wider than its predecessors.

With a strength I didn't know I possessed, I kicked out at the man, catching him full in the face and causing him to fall back upon his companions. Quickly, I vaulted across to the adjoining roof where I realized that Miss Culbertson had led us to a steep, narrow stairway leading to the alley below. Standing at the foot of the stairs were Gum Toy and Hi Gim—the child we'd rescued clutching the frightened man tightly about his neck.

"Go. Quickly!" Miss Culbertson ordered.

She didn't have to tell me twice. Scurrying down the rickety stairs as quickly as I dared, I half stumbled onto the street, followed a moment later by Miss Culbertson. She led us at a run toward the corner where we'd left our carriage. Lungs gasping for air, I had no need to look over my shoulder to know that the *bow hop doy* were following much too closely upon our heels.

I had just reached our waiting carriage when it happened. One moment I was lifting myself onto the rig, the next instant unseen hands had grabbed me from behind and were pulling me down the alley. Before I knew what was happening, I'd been dragged inside an unlit room and the door had been slammed closed behind me.

"Unhand me this instant!" I demanded, fighting to pull away from the assailant who held my arms pinned tightly to my sides.

The room was so dark I could see nothing. When I heard more than one voice whispering in Chinese, I realized I didn't even know how many villains I was up against. This so unnerved me, I lashed out with the only part of my anatomy I could still move, my feet. Judging by the howls this elicited, I knew I'd been at least partially successful. But when I drew breath to demand to be released, a hand clamped across my mouth so roughly my head whipped back with a painful jolt. Under the circumstances, I feel no need to apologize for employing my last remaining weapon. Maneuvering my body sideways, I kicked as hard as I could in the direction of what I hoped was my captor's groin.

I was rewarded by a bellow of pain and the offending hand was momentarily removed. But before I could call out, a piece of cloth was stuffed into my mouth and my arms were bound, none too gently, with what appeared to be another length of cloth.

"Be still!" a man's voice growled in my ear.

Outside the door, Miss Culbertson called out my name, but my gag silenced any attempt to respond. I had to fight back silent tears of frustration. The group from the mission was mere feet away, yet they might as well have been on the moon for all the assistance they could render. Then I heard running feet and knew the highbinders would soon be upon them. My companions had no choice but to make good their escape while they could, yet my heart sank to hear their departing carriage.

When the street was finally quiet, one of my captors opened the door a crack and a thin ribbon of moonlight penetrated the room. I saw that there were two of them, both muscular and unusually tall for Chinese. One villain scouted the street while the other wrapped a piece of silken material over my eyes as a blindfold. Then silently they slipped out of the room, holding me wedged tightly between them.

We moved forward in this uncomfortable fashion for what seemed like miles, but was probably no more than four or five blocks. Several times I was aware of being led around obstacles in the street, and once when I started to stumble, strong hands helped me to my feet. All of which added to my growing confusion. Where were they taking me? And why? Wouldn't it have been simpler to finish me off in the room we'd just vacated, leaving my body to be discovered at a later time?

I was roused from these depressing thoughts when the men stopped and knocked on a door. A moment later, the door opened and I was ushered inside some sort of building. My captors spoke briefly in Chinese to another man, then escorted me into what I guessed to be an entryway and through yet another door.

Still blindfolded, I was guided up a flight of stairs and finally eased into a chair. Immediately, my hands were released from their bonds and, much to my relief, the cloth was pulled from my mouth. While I fought to catch my breath, the silk was removed from my eyes and, wordlessly, my kidnappers slipped away.

Although a blindfold no longer obstructed my sight, it was several moments before my brain could take in the images bombarding my senses. For reasons I couldn't begin to fathom, I'd been deposited in the most amazing room I had ever seen. The decor represented neither East nor West, Tajmahal nor English manor house; in truth it was all of these at once. Across from me stood a marble statue of the Greek goddess Diana, which would have been at home in Leland Stanford's foyer. On the opposite wall hung what looked to be an early Van Gogh and next to that a splendid Goya. On another wall I spied a Courbet, a Barye and a classic

Rousseau. The magnificent carpet was Persian, its exotic weave and rich colors perfectly enhancing an eclectic collection of furniture.

There were, of course, the expected Chinese pieces, most notably some exquisite jade carvings and a lovely old *hua-li* sideboard, similar to one I had seen while visiting London's British Museum. Amazingly, these Chinese pieces sat side-by-side with equally fine examples of English Tudor and French Provincial. Aside from the monetary value of the collection, this meeting of East and West managed to achieve a strangely harmonious environment, a sharp contrast to the dichotomy that existed beyond these walls.

I was drawn from these musings by a movement to my right, and was startled to realize someone had soundlessly entered the room. A distinguished-looking Chinese man sat regarding me with polite interest from a square-backed, *kuan moa* chair, which rested on a small dais placed in the center of the rear wall. It reminded me of a small throne, such as a Chinese dignitary might use while conducting a formal audience.

The man inhabiting the chair-of-state did, in fact, possess a regal bearing. Even seated I could see he was tall for a Chinese, and his clothes bore out this air of nobility. The tunic of his blue satin robe was patterned in a rich, black velvet overlay, and the face that regarded me above the embroidered collar was unlined and finely chiseled. The man's coal-black hair—shaved and oiled into a long queue—showed little gray, yet I felt certain he was not young. It was his eyes, I decided, that betrayed his years. Dark and penetrating, they held a wisdom and perceptiveness that can only be acquired over time. It was the unmistakable glint of ruthlessness I saw there, however, that chilled my blood. Intuitively I realized that this man was accustomed to getting what he wanted, regardless of the cost.

"My modest home pleases you?" he asked in flawless English.

"It's—quite extraordinary," I replied, realizing even as I spoke that these words hardly did justice to such magnificence.

He seemed amused. "But you are surprised by my choices?"

"They're unusual certainly. But the effect is pleasing."

It was true. Within these walls time seemed to stand still, and I felt an unexpected sense of calm. Here, I thought, one might find sanctuary from the disquiet of the outside world.

Even as these thoughts crossed my mind, I recognized their incongruity. I was a prisoner, I reminded myself, taken against my will for heaven only knew what reason. Indeed, despite this serene Chinese conversing with me as if I were an honored guest, my life might still be in danger.

"Please, do not distress yourself," the man said, as if reading my thoughts. "I mean you no harm. Furthermore, I regret the treatment you received at the hands of my men. They have informed me that you fight like a Yan Wo, which, you may know from your research into our customs, is a particularly vicious tong. My men meant this as high praise, but it does not excuse their ineptness. I offer my profound apologies, Miss Woolson."

I looked at him in surprise. "You know my name?"

"You are the only daughter of the Honorable Horace Woolson. Your eldest brother, Frederick, recently announced his intention to run for state senate. Another brother, Charles, is a skilled, if underpaid, physician." He smiled. "Your brother Samuel, or should I say Ian Fearless, is a talented writer. I found his article on Tangrenbu last year interesting, if a bit overdramatized."

If it had been my host's intention to startle me, he'd succeeded. "In at least one respect you know more about my siblings than my own parents," I said, trying to keep my voice calm. "But I don't understand. Why have you taken the trouble to learn so much about my family?"

"I find it prudent to know as much as possible about those who show an interest in me, Miss Woolson."

"Show an interest! But—" Suddenly my situation, as well as the identity of this surprising man, become clear. "You're Li Ying."

He inclined his head. "I have neglected to introduce myself. An oversight for which I must again beg forgiveness. You are correct, Miss Woolson. I am Li Ying."

I forgot my manners and stared frankly at this alleged God of the Golden Mountain, the most powerful and feared tong lord in Tangrenbu. I'm not sure what I'd expected, but certainly not this refined, obviously educated man who lived in a house that would have made the Astors proud.

A manservant noiselessly appeared, bearing a tray containing a pot of aromatic China tea, as well as a selection of very Western sandwiches and cakes. To my surprise I found I was hungry.

"I hope you will enjoy this modest refreshment." He waited until I had sampled my tea before raising his own cup.

"It's delicious. Thank you." It was, in fact, the finest tea I had ever tasted.

"You honor me." He went on to make polite, but insignificant, conversation while we ate. It wasn't until the servant collected the remains of our meal that he came to the heart of what I now knew must be the reason for my abduction. "I am most curious to learn, Miss Woolson, why you have been inquiring about me."

Anticipating the question, I had been turning over in my mind how best to answer. In the end I decided that any attempt to deceive this man would not only be foolhardy, but would surely fail. Consequently, I told Li Ying the circumstances surrounding Hanaford and Mills's deaths, and how his own name had come to my attention. When I described finding his note to the banker, he raised an eyebrow.

"I am disappointed that Mr. Hanaford was so indiscreet."

"So you admit you wrote the letter."

"Oh, yes. And several others like it."

"But why?" I asked, then realized the tong lord was hardly likely to satisfy my curiosity. Again he surprised me.

"Because I was blackmailing him," he replied without the slightest hesitancy. "I had been doing so for a number of years."

This time I was at a loss for words.

"I see I have shocked you, Miss Woolson." He smiled. "Perhaps it would help if I told you something of myself and the events that led to my association with Mr. Hanaford."

"Yes. I would like that very much." I realized I had moved forward expectantly in my chair and consciously sought to relax.

"You have undoubtedly heard stories about me," he began. "While some of them are true, you must not believe them all."

I was unsure how to respond to this, so I said nothing.

"My family comes from Canton," he continued. "My father was a scholar-official, a ruling mandarin of some distinction. In time I, too, passed the Confucian examinations and prepared to devote my life to the service of my country." He paused, and when he went on, his voice was tinged with regret. "Unfortunately, that was not to be. The turbulent political situation in the south forced me to leave my country. After working as a seaman aboard a clipper ship, I traveled to Nevada because I had heard stories of great riches to be found in the silver mines."

He noted my heightened interest. "Yes, Miss Woolson, it was there that I first met Mr. Hanaford and his three partners. You must understand that many of my countrymen were leaving China at that time in search of a better life in America. Circumstances for the Chinese in Virginia City, however, were not easy. We faced bigotry and fierce competition from other miners. We were considered a subspecies and were not allowed to stake our own claims, but were forced to take the white man's leavings. I was more fortunate than most and managed to acquire a mine that had been abandoned by two white men who cared more for alcohol than wielding axes. I worked the mine for many months, convinced that valuable minerals lay hidden in its tunnels. In the end I was proven correct. The mine turned out to be extremely rich."

"That's how you acquired all this, then?" I asked, looking about the extraordinary room.

His mouth tightened and he regarded me with undeviating frankness. "I am afraid not. When the value of my mine became known, Mr. Hanaford and his partners relieved me of my claim."

"Relieved you of your—? You mean they stole it? But how?"

"It was childishly simple. It was, after all, my word against theirs." His smile was ironic. "And I was Chinese."

"You must have had recourse. Surely the law protected you—"

His laughter cut through my words. "We are speaking of Virginia City, Miss Woolson. You are presuming a system of equality under the law that does not yet exist in San Francisco. Only last year the men of this city voted to exclude Chinese from entering the state. Those who are already here are barely tolerated. We cannot become naturalized citizens, nor can we marry a white person. We have been driven from many occupations because of our perceived threat to the white worker. All this in a so-called civilized city. Imagine, then, the situation facing us in a remote mining town with virtually no laws, and no one to enforce what few there were.

"It's reprehensible!" I exclaimed, incensed by such discrimination.

"No, it is reality," he replied with a quiet smile. "That was what I learned, you see. In order to succeed, I would have to make the white man's rules work for me."

"So you left the mines and came to San Francisco."

He nodded, but did not elaborate further. Once again his erudite face became unreadable. Was this all he was going to tell me? There was so much more I longed to know.

"You had good reason to resent the men who took so much from you." I realized this statement was hardly as subtle as I would have liked. On the other hand, I knew of no good way to ask someone if he was a murderer. Especially a man like Li Ying.

Again, he smiled. "If you are asking whether I killed Cornelius Hanaford and Rufus Mills, Miss Woolson, the answer is no. While it is true I bore no love for either man, they were worth a great deal more to me alive than dead."

"You mean the blackmail money." I had an unexpected thought. "Were Mr. Wylde and Senator Broughton paying you as well?"

His face was calm, but his eyes burned like black coals. I suddenly felt lost, without any real idea where I was going. I had allowed Li to lull me into believing he meant me no harm, but that trust was suspect. Despite the feeling that I was standing at the edge of a precipice, I boldly pressed on.

"Mr. Hanaford and Mr. Mills were two of the most influential names in San Francisco," I said. "How was it possible for you to wield control over such men?"

Li considered this. "You have a saying, Miss Woolson, that one must not speak ill of the dead. The path to achieving the power and influence of which you speak is not always smooth. Nor is it always honorable. Let us say that when I was presented with an opportunity to collect on a debt long overdue, I was fortunate to possess the knowledge and ability to do so."

"The authorities may view that as a motive for murder."

"Undoubtedly." His mouth moved into a half smile. "Do you plan to tell them, Miss Woolson?"

I'm not ashamed to admit that my heart pounded as I looked into that enigmatic face. In truth I hadn't fully considered what I would do if and when I was released from Li's house. Yet again my host surprised me by breaking into laughter.

"Please, do not look so aggrieved. Of course you will inform your brother's friend on the police force what has happened. I assure you it is of no consequence. The authorities cannot harm me, nor have they the power to disrupt my organization. They are, however, understandably concerned for your safety. They have been combing the quarter since you became separated from Miss Culbertson after rescuing little Chum Ho from the opium den. Again, I apologize. I regret having caused you and your friends distress. It was necessary, however, that we have a chat."

His mouth twitched slightly and his black eyes twinkled.

"You are known for your candor, Miss Woolson, and now that I have had the honor of meeting you, I see that the reputation is justified. In your innate honesty, I am certain you will acknowledge that tonight's discussion has been to our mutual advantage. If anyone can prove Mrs. Hanaford innocent of murdering her husband, I do not doubt that it will be you."

CHAPTER NINE

Any hope I had entertained of sneaking into my house the next morning was dashed when my parents pounced on me the moment I opened the door. The alarm had been raised when Mama discovered I hadn't slept in my bed the previous night. I gather I had returned just in time to prevent Edis from summoning the police.

Papa's tirade was mercifully forestalled when my mother realized I was painfully favoring my left foot. Charles examined the afflicted appendage, then tersely informed me I was lucky to have escaped my night's folly with nothing more serious than a sprained ankle. I was duly bandaged and hustled off to bed. There, surrounded by my befuddled family, I was at last forced to offer an explanation for my behavior.

In doing so, I was careful to include as few details as possible. The fact that I had been returned to my front door by two of Li Ying's men, however, made it difficult to deny in which part of the city the accident had occurred. Even a considerably watered-down version of my adventure with Miss Culbertson had been enough to drive my mother to tears and cause my father to threaten a nunnery if I ever again did anything so irresponsible.

Only Charles's insistence that I must rest—in fact that I would need to stay in bed until the swelling in my ankle receded—finally brought a blessed end to parental censure. Before my father left the room, however, he bent down to whisper, "You haven't told us half of what happened to you last night, my girl. I won't press the matter now, but when you're feeling better we're going to have a little chat."

"You may not like what you hear, Papa," I answered guiltily.

"No, I probably won't," he said, planting a kiss on my forehead. "Nevertheless, I can't wait to hear it."

To my surprise I slept until mid-afternoon, awakening when Mama entered bearing a late lunch. She plumped my pillows, then laid the tray on my lap. It was only after I'd taken a bite of Cook's excellent beef sandwich that I realized I was famished.

My mother watched me for a moment, then said, "What you did last night was very reckless, Sarah."

"It was necessary, Mama. And I didn't go alone."

"I know. You went with that woman from the Presbyterian Mission. I've long admired Miss Culbertson's work. Still, her raids are dangerous."

"I'm sure she would tell you that saving even one girl from white slavery is worth the risk."

"Yes," Mama said wearily, "I'm sure she would." She fussed with my bedclothes, then surprised me by saying, "You should have been a boy, Sarah. Lord knows I've tried, but I begin to despair of ever seeing you properly settled."

"By that I assume you mean married with a house full of children." My mother and I had had this discussion before.

Mama ignored my ironic tone. "I know you'll find this hard to believe, but I have some idea how you feel. There was a time when I, too, had ideas of what I wanted to do with my life."

I stopped chewing. "You mean other than marrying Papa?"

"This was long before I met your father—I couldn't have been more than six or seven. I'd had a fight with my older sister, your Aunt Eloise. She'd received a lovely white porcelain horse for Christmas, and I thought it was the most beautiful thing I'd ever seen. I offered to trade her my new skates for it, but she refused. After days of pouting, my governess suggested I write about the horse. If I couldn't own it, I could make up stories about it to my heart's delight."

"And did you?" I asked, intrigued by this rare glimpse into my mother's childhood.

"Oh, yes. Pages and pages—in a little notebook. At first I wrote about the anger I felt toward my sister. Then, gradually, it became a story of a real horse."

I lay still, afraid to break the spell. My loving but reticent mother rarely shared her more intimate thoughts.

"It sounds silly, but my horse became very real to me. Soon my sister's porcelain pony paled next to the lively creature of my imagination. That was the beginning. For years I wrote all sorts of stories. I don't know how many notebooks I filled."

I was struck by the similarities between Mama and Samuel, who was driven by the same dream. What would Mama say if she knew her youngest son had inherited her passion? In addition, that he was making a name for himself—even if it wasn't the name he'd been christened. I was sorely tempted to share this with her, but in the end I knew I couldn't break Samuel's confidence.

"Do you still have the notebooks?" I asked.

"Do you know, I have no idea," she said, looking surprised by my interest. "I haven't seen them since we left Williamsport."

"Look for the stories, will you, Mama?" I said, squeezing her hand. "I'd love to read them."

Mama looked pleased, if a little self-conscious. "They're just the ramblings of an overimaginative child, Sarah. Still, if you'd like, I'll try to find them. There are some old chests in the attic. I might look there."

"Good." I started to get up. "I'll help you."

Mama gently pushed me back onto the pillows. "You'll do no such thing. If I find my funny little notebooks, I'll bring them to you. Perhaps they'll help pass the time while your ankle mends."

She hesitated. "There was a reason I told you this story, Sarah. When I said you should have been a boy, I meant that your dreams, like my childhood fancies, are better suited to a man. I don't doubt your ability to become a fine attorney, but have you considered the price you'll have to pay? You'll be the subject of gossip, spurned by other women, and you'll be mocked by men in their clubs. You'll find it difficult, if not impossible, to make a suitable match, or have a home of your own." She took my hand. "My dear, are you willing to make such a sacrifice?"

I had thought of these things, of course. Truth be known, I didn't relish a life alone, and it pained me to think I might never bear children. But there was a price to pay for marriage and motherhood, as well, perhaps one even more costly than that demanded of me by the legal profession.

"I do want those things, Mama, and if I knew of a way to have them both, I would. But as you just pointed out, it must be one or the other."

She sighed, then rose and picked up my tray. "It's not the life I would have chosen for you, Sarah, but I realize nothing I say is likely to change your mind. It never has. You were always the most headstrong of all my children. I only pray you won't live to regret your choice."

"If I do, I'll have no one to blame but myself." I looked up at her. "You could still do it, you know, Mama. Write, I mean. We're all grown now. You could find the time if you tried."

She looked horrified. "Your father would never permit it. You know his feelings about writers."

I smiled. She didn't realize it, but she had just proven my point. To be a married woman in this world meant having a man make choices for you. He could decide how your money was spent, how many children you had, where you lived and in what kind of house, even in what church you would worship.

No, I thought, as my mother carried the tray from the room. I had made the right decision. For better or for worse, I would have to live with it.

The next morning, I convinced Charles that it would do no harm if I sat in the back parlor, my ailing foot propped upon a stool. Because it afforded a magnificent view of the Bay, this had long been my favorite room in the house. Since childhood I had happily escaped to this retreat, never tiring of the ever-changing panorama of sea and sky and hills framed in our large bay window.

Today the scene was idyllic: there were few clouds and the water reflected a moving mirror of blue and silver. It was so clear that I could see Yerba Buena—or Goat Island, as it was usually called—as well as graceful coasting schooners and the small fleet of Italian fishing boats that serviced Fisherman's Wharf.

There I remained for hours, looking out at the Bay and reading the stories in the little notebooks Mama had unearthed in the attic. Charming in their innocence, the tales were told with a spirited imagination I never would have guessed my mother possessed. What a shame, I thought, that such a talent remained unfulfilled because of the outdated dictates of society.

Shortly after lunch I received a surprise visit from Miss Culbertson. The poor woman seemed pathetically relieved to find me in more or less one piece. She regretted my sprained ankle but, like Charles, was happy I had come to no more serious harm. She was considerably taken aback when I told her of my visit with Li Ying, especially when I described his remarkable home. Since client confidentiality did not permit me to discuss the reason for my abduction, the poor woman was genuinely bewildered as to why I'd been singled out for such a dubious honor.

"I'm just grateful you're all right," she said when I'd ended my tale, then went on to thank me for what she generously termed my "invaluable help" in the raid. Chum Ho had been taken in by a Chinese family to be raised as their daughter. There was no use sending her back to China, she said sadly, since the girl's family would almost certainly sell her right back to the slave traffickers. Poverty in some of China's southernmost districts was extreme. Here, Chum Ho would have a good home and a chance for a brighter future than she could expect in her native land. ·

After Miss Culbertson's departure, I went back to reading my mother's stories until my reverie was interrupted by the sound of a voice that could belong to only one person. Our butler's usually unflappable expression registered mild surprise when I instructed him to show Mr. Campbell in.

Robert was untidily dressed, even for him, and he looked cross and out of sorts. Not bothering with even a token show of good manners, he immediately denounced what he charmingly termed "the stupidest stunt he'd ever heard of."

"Shepard is livid I let you out of my sight. I'll be damned if he doesn't blame me for the whole fiasco. What in the name of all that's holy were you thinking of, risking your life like that?"

Without waiting to be invited, he pulled up a chair and sat down, then ordered me to report everything that had happened on the raid, including how I had injured my ankle—which he'd been eyeing ever since walking in the door.

I felt a wave of resentment. How dare the odious man march into my home and toss about demands as if he owned the place!

"How did you hear about the raid?" I demanded.

His laugh was derisive. "You're even more naive than I supposed if you think a white woman can be abducted in Chinatown without it becoming public knowledge. Miss Culbertson had half the police force out looking for you." His eyes bore into mine. "I know this has something to do with that confounded note we found in Hanaford's desk, so you might as well tell me everything."

He looked so incongruous sitting there in Mama's fragile armchair—like some oversized Chief Sitting Bull—that despite myself, my anger turned to amusement. Clearing my throat to cover a strong urge to laugh, I described my Chinatown adventures, concluding with Li Ying's assertion that Hanaford and his partners had jumped his claim in the Comstock Lode, a name commonly used to refer to the Virginia City Silver Mines.

"He admitted to blackmailing them for years," I finished, "without the least embarrassment or guilt."

Robert said thoughtfully, "I can't see why Li would want to kill the geese laying the golden eggs. On the other hand, what if

Hanaford and Mills refused to make any more payments? Maybe Li decided to kill them as an example to the other two."

"Somehow I can't see Hanaford or Mills defying a man as powerful as Li Ying. I certainly wouldn't want him as an enemy." Then, reluctant as I was to tell him what I'd learned about Fowler's identity, I decided he'd better know that, too.

"You're telling me that Fowler is Rufus Mills's illegitimate son?" he exclaimed when I was through. "Can you prove it?"

"No, of course not. But you're missing the point. I was able to verify that Jessie Gooding did work for the Mills family as a hired girl. And the dates of her employment match up with the time Peter must have been conceived. The important thing is that Jessie raised her son to believe Mills was his father. That's what the prosecution will claim if they unearth this story."

Robert stared at me. "You realize this puts the final nail in Fowler's coffin. Probably in Mrs. Hanaford's as well."

"I know," I admitted morosely. "That's why I'm telling you. I need your help to get to the bottom of this mess before the story becomes public knowledge."

He sniffed dismissively and his expression spoke volumes.

"Don't say it. I know who you think is guilty." My ankle had begun to throb and I shifted it to a more comfortable position on the stool. "I admit I could be wrong about Peter, but I'm not mistaken about Annjenett."

"We've been over this before, Sarah. Even you must see how well it fits together: Fowler helps Mrs. Hanaford murder her husband in order to inherit his estate. In return, Mrs. Hanaford helps Fowler plan Mills's death to avenge the wrong done to his mother."

I stifled a groan. Stated like that, Robert's bald reasoning painted a bleak picture for my client.

He gave a sardonic laugh. "You should be working for the prosecution, Sarah. You're handing them an ironclad case."

I shot him a look, but I knew he was right. Instead of helping my client, I was tightening the noose around her neck.

"Fowler knows more than he's telling," I said, hating my defensive tone. "It's time we had the truth out of him."

"Assuming the man is capable of telling the truth—which I seriously doubt."

"We have to make him understand it's his only chance of avoiding the gallows. I know he isn't our client, but—"

"All right, all right," he broke in, holding up a hand. "When do you want to visit the jail?"

"So you're willing to help?"

"What choice do I have? You've made up your mind. Changing it would be like trying to stop a herd of stampeding buffalo."

"Excellent," I said, ignoring the unflattering analogy. "I'll see you at the jail, then, first thing Monday morning."

He stood and fixed me with those clear, blue-green eyes.

"Just remember, Sarah, this was your idea. Once we're inside that cell, I mean to have the truth out of Fowler. If necessary, I'm prepared to wring it out of him!"

Samuel had spent the weekend in the country, so I didn't have a chance to speak to him until Sunday evening. Before he could start in on the business with Miss Culbertson, I told him what I had learned about Fowler's probable parentage, then recounted the raid we'd staged to save little Chum Ho from the highbinders, including my unwilling visit with Li Ying. To my surprise, he seemed more intrigued than angry.

"What a wonderful story this would make," he said, journalistic eyes alight.

"Don't even think about it!"

He laughed. "Relax, Sarah, your secret's safe with me. At least for the time being. I'd give a lot to meet this Li Ying, though. You don't suppose—"

"No, Samuel, I don't. Besides, I was blindfolded. I could walk down every street in Chinatown and still have no idea where I was taken."

There was a sudden burst of laughter outside the library door. Samuel waited until the voices had passed before saying, "Speaking of Chinatown, I had a chance to speak to my contacts before I left town. It seems you were right about Mills, little sister. Evidently he'd been using opium for at least a year, perhaps longer. I don't know what this does for your case, but it might explain why he was in Chinatown the night he was killed. Unless, of course, he was delivering a blackmail payment to Li."

"No, I don't think that was it. As Robert pointed out, why would Li want to kill off a good thing?"

He sat for several minutes, thinking. "You know, Sarah, maybe we're overlooking the obvious. There's always the possibility Mills was murdered because he owed money to his opium dealer."

I considered this. "As far as I know Mills wasn't facing financial difficulty, although I suppose I should check at his bank. But wouldn't it make more sense for his supplier to simply withhold the drug until Mills paid? Besides, it seems too much of a coincidence that a Chinese opium dealer would just happen to stab Mills in the same anatomical region as Hanaford's killer."

"Stranger things have happened, but it does seem improbable." He pulled out his watch. "It's six. I'm late for an engagement."

"With Hortense Weslyum?" I said with a wry smile. Hortense

was Samuel's latest lady friend, a young woman I found particularly silly and superficial. Hortense, however, had two important qualities to recommend her to my brother: she was very pretty, and her father published the *Morning Chronicle,* a valuable connection for an aspiring journalist.

Samuel grinned. "As a matter of fact, I've been invited to attend the opera with Hortense and her parents."

"Given Hortense's intellect and sparkling wit," I said with thinly veiled sarcasm, "I'm sure you'll have a stimulating evening. Do please give my regards to Mr. Weslyum. I understand the *Morning Chronicle* is searching for a new true crime serial. I'm sure he'll find your ideas fascinating."

Samuel pulled a face at me—the same one he'd used to tease me since we were children—then hurried off, leaving me alone to contemplate the ruinous case against my client.

I spent a restless night filled with nightmares about Annjenett being led to the gallows, and awoke the next morning tired and mildly depressed. I was pleased to note, however, that my injured ankle felt a good deal better. Confident I'd be able to hobble about, I dressed and slipped out of the house before anyone could raise a fuss.

True to his word, Robert was waiting for me at the jail. My heart sank, however, at the sight of his dour expression.

"The police have found out about Fowler's connection to Rufus Mills," he bluntly announced. "There's no point looking so stricken, Sarah. You said yourself they were bound to stumble onto Fowler's questionable paternity."

"Yes, but not so soon. We need more time!"

"Well, we aren't going to get it. The police have been questioning the two of them all morning. They're being allowed no visitors." He looked glumly at a passing jailer. "Paulson was right. Our only hope now is to plead insanity."

"No! Annjenett did not kill her husband. I refuse to give her up to the wolves without a fight."

Robert threw up his hands. "Oh, for god's sake! Why is it so hard for you to admit defeat?"

Realizing the futility of trying to make him see my point of view, I turned to leave only to run headlong into Thomas Cooke. The change in Annjenett's father since his daughter's arraignment was startling: his face was ashen, his eyes sunken, and clearly he had lost weight. His eyes lit with recognition when he saw us, which was surprising since we had never been formally introduced.

"Excuse me, but I believe you are Miss Woolson," he said. "And you're Mr. Campbell, are you not, sir? You were in court with my poor girl." His overbright eyes were pleading. "Please, you must help me. They refuse to let me in to see her."

"I'm sorry, Mr. Cooke," I told him gently. "Evidently she's being questioned. Perhaps if you come back later—"

"Why won't anyone tell me what's happening?" he broke in, taking hold of my arm. "I've been hearing wild stories about that man, Fowler. It's all lies, I'm sure of it! My daughter was a good wife. She would never have been unfaithful. And with an actor, of all people."

As I tried to extricate myself from his painful grasp, Robert stepped in and gently pried the man's fingers from my arm.

"There's no need to excite yourself, Mr. Cooke," he said, guiding the distraught man toward the door. "I'm sure they'll let you see your daughter as soon as she's back in her cell."

"You don't understand," Cooke cried, "it's all my fault. If I hadn't been such a fool, my poor girl would never have had to marry that man. She didn't love him. I knew that, yet—" His voice caught in a half sob. "Oh, lord, if I hadn't been so selfish, none of this would have happened! There must be something I can do."

"We're doing everything possible," Robert assured him.

I watched openmouthed as the distressed man allowed himself to be led outside. This was a totally unexpected side to Robert Campbell. Who could have guessed that the voice capable of stopping wild horses in their tracks could be so gentle?

Flagging a cab, Robert helped Cooke inside. When he turned back and found me watching, he frowned, as if daring me to comment on his behavior. I started to speak, then decided it would be best to act as if I hadn't noticed. Instead, I hailed my own cab.

"Now where are you going?" he asked, jumping in behind me.

"If you must know, I'm going to Hanaford's bank. Since there's no way I can get into 'trouble' there, you're free to go about your own business."

In truth, I wanted a private word with Eban Potter concerning Mills's financial situation. Since this was a delicate subject, I feared that Robert's presence would only complicate matters. But when the irritating man made no move to leave the cab, I resigned myself to suffering his company, at least until I could find some way to be rid of him.

We arrived at San Francisco Savings and Trust shortly after noon, but were told that the manager was out. When I explained the importance of our business to the clerk, he finally relented and informed us that the bank manager sometimes ate his lunch in the small park across the street.

Ignoring Robert's grumbles that he could use a bite to eat himself, I led the way through the rush of lunch-hour traffic to a small but charming oasis set, like a rare gem, between two solid walls of mortar and brick. It was delightful to find natural beauty left undisturbed in the center of town. I have long maintained that San Francisco must act soon to preserve our city's natural flora and fauna from careless urbanization. It's city parks such as these that we must save before they are sealed beneath a sea of concrete. Entering the quiet retreat, I was pleased to spy tall oak and arroyo trees, as well as a wide selection of native fern, Douglas Iris and the colorful California Poppy.

Robert brought me back to our errand when he spied Eban Potter sitting alone on a bench in front of a small pond. Beyond the water was an interesting outcropping of rock that formed a pleasing grotto. A dozen or so birds fluttered about the bank manager's feet, feasting on the remains of his lunch. Potter looked up, startled to see us, and for a moment I regretted that we'd intruded upon such a tranquil scene. His smile and gracious greeting, however, quickly set me at ease.

"Miss Woolson, what a delightful surprise," he said, rising. I performed the introductions, then begged him to sit down again as Robert and I settled on an adjoining bench.

"You've chosen a peaceful spot, Mr. Potter," I told him.

Potter threw more crumbs to the greedy birds, then smiled. "I used to bring my daughter here when she was a little girl. She loved to feed the birds and pick flowers. She'd make up a little bouquet and insist I take it back to the bank and place it on my desk so I would remember her while I worked."

"Oh? I didn't know you had a daughter." For some reason I had assumed the baby had died in childbirth with her mother.

"Louisa died of a fever, Miss Woolson. It's been nearly two years now. I come here to remember the happy times we enjoyed together." He tossed out the last of the crumbs and brushed his hands. "But you didn't come here to listen to a rambling old man." His eyes grew very large and looking around, he lowered his voice.

"I've been hearing the wildest rumors, Miss Woolson, about you and that woman from the Presbyterian Mission. You didn't—I mean you couldn't really have accompanied her on one of her raids?"

"Actually, I did, Mr. Potter. Miss Culbertson is a most courageous woman."

"But it must have been dangerous." He gave a little shudder. "Especially if what they say is true about the tong lord. Did he—I mean, were you actually kidnapped?"

Without going into details, I briefly sketched my late-night visit with Li Ying, finishing with Li's assertion that the four mining partners had stolen the claim to his Comstock silver mine.

"Did Mr. Hanaford ever mention this to you?" I asked.

Potter looked taken aback. "What an astonishing story. I know little about this Li Ying, but I have a difficult time believing his accusations can be true."

I had been prepared for the bank manager's loyalty to his slain employer and decided to change tactics. As delicately as possible, I broached the subject of Peter's possible relationship to Rufus Mills. This time he didn't appear surprised.

"I remember the incident, of course. It was in all the newspapers." He stopped, looking embarrassed.

"What is it, man?" asked Robert, leaning forward on the bench.

"Well," Potter said hesitantly, "At the time of the scandal I had reason to doubt Mr. Mills's denials of paternity. Quite by accident, I overheard a conversation he had with Mr. Hanaford in which he all but admitted to being the boy's father. It was right after the stories began to appear in the papers. Mr. Mills was very upset. He accused the woman of being a scheming opportunist, and said he'd had better, that is, more obliging women at houses of—I mean—" His face colored.

"We get your meaning, Potter," Robert told him.

"It was no secret that Mr. Mills longed for a son," the manager went on, "but sadly Mrs. Mills did not seem able to give him children. I think he secretly believed the Gooding woman's child was his, but he didn't dare claim paternity for fear of bad publicity. He was just beginning to make a name for himself, you see. The scandal could have ruined him."

Maddeningly, a young couple strolling through the park stopped a few feet from where we sat and admired the birds clustering around their feet in hopes of another meal.

"Go on, please," I prodded, when the couple finally moved on.

"There's not much more, except for the boy himself. The Gooding woman brought him to the bank once—he was ten or eleven, I believe. Anyway, the child was the spitting image of Mr. Mills. I don't see how anyone could have doubted his paternity once they'd seen the lad." He sighed. "But in the end, the court ruled in Mr. Mills's favor. I felt sorry for the boy and his mother. But there was nothing I could do."

"You weren't called as a witness?" I asked in surprise.

"No. Strange, isn't it? When Miss Gooding's lawyers questioned me, I told them everything I knew, including the conversation I'd overheard between Cornelius and Mr. Mills. This may sound fanciful, but I got the impression they didn't particularly care whether their client won her case or not. They thanked me, but said my testimony wouldn't be necessary."

Robert and I exchanged glances, each of us, I suspected, thinking the same thing: Jessie Gooding's own lawyers had been bought off. I thought of the pathetic old woman living in the house on the Barbary Coast and wondered what kind of man would reduce a woman to such circumstances, especially if he suspected he was the father of her child. I could only imagine how hard it must have been for Peter, struggling to survive on the streets while the man he believed to be his father lived as a millionaire. But this was no time for moral outrage, not while my client languished in that miserable cell. Pressing on with the business at hand, I asked if Potter had any reason to believe that Mr. Mills was experiencing financial difficulties before his death.

"It would be unethical for me to discuss a client's account, Miss Woolson," he replied soberly. "But I don't think I'd be breaking a confidence to assure you that Mr. Mills's financial affairs were in very good order."

"I suppose that will have to do." I was disappointed but not surprised that he couldn't be more specific. There was, however, one last thing I wanted to know. "I saw Mr. Wylde at the theater last week, in the company of a lovely young woman. She was tall and slender and had golden hair dressed in the latest French fashion. Do you happen to know who she might be?"

"You must be referring to Yvette, Mr. Wylde's daughter," Potter replied with a smile. "I wasn't aware she was in town."

It was my turn to look surprised. "Mr. Wylde's daughter? I didn't realize he was married."

"It was many years ago, shortly after his return from Virginia City," Potter explained. "His wife was French and very beautiful. Not long afterward, Yvette was born. Unfortunately, Mrs. Wylde seemed unable to adjust to life in San Francisco and begged to return to her native country. I assume Mr. Wylde didn't care to leave the city, for in the end his wife went back to France without him, taking the little girl. I believe Yvette recently finished her schooling abroad."

"Were the Wyldes divorced?" I asked.

"If they legalized their separation, I didn't hear of it. I do know that Mr. Wylde makes frequent trips to Paris to visit his daughter. I believe they've remained close. I can't presume to know the nature of his relationship with his wife."

"Of course not," Robert answered, giving me a hard glare. It was clear from his expression that he not only saw little purpose to these questions, but that he was anxious to be off.

Realizing there wasn't much more to be learned from the bank manager, I thanked him for his time and Robert and I walked out to the street where, predictably, he began ranting about my ankle, admonishing me to go home and get some rest. Since my foot was clearly none of his business, I insisted on accompanying him to the office. There, I was forced to endure yet another lecture about my involvement with Miss Culbertson, this time from my tedious employer. When the fountain of his ire finally ran dry, I retired to my office where I closed the door, propped up my throbbing foot, and stared gloomily at the gray walls. Then, for lack of something more productive to do, I proceeded to write out a detailed list of everything we had so far learned about the case.

When I had finished, I studied the page. It was disappointing to see how little solid information we'd managed to accrue. Assuming Annjenett and Peter's innocence, the only other people I could think of who would profit from Hanaford and Mills's deaths were Wylde and Senator Broughton. If this deduction was true, then one of these men was a murderer, while the other man's life was in mortal danger. The problem, of course, was which one was which?

Then there was the unusual way Hanaford and Mills had been killed. Why attack their genitals? I asked myself. I simply could not believe this had been coincidental, or that the choice had been random. Striking at the heart or the throat would have been a much quicker and more efficient way to ensure death. Why had the assailant chosen that particular area of the anatomy?

Which led me—however unwillingly—back to Annjenett and Peter. Although loath to admit it, I could imagine Fowler choosing to kill Hanaford in this manner because of the abuse Annjenett had suffered at his hands. Likewise, he might have felt Mills deserved the same fate because of the way he'd mistreated his mother.

I leaned back in my chair, unhappy with where this was leading. Robert was right, the more evidence I uncovered, the more it seemed to seal Peter Fowler's fate. Was it possible Annjenett had been so deceived by the actor that she'd been willing to provide him with a false alibi the night of her husband's death? Had she really gone downstairs with him to confront Hanaford? Or had she stayed in her room while Peter faced her husband alone?

I threw down my pen in disgust. Even to me this explanation seemed the most plausible. If I couldn't be sure of my client's story, how in the world could I expect a jury to believe it?

That evening, I remained in the parlor mulling over the case long after the rest of the family retired. I expected Samuel—who was again out with Hortense Weslyum—to be home soon. I kept telling myself that if we could only put our heads together, we might begin to make sense of this mess.

I don't know how long I'd been dozing in my chair when I was startled awake by a soft knock. Hurrying into the hall, I opened the front door a crack and was startled to find George Lewis, in full police uniform, standing on the stoop.

"I beg your pardon, Miss Sarah," he said, looking surprised to see me. "I saw the light in the window and thought Samuel might still be up."

Something about the man's manner alarmed me. I knew he would never call this late at night without serious provocation.

"What is it, George? Has something happened to Mrs. Hanaford?"

"No," he said quickly, sensing my distress. "It's Senator Broughton. He was attacked this evening—outside his club."

CHAPTER TEN

I stared at George, too stunned to speak. Before I could gather my wits to ask what had happened, a carriage reined up on the street in front of us and Samuel alighted. Not surprisingly, he looked startled to see his friend and I conversing outside the front door.

"George? What in god's name are you doing here at this hour?" he asked, taking the steps two at a time.

Before George could answer, I motioned both men inside. This was hardly the place to conduct a conversation with a uniformed policeman, especially after midnight. Already several lights had been lit in adjoining houses. It would be the scandal of the neighborhood if curious eyes observed our incongruous little group from behind drawn shades. Leading the way into the parlor, I turned up the gaslight while Samuel stoked the dying embers in the hearth. When the fire crackled back to life, he threw on a fresh log and turned to George.

"All right, man, out with it. What's happened?"

George looked self-consciously from my brother to me, then with a slightly flushed face began the surprising narrative.

"An elderly couple were walking their dog shortly after nine this evening, when they saw Broughton leave the Bohemian Club. He tried to hail a cab, but when none came by he started to walk. He'd taken no more than a few steps when a man jumped out of the shadows and began striking at him with a knife. When the couple shouted for help, the man ran away. Their cries probably saved his life. As it was, he suffered only minor cuts and bruises."

Samuel considered his friend for a moment, then said, "It must have been an attempted robbery."

"Not according to the senator," George replied. He leaned forward, his boyish face earnest. "In fact—now here's the strange part—Broughton claims the attack was an accident."

"An accident?" I stared blankly at the young man. "But that's ridiculous!"

"Yes, that's what I thought," George agreed. "But the senator insists the man meant him no harm."

There being no rational response to such an irrational statement, the three of us sat for a time in silence. I was about to question George further, when the door suddenly opened to reveal Celia, dressed in a pale-colored dressing gown and carrying a lighted candle. Her eyes went from Samuel to me, then grew very wide at the sight of the uniformed policeman calmly sitting in our front parlor.

"I heard voices," she said in growing alarm. "Is something wrong?"

I drew my sister-in-law into the room before she could rouse the rest of the house. Keeping my voice low, I introduced George, then briefly explained the reason for his visit.

Celia put a small hand to her mouth to stifle a gasp. "But that's horrible! Was the senator seriously injured? Have they caught the assailant?"

"The man's face was covered, Mrs. Woolson," George told her, sounding a little abashed. "I fear we have little to go on."

Celia's face creased with concern. "It's a terrible thought, but do you think the attack on Senator Broughton can have anything to do with the murders? It seems, well, too much of a coincidence otherwise."

"I couldn't agree more," I said, looking pointedly at George.

He shifted uneasily. "It won't be the official police position, mind you, but yes, I'm beginning to think you may be right."

"If it is connected," Celia said eagerly, "then surely the police will be forced to release Mrs. Hanaford and Mr. Fowler. They couldn't have attacked the senator from their jail cells."

"I'm afraid it's not that simple," George told her. "The prosecutor's put together a strong case against those two. It'll take a lot to get him to change his mind. It doesn't help that Senator Broughton insists tonight's attack was an accident."

"How can a knife attack be an accident?" I said in disdain. "I still don't see why he'd make such a ludicrous statement. Unless—" I looked at George. "Is it possible Senator Broughton recognized his assailant and for some reason feels the need to protect him?"

It was clear from George's face that this possibility hadn't occurred to him. "The senator claims it happened too fast to get a good look at his attacker, which agrees with the witnesses' account. According to them, the man wore a dark topcoat, and his hat was pulled down so low it was impossible to see his face."

A log fell in the fireplace. Samuel picked up a poker and prodded it back into place, then stood with his back to the hearth. "So, what now?"

"I don't think we have a choice," I said matter-of-factly. "Since the authorities don't see fit to investigate, we'll have to do it ourselves." Three sets of eyes watched as I reached for a notebook and pencil. On the first page I wrote: "To Discover." "First," I said, "we need to know where Benjamin Wylde was at the time of Senator Broughton's attack."

"Benjamin Wylde?" Celia looked bewildered. "What can he have to do with this?"

George coughed discreetly while Samuel rolled his eyes. Ignoring them, I explained the partners' tontine agreement, adding that the fund had by now grown into a very sizeable sum of money.

"But surely you can't suspect Mr. Wylde!" Celia exclaimed.

"It's a possibility we must at least consider," I said, daring my brother to contradict me. Samuel gave me one of his looks, but said nothing. "All right then. The second thing we have to determine is Mr. Wylde's financial situation."

"And just how do you propose to do that?" asked my brother, a challenging twinkle in his eye.

I chewed thoughtfully on my pencil. "We can hardly ask Wylde to show us his books, so I guess I'm going to have to manage another look at his file."

Samuel snorted. "God help you if Shepard catches you pulling a fool stunt like that. You're treading on thin ice as it is."

Celia was shaking her head doubtfully. "I just can't imagine Mr. Wylde as a murderer."

"Unfortunately, money and influence do not render a man incapable of violence," I told her grimly.

Celia nodded, but I could see her misgivings mirrored in George and Samuel's eyes. Clearly I was outnumbered.

"All right," I said with a sigh. "If Wylde can account for his time the night of either murder—or tonight when Senator Broughton was attacked—I'll concede his probable innocence.

There, I can't speak fairer than that. But keep in mind he already lied about his whereabouts the night Mills was killed."

George and Celia looked at me in surprise, and I realized that only Samuel knew about my visit to Wylde's office. Deciding it would be foolish to hold anything back at this stage, I related everything I'd learned to date concerning the case, including Mills's opium addiction and my abduction by Li Ying. When I finished, Samuel was leaning back on the sofa, eyes closed, an enigmatic smile on his face. George and Celia were regarding me in openmouthed astonishment.

"This must be held in the strictest confidence," I told them. "Particularly by you, George. At least until we've had an opportunity to discover the truth. After that, you can take our findings to your superiors. Do you agree?" I stared hard at the young man until he reluctantly nodded.

"If this comes out, I could lose my job," he said unhappily. "But you're right, Miss Sarah. If I went to them with a story like this, they'd not only deny it had anything to do with the case, they'd think I'd lost my mind in the bargain."

Celia, who'd been listening quietly, said, "I can't stop thinking about Mrs. Hanaford. I don't know how she manages to survive in that awful place. Thank goodness she has you, Sarah, or she'd have little reason for hope." Her small jaw hardened. "I want to do all I can to help the poor woman. If I found myself in her place, I fear I wouldn't be able to bear it."

"Adversity often brings out the best or the worst in us," I told her gently. "Given the same situation, I'm sure you'd discover a reserve of strength you didn't know you had." Then, in an effort to mask how much Celia's sentiments had moved me, I went back to my list. "Now, how are we going to check on Wylde's whereabouts?"

"If you're really set on doing this, Sarah, I think we should hire a professional," Samuel said. "Perhaps a man who's had experience on the force. George, you must know of someone."

George didn't look hopeful. "Most of the private inquiry agents I know left the department under dubious circumstances. I wouldn't trust them to find a wrench in a toolbox, or if they did, to keep it to themselves. The few who are reputable receive the bulk of their incomes performing work for local attorneys."

"Including Wylde?" asked Samuel.

"Particularly Wylde," George said. "I can't think of anyone we could count on not to go to him and reveal what we're doing."

"And be paid a handsome reward for his efforts," Samuel added.

"Exactly. As I said earlier, it appears we must do this on our own." I turned to my brother. "Samuel, couldn't you make inquiries about Wylde at your club? There's always the possibility he was seen by someone on the nights of the murders."

"I could try," he said a bit doubtfully. "We share few mutual friends—and of course I don't know which clubs he belongs to—but I'll see what I can find out."

"Excellent." I noted this on the paper. "Now, if we only had some way of asking a few discreet questions at his home." I looked hopefully at George, whose eyes widened as he took my meaning.

"Oh, no, Miss Sarah. It would be worth my job if I went around questioning people on my own. Especially a man like Mr. Wylde." He reddened, as if afraid of being perceived a coward. "But I'll see what I can find out at the station. Maybe it will occur to the lieutenant to question Mr. Wylde or his servants."

I thanked George but thought it unlikely anyone on the force would be brave enough to face the wrath of a man as powerful as Benjamin Wylde, especially when the attorney possessed the skill and wherewithal to press his grievances in court. Moreover, the police had no reason to question anyone else when they were convinced that the real killers were already in custody.

"It's too bad we can't plant someone in Wylde's household," I mused, more to myself than to the others.

Celia looked up. "Oh, but I think we already have someone there. If I'm not mistaken, one of Ina's sisters works for Mr. Wylde."

Celia was referring to our maid, Ina Corks, who came from a large Irish family. Most of her brothers worked in shipyards or on the docks. The majority of her sisters were, like herself, employed as domestics.

"Of course we'd have to offer Ina a plausible reason for doing such a thing," she went on. "We certainly can't say we suspect Mr. Wylde of being a murderer."

"Good lord, no," Samuel said, laughing. "She's a frightened little mouse as it is."

The four of us sat thinking for several moments, then I turned to Celia. "What if we told Ina that one of your friends was taken with a man she saw while riding in Golden Gate Park. From his description, you thought the man might be Wylde. But before you mention his name to your friend, you wondered if she'd make sure he was actually in town on the dates she saw him." I looked around for a response. "Well, what do you think?"

"It might work," Samuel said thoughtfully.

"That's a splendid idea," pronounced Celia. "It's sure to appeal to Ina's sense of romance. If Mama-in-law can spare her, I'll invite her to come along when I take the children to the park tomorrow. That way we can talk without being overheard."

"Excellent." I jotted this down below Samuel's contribution.

"Even if we establish that Wylde was in the city, we still won't know if he went out on the nights in question, and if he did, where he went," George put in. He looked at Celia. "Surely obtaining such personal information is asking too much of your maid's sister."

"Not if she's clever," Celia told him. "Mind you, she couldn't ask Mr. Wylde such questions. But if she's careful, she could query the other servants. Certainly the butler and Mr. Wylde's valet would know his movements on any given night, and perhaps one or two of the maids. There's a great deal of downstairs gossip in any household, Mr. Lewis. A resourceful girl can learn a great deal."

"Even if Wylde got word of the nosey maid," I said as George continued to look doubtful, "he'd just think himself the target of a lovesick female. But chances are, he'll hear nothing. He's probably as oblivious to the internal workings of his own house as Samuel is about his."

Samuel started to object but, glancing at my timepiece, I cut him off. "It's late. Unless there are any more suggestions, we'd better get to bed." Actually, I wanted to break up our meeting before further objections could be raised. I needed no one to point out the flaws—as well as the risks—in our plan. On the other hand, no one had come up with a better strategy and Annjenett's trial would start in a matter of days. If we weren't prepared to gamble now, it might soon be too late.

A quarter of an hour later, lying beneath my quilt, I thought back to Celia's concerns about Annjenett. No clean sheets and soft blankets for my client, or the warmth of coals glowing cozily in the hearth. Did she despair of returning to her own home and enjoying the simple creature comforts, which like most of us, she'd always taken for granted? In the dead of night, did her jailers trouble themselves to speak encouraging words to allay her fears? Or did she lie in her cold cell feeling abandoned by the world?

Despite the warm bedclothes tucked about my neck I shivered, not from the cold, but from fear. Celia said that Annjenett was fortunate to have me, that I might represent her only hope. But what if I failed in my quest to find the real murderer? What if, in the end, I was unable to set her free?

In the dark loneliness of my bedchamber, it was a fear I could no longer keep at bay.

The following morning I arrived at the office early, hoping to speak to Robert before Shepard and the other senior attorneys made an appearance. I was surprised to find him already ensconced behind the cluttered desk in his office.

"Thanks to you I'm days behind in my work," he grumbled, sweeping out a hand to indicate a pile of books and papers so high they nearly hid his disapproving face.

"It wasn't my idea that you follow me like a lost dog all over town." Ignoring his mostly unprintable retort, I seated myself on the only other chair in the miniscule room and proceeded to tell him about the attack on Senator Broughton. When I finished, he looked at me with narrowed eyes.

"Naturally, you think this has something to do with Mills and Hannaford's deaths."

"Of course they're connected." I regarded him in exasperation, then decided that, despite his obtuseness, I had no choice but to press on. "Look, Robert, I didn't come here to argue. The fact is, I need your help."

He raised a suspicious brow. "To do what?"

"I need information about Benjamin Wylde's financial situation."

I sat silently through the anticipated explosion. When Robert finally ran out of steam, I calmly continued, "Since Shepard has forbidden me to go into the file room, I thought you might look up the pertinent data for me." I stared pointedly at his cluttered desk. "Surely some of these cases require you to access the files. It shouldn't present a problem."

"Of course not. No problem at all. Other than the fact that I'd be fired on the spot if Shepard, or any of the partners, caught me giving you personal information from a client's file."

I noted the stubborn tilt of his square jaw and the disdainful glint of those penetrating eyes, then stood and straightened my skirt. "All right, have it your way. I'll have to find a way to get the file myself. Shepard's in the office this morning and I'd hoped to avoid a possible confrontation. However, needs must."

"Oh, good lord!"

He was out of his chair before I could reach the door. I gave a little gasp as he took hold of my arm, but I didn't attempt to pull away. In truth, my threatened departure had been a bluff. I badly needed Robert's help. It would be far more difficult to carry out the mission on my own.

"You little fool!" he said sharply. "Don't you know that Shepard is looking for any excuse to throw you out of here? I'm not the only one he's spoken to. Everyone in the office has been instructed to keep an eye on you. You haven't a prayer of slipping into the file room unnoticed."

For some inexplicable reason, my heart had begun to pound in my chest. No doubt, I reasoned, it was because I sensed his weakening resolve. I took a deep, calming breath, then looked up at the ruddy face so close to my own.

"Well, well, Mr. Campbell," I said, trying to keep my tone nonchalant. "I'd have expected you to cheer the possibility of seeing the last of me in this office."

"I'm not saying I wouldn't, you annoying woman—" I watched as he glanced through the glass portion of his door. By now, most of the clerks had arrived and were staring curiously at us from their desks. Hastily, he let go of my arm and moved back a step. "Damn it all, Sarah, you're going to get us both fired!"

For a moment our gazes locked. I don't think I'd fully appreciated what an intense shade of turquoise his eyes were, or how they seemed to bore straight through me. I had no idea what he saw in mine, but it was easy enough to read in his the fierce internal battle he was waging.

Finally, he expelled the breath he'd been holding and said, "For god's sake, Sarah, don't do anything stupid. Shepard's due at court after lunch. I'll wait until then and see what I can do."

"Thank you, Robert. You won't regret helping me."

He gave an abrupt snort. "That remains to be seen. It's far more likely I'll regret it a great deal."

It was hard to fill the hours before lunch. Augustus Paulson had scheduled another strategy meeting for the following week, but until then there was little work I could do on the case. At any rate, I couldn't plan my next move until Samuel, Celia and George had completed the assignments we'd agreed upon the night before. Most irritating, of course, was the fact that I couldn't complete my own part of the scheme until Robert secured Wylde's files. I'm not used to relying on others to carry out tasks that, at the risk of sounding immodest, I'm best qualified to perform on my own. The enforced inactivity was maddening!

Several times I walked past the closed file room, my fingers itching to open the door. But each time I reached for the knob, a clerk or associate attorney always seemed to happen by. After several aborted attempts, I began to believe that Robert had spoken nothing less than the truth. It seemed that my employer had enlisted everyone in the office to keep an eye on me!

Furious to be treated with such condescension, I boldly marched into Joseph Shepard's office and demanded that he consign some of the firm's work to me.

"I'm well aware that you've ordered Robert Campbell to dog my every step," I told him. "Now you've set the rest of the office to spying on me as well. If you really want to keep me out of trouble, then give me some bona fide work to do." He stared, small eyes bulging, while I went on to state that I had a particular case in mind. "Mrs. Rebecca Carpenter's suit against Mr. Howard Brooks has come to my attention."

He looked at me blankly and I saw I must refresh his memory.

"It concerns a vehicular accident some months ago. Mrs. Carpenter was returning home from her employment as a room maid at the Baldwin Hotel when she was hit by Mr. Brooks's carriage. She claims he drove without care to her person, indeed without concern for the safety of any pedestrian."

He made a dismissive gesture. "Yes, yes, I remember," he said, although it was plain he hadn't the slightest recollection of the event. "And just what do you feel you could bring to this case?"

"The defendant counters that he was in no way negligent. What is more, he argues that Mrs. Carpenter cannot use loss of wages as evidence of personal damage suffered as a result of the injury."

"Those arguments seem perfectly sound. This woman, er—"

"Mrs. Carpenter," I prompted, praying for patience.

"Yes, yes. Mrs. Carpenter must realize that a wife's time and services belong to her husband. For loss of such service and expenses, the husband alone has the right to sue. The law is perfectly clear on this point. I can't imagine what you think you can do to change it."

"It has already been changed," I told him, enjoying the look of surprise on his pudgy face. "Or, at least it's been altered. By the Earnings Act of 1860."

He rejected this with a wave of his hand. "A ridiculous piece of legislation, for which we can thank a bunch of ignorant busybodies who think that if they make enough fuss they'll be accorded 'women's rights.'" These last words were uttered in a voice laden with sarcasm. "It's all so much nonsense. Besides, that act has yet to be satisfactorily tested in court."

"Exactly! Which is why we must seize the opportunity to do so now. To date, the judiciary has chosen to interpret the intent and spirit of the act as narrowly as possible. Mrs. Carpenter has four small children. Her husband is a drunkard and currently unemployed. Because of Mr. Brooks's carelessness, she'll be unable to work for weeks, perhaps months. We must do everything we can to see that she receives a fair settlement."

My employer held up a protesting hand, more to get rid of me, I suspected, then because he agreed with my sentiments.

"All right, Miss Woolson, you've made your point. If it will keep you out of my office, you may inform Mr. Ackroyd that I've given you leave to write a brief on the case. Now, please, I must prepare for court this afternoon."

Delighted, I set off to find Eugene Ackroyd, one of the firm's junior associates. As Ackroyd, too, appeared to have forgotten poor Mrs. Carpenter, he seemed happy enough to pass her on to me. Carrying her pitifully thin file into my office, I set to work. Thanks to Mrs. Carpenter's excellent recall of the accident— as well as the accounts of one or two apparently reliable eyewitnesses—I was able to compose a legal brief that I felt confident would force the most narrow-minded judge to consider my client's position.

I was so engrossed in my work that I was startled when Samuel entered my office late that afternoon, with Robert following close upon his heel.

"A funny little clerk told me I'd find you back here," my brother explained, then looked inquiringly at Robert.

Realizing the two hadn't met, I performed the introductions, then told Samuel that Robert was also helping with Annjenett's case. Predictably, Robert instantly started to protest my version of his role in our unofficial investigation, when Samuel grinned broadly and reached out his hand.

"So you're Campbell. Sarah's spoken of you. I'm pleased to make your acquaintance at last."

Robert seemed momentarily taken aback by Samuel's congeniality, then reached out and returned the handshake. I watched Robert's reaction with amazement; I never fail to marvel at the easy way Samuel has with people—men as well as the women who flutter about him like bees on a honeycomb. I've heard Papa proclaim more than once that Samuel could charm Beelzebub himself if he had a mind.

"My pleasure, Mr. Woolson," Robert said, studying Samuel. He appeared to like what he saw, for he returned my brother's smile. "I understand you're also a lawyer?"

"I haven't taken the bar examination yet," Samuel hedged, loath to admit, I knew, that he had no intentions of trying—at least not in the foreseeable future.

"Will you two please come in and close the door?" I said, not anxious to be overheard by the prying ears that I now suspected were lurking in every corner. Fortunately, I had moved a third chair into my office. We were crowded, but no one need stand. "First you, Robert? Did you find Wylde's file?"

"I found several," he answered. "I didn't dare remove them from the file room, but I had time to give them a cursory look."

"And?" I prodded.

Robert answered with obvious reluctance. "It seems that some of Wylde's investments haven't been doing well. He lost a significant amount of money in the crash of '79."

"Are you saying that he's bankrupt?" Samuel asked in surprise.

"Not at all. He's just suffered one or two financial reversals." He darted me a look. "I'm reluctant to pass this on to your sister. She has an unfortunate tendency to make mountains out of molehills."

Samuel laughed. "That's an understatement."

I ignored them, concerned only with how this information might affect our case. "So, it's possible that Wylde viewed the tontine as a way out of his financial difficulties," I mused aloud.

Robert threw up his arms. "There, you see what I mean? We don't know enough about Wylde's situation to jump to such an outrageous and potentially litigious conclusion. The western stock market is always volatile. For all we know, he may have a fortune in reserve and invest only what he can afford to lose."

"That's true," I admitted calmly, surprising both men, I'm sure, by refusing to let them ruffle my good nature. "It's one more piece to the puzzle, though. We'll have to obtain more precise figures in order to form a more educated judgment, but you've made a good start, Robert."

For some reason, my innocently offered gratitude seemed to ruffle the attorney's ever-explosive temper. Before he could gear up to a full assault, however, I turned to Samuel.

"Were you able to find out anything at Wylde's clubs?"

"Not much. Wylde claims membership in the Bohemian

Club—to which I also belong," he added for Robert's benefit. "But I rarely see him there. Evidently, he spends more time at the Pacific Union Club. Too bad we can't enlist Frederick's help," he added, alluding to the family joke that our eldest brother spends more time at his club than he does at his own home. On this point, at least, I can't bring myself to cite Frederick. If I were married to Henrietta, I might well move into my club, bag and baggage."

"Do you know if he was at either club when the murders were committed?" I asked, moving to the heart of the matter.

"I know he wasn't at the Bohemian," Samuel answered. "Checking the Pacific Union will be more difficult, since I have no membership there. However, several of my Bohemian colleagues who belong to both clubs have promised to make some discreet inquiries."

"Which may take more time than we have at our disposal," I said, then wondered aloud if Celia had had any luck with Ina.

"Who's Celia?" asked Robert. "And what role does she play in this melodrama you've concocted?"

Briefly, I described our household, then related the strategy Samuel, George, Celia and I had agreed upon the night before.

"I just hope these wild speculations of yours don't result in a libel suit," said Robert gloomily.

"Nonsense," I said, then added with blissful naiveté, "Benjamin Wylde need never learn of our inquiries."

As it was nearly five o'clock, Samuel and I bade farewell to Robert and left for home. Eager to learn how Celia had fared with our little Irish maid, I was disappointed to learn that she and my mother were not yet back from paying social calls. While I waited for them to return, I spent a more or less unproductive hour in my room updating the list I'd drawn up concerning the case.

When I was finished, I looked over my short list of suspects. In addition to Peter Fowler—who in all honesty I couldn't rule out—it included Benjamin Wylde, Senator Broughton and Li Ying.

I forced myself to examine these men with a dispassionate eye. Had I been overeager in casting Benjamin Wylde in the role of villain, I asked myself? Had I allowed my personal dislike of the man to cloud my judgment? Or was it the stubborn belief in my ability to judge character that led me to gloss over suspects I found more personally appealing? While it was true that Wylde had a strong motive for wishing his partners dead, we had yet to establish whether he also had the opportunity. Besides there might be heaven only knew how many others who possessed motives for killing the former mining partners.

Starting with Li Ying.

In hindsight, I was dismayed by how easily I'd been taken in by the man. Discounting his imposing appearance and lifestyle, what did I actually know about Li Ying? He was a feared tong lord, the acknowledged God of the Golden Mountain. He was also a self-proclaimed blackmailer. Was it such a leap from blackmail to murder? Assuming the veracity of his story about a stolen mining claim, he had ample motive for wanting to see the four mining partners dead. His assertion that killing them would be self-defeating was suspect. There was always the possibility—albeit remote—that Hanaford and Mills balked at paying further extortion money. Even in today's world, Li would find it next to impossible to prove that four of the city's most respected men had callously robbed him. In the end, it would come down to the partners' word against a Chinese, which in reality meant no contest at all. Had Li become so irate that he'd finally decided to make the four men pay the ultimate price for their treachery?

I put a check by Li's name, then moved on to Peter. Here again personal bias intruded. I had difficulty imagining the affable actor as a murderer, despite the fact that he had ample motive and no apparent alibi. As Annjenett's lover, he would understandably wish to remove the obstacle to their happiness—and his financial freedom. Hanaford's money would also enable him to move his mother out of Bertha's bawdy house. As for Mills, well, Peter believed the industrialist to be his father, a man who had selfishly used, then deserted, his mother. Who could say what desperate lengths any of us would be driven to given those circumstances?

Drawing a check beside Peter's name, I moved on to ponder Senator Broughton. True, he'd been attacked outside his club, but I couldn't ignore the possibility that the incident had been staged. It could have been an ingenious ploy to shift suspicion from himself if word of the tontine agreement became public, as it must sooner or later. No, I decided, I couldn't rule out Broughton, and placed a check by his name as well.

I was still pouring over my notes when Celia knocked lightly on my door, then burst in before I had time to answer.

"I spoke to Ina," she said breathlessly. "She's agreed to talk to her sister, Lotty, about Mr. Wylde."

"Was she suspicious?" I asked anxiously.

"Not at all. In fact, she thinks it's quite romantic."

"That's wonderful, Celia. When will Ina be able to speak to her sister?"

"Not until Monday afternoon. That's Lotty's next half-day off. I know it's hard to wait, but I can't think of a way to get them together any sooner."

"No, we don't want to arouse suspicion." Still, it was frustrating. It would be five days before the sisters could meet. Then we'd have to wait heaven knows how long until Lotty could get back to Ina. Unless—

"What if Ina delivered a message to her sister?" I proposed. "Something personal—about her family, perhaps?"

Celia looked delighted. "Yes, that would work. It's unlikely anyone would question Ina reporting some sort of minor domestic emergency. I'll ask her about it tonight." She lowered her voice. "What about you, Sarah? Were you able to find out anything useful about Mr. Wylde's financial affairs?"

Briefly, I related Robert's discovery of Wylde's monetary setbacks, then Samuel's report concerning the attorney's clubs.

"It's all so frustrating," I said, rising from my chair and walking to the window. The sky outside was overcast and it looked like rain. I drew the drapes and turned back to Celia. "Subterfuge is so time-consuming. And so subject to failure."

"Yes, but it's the best we can do under the circumstances." She crossed to me and touched my arm. "I understand your concern, Sarah. It's hard to be patient. But remember, our cause is just."

Celia looked so earnest, I couldn't help smiling. I wished I could share her certainty that a just cause was enough to ensure success, but I knew all too well that life doesn't always supply a happy ending. After she left, I prayed that hard work and perseverance would bring results, even if a just cause failed.

That weekend, Mama, Papa, Samuel and I were to attend a performance of Verdi's *Aïda* at the Opera House. At the last moment, however, Hortense Weslyum asked Samuel to take her to a cousin's engagement supper, which, of course, left us with a spare ticket and me without an escort. Personally, I had no objections to attending the opera alone, but Mama insisted it was out of the question and suggested we invite Ulysses Lyman, one of Freder-

ick's fatuous friends. In hindsight, I'd like to believe it was this unhappy prospect that led me to do the unthinkable.

Actually, the opera was the last thing on my mind as Robert and
I sat in my office the next day discussing our progress—or lack of
it—with Annjenett's case. I was disappointed that after exhaustive
inquiries, Samuel had been unable to learn anything more about
Wylde from his fellow Bohemians, and my patience was wearing
thin waiting to hear back from Ina's sister.

"So, here we sit," I told Robert dejectedly.

I was prepared for one of his derisive comments. Instead, he
surprised me by saying, "You've done everything possible, Sarah.
Paulson tells me you've been to the jail to visit Mrs. Hanaford
every day this week. No one could do more."

I still say it was the fear of spending an evening in the company
of a man even more boring than Frederick that led to what I can
only describe as a temporary lapse of sanity. Having said this, I have
to admit that Robert's unexpected display of sensitivity threw me
off balance. Without taking time to consider what I was saying, I'd
blurted out an invitation for him to accompany my parents and
myself to the opera the following night. He looked momentarily
taken aback, then, much to my surprise—and probably his own—
he accepted.

"Good," I said, then realized I had no idea what to say next. I
was already regretting my impulsiveness, but could think of no civil
way to retract my words.

The feeling of awkwardness grew. I'm sure Robert felt it, too,
for after several bleak attempts at conversation, he rose, ran a hand
through his thick mop of hair, then left, promising to meet us at
the Grand Opera House in time for the performance.

He was as good as his word. The next night we found Robert

standing in front of the theater, a red-brown bear surrounded by the cream of San Francisco Society. It was difficult not to smile at the sight of the testy attorney, fashionably attired in top hat and tails, the snug coat and trousers betraying the fact that they must be borrowed. I only hoped the straining seams were up to the task of holding in his muscular six-foot-four-inch frame.

The Opera House was packed as we took our seats in the dress circle. Above us glittered the brilliant chandelier boasted to be the largest and grandest in the country. All about us sat men in elegant nightclothes and women resplendent in silks, laces and fine jewels. Seated in a box to our right, I was interested to spy Senator Broughton and his wife, Martha. I studied the politician from behind my program, but could detect no outward sign of the injuries he'd sustained from the attack the previous week. His mood, however, did not appear affable; at one point he spoke sharply to his wife and I saw her recoil from the sting of his words. After that, they sat in stony silence, each seemingly engrossed in their program. Through my opera glasses, however, I could detect tears shimmering in Mrs. Broughton's eyes.

I thought back to the night of Frederick's party and the scene that had played out between the couple after Mills's abrupt departure. Despite the devoted faces the Broughtons put on for the electorate, I wondered about the true nature of their relationship. They'd been together twenty years, but that didn't mean it was a happy marriage. Too many couples, I thought sadly, continued on rather than face the harsh judgment of a society that considered divorce not only a scandal, but also a failure of character.

"If you stare any harder at that man, you'll bore a hole through his head," Robert said, startling me out of my thoughts.

"That's Senator Broughton and his wife," I explained softly.

"I know well enough who it is. I also know why you're study-ing him like a bug under a microscope. You're still trying to con-nect his attack last week to his partners' deaths."

"I refuse to argue the obvious. Especially to someone too thick-headed to know the truth if it—"

"You're a fine one to talk," he cut in, his elevated voice attract-ing Mama's attention. She raised a cautionary eyebrow, but Robert was oblivious. "The blinders you wear prevent you from seeing any further than your own biased—"

"Oh, do be quiet!" I told the irksome man. "The performance is about to begin."

The house lights dimmed and the orchestra struck its opening chords, causing me to forget my irritation. As usual with Verdi, I was swept away by the natural force and spontaneity of his music. Unlike Wagner, whom I admire but occasionally find too deliber-ate, Verdi's simple directness spoke to my soul. When I glanced sur-reptitiously at Robert, I was amazed to discover that he, too, seemed mesmerized by the performance. I looked quickly away, ashamed to admit that I hadn't expected him to understand, much less appreciate, Verdi's mastery. It was annoying to discover I'd been wrong, and for a brief moment I wondered what other surprises he was hiding.

During intermission, we enjoyed champagne with friends of my parents, and it wasn't until after the performance that I again caught sight of the Broughtons. Papa saw them, too, as we left the theater and called out to the senator, but Broughton appeared not to hear. Without slackening his step, he took his wife's arm and started across the street toward their waiting carriage.

What happened next was over so quickly that even now it's dif-ficult to recall the event with any real clarity. I remember com-menting to Papa that finding a cab in this crowd wasn't going to be easy when I saw the blur of a four-wheeled phaeton rounding the corner. To my shock, it made directly for Senator Broughton and his wife. I expected the driver to slow his horse, then watched in horror as the animal accelerated, spurred on by a man dressed entirely in black, with a dark hat pulled low over his eyes. I could see nothing of his face, only the snapping of the reins in gloved hands, urging the horse ever closer to the couple.

Belatedly, the senator spotted the phaeton and tried to hurry his wife across the street and out of its path. But Mrs. Broughton stood frozen, her eyes fixed on the carriage like a frightened deer. With a cry, her husband tugged on her arm. At the same moment, the driver swerved the phaeton toward the spot where, a moment before, Broughton had been standing, but where he had now pulled his wife.

I'll never forget the look of terror on Martha Broughton's face as the carriage bore down upon her. She made no sound; at least I can remember none. Even if she had, it's doubtful I would have heard it over the screams of horrified bystanders. Robert claims that my own screams were loudest of all, and that he had to physically restrain me from rushing headlong into the street.

As I say, it was over in a minute, but it's a minute that will remain forever etched in my mind. To this day I relive the horror in my dreams, watching helplessly as the phaeton bears down upon the terrified woman until my cries awaken me.

I realize that the guilt I feel is irrational, yet no matter what I do it won't abate. I'd been so close—mere feet away—yet I had been powerless to avert the tragedy.

CHAPTER ELEVEN

Mrs. Broughton's death sent shock waves through the city. As a senatorial candidate, Frederick pounced on the opportunity, demanding that laws be passed to ensure that San Francisco's populace was safe on its increasingly congested streets. While it was true that traffic mishaps were growing at an alarming rate, there was no doubt in my mind that Mrs. Broughton's death had been intentional. Everything had happened in a few blurred moments, but I was certain that at the last minute the phaeton driver had deliberately swerved his horse toward the senator. If Broughton hadn't moved, he would very likely have received the brunt of the carriage's force and his wife might have escaped serious injury. The act had been premeditated. Someone had wanted to see the Broughtons dead. But had the object been to kill them both, I asked myself, or just one?

I thought I knew, although so far I'd found no way to prove my theory. Indeed, reports of the incident were considerably muddled. Robert and I appeared to be the only witnesses who had actually taken note of the driver; everyone else's attention had been focused on the Broughtons and the carriage bearing down upon them. And while he and I agreed on the driver's appearance, the authorities once again seemed maddeningly incapable of seeing the truth. They refused to connect the phaeton driver with the man who had earlier assaulted Senator Broughton, despite the fact that both descriptions matched perfectly.

My entire family, save the children, attended the funeral, arriving in two carriages hired by Papa for the occasion. A crowd had already formed in front of the church by the time we made our appearance. I spied Joseph Shepard, and not far from him, Thomas Cooke, Annjenett's father. His face was gray and deeply lined and he seemed even more distracted than when I'd last seen him at the jail. I thought of going over and speaking to him, but what could I say? Despite all my grand promises, his daughter remained locked up in city jail.

My gaze moved on and I saw Eban Potter standing alone on the church steps, looking uncomfortably out of place in such distinguished company. Excusing myself to my parents, I moved to speak to him.

"This is horrible, horrible," he said, mopping his head with a handkerchief.

I silently agreed. Sudden, unexpected death like that was always tragic, especially when it was likely a monstrous mistake.

"Were you acquainted with Mrs. Broughton?" I asked.

"Not much of late, but when Cornelius—Mr. Hanaford—and the others returned from the mines, I saw rather more of her. She was a fine woman—a credit to the community."

"Yes, I'm sure she was." I lowered my voice. "You're convinced then that Mrs. Broughton's death was accidental?"

His gray eyes widened in surprise. "My dear Miss Woolson, what else could it be?"

The time to equivocate was long passed. "Don't you think it's odd that this should happen so soon after the knife attack on Mr. Broughton? Have you considered that he might have been the intended victim and not his wife?"

He stared at me in seeming astonishment. "You think the driver of the phaeton meant to kill Mr. Broughton? But why?"

"There's the matter of the tontine," I reminded him, and watched his face light with comprehension.

"But that would mean——" His voice trailed off as he looked over my shoulder. Following his gaze, I saw Benjamin Wylde alight from a carriage, then turn to assist his daughter, Yvette.

"No," he went on, shaking his head. "I can't countenance such a thing. Without divulging particulars, I assure you that Mr. Wylde's affairs are in perfect order. He'd have no reason to resort to such desperate measures."

"What if I told you that over the past year he's experienced financial reversals?"

He regarded me sharply, as if wondering how I might have obtained such confidential information. "I would be very shocked indeed, Miss Woolson. Where did you hear such a thing?"

"I'm afraid I'm not at liberty to say. But my source was reliable. You must agree it lends credence to my theory."

His skeptical gaze traveled once more to Wylde and his daughter as they stood speaking to Frederick and Henrietta. To my disgust, I saw that my brother was taking advantage of the meeting to pursue his senatorial cause. This was hardly the place for levity, but I couldn't help smiling at the dazed look on Wylde's face. For once the unpleasant attorney and I agreed; I often had the same reaction when forced to listen to one of Frederick's rambling dissertations.

"Regardless of your source, Miss Woolson," the banker said, recalling me to the business at hand, "I can't believe such a thing. There must be another explanation."

"There may be," I admitted truthfully. "But for Mrs. Hanaford's sake I have no choice but to examine every possibility."

Instantly, his face grew pained. "Surely the police can't still think her guilty."

"Unfortunately, they do. At the very least they consider her an accessory to murder."

"But that's monstrous!" When I nodded agreement, his face softened and he took hold of my hand. "I know you're doing all you can for the poor woman, but you must exercise the utmost care." His intense eyes bore into mine. "Trust me, Miss Woolson, there are forces of evil at work here. Promise me you'll be very cautious."

The passion of his words took me by surprise. His pale face had drained of color as he squeezed my hand almost painfully.

"I'm not sure I understand, Mr. Potter. What do you mean by 'forces of evil'?"

"You're very young, my dear. I pray you'll never experience the evils of which I speak." He gave me a weak smile and released my hand. "Come, it's time. We must go inside."

Looking around, I realized we were among the last few mourners remaining outside the church.

"I have faith that right will triumph and that Mrs. Hanaford will soon be proven innocent," he added with conviction.

He turned away before I could reply and entered the church. I followed, to find that my family had reserved a seat for me in a pew several rows behind Senator Broughton and an elderly woman whom Celia whispered was his late wife's mother. The senator sat ramrod straight, head facing the altar. I couldn't see his face, but I sensed that he was holding himself tightly in check. Was he afraid his emotions might prove an embarrassment, I wondered? Surely at such a time it was forgivable to show one's bereavement. No one would fault him for publicly betraying his grief.

But were his emotions those of grief? I remembered the man's behavior toward his wife the night of the opera, and realized again how little I knew about their personal life. I forced myself to consider the possibility that, for reasons I couldn't begin to guess, Broughton had hired someone to injure his wife. The idea was so appalling that I was instantly ashamed. Besides, it made no sense. Even if the senator had wanted to see his wife dead, surely paying a man to hit her with a carriage was too risky, not only to himself but to innocent bystanders.

My gaze moved to Benjamin Wylde, who sat with his daughter across the aisle. The girl was crying softly into a handkerchief, her lovely face a mask of grief. Her father, dressed in a dark suit and a starched, high-winged collar, stared unblinkingly at the pulpit as the minister eulogized Mrs. Broughton. Studying that sharply chiseled face, I again found myself wondering if it was because of this man that three people were dead. What was going on in his mind, I asked myself? Was he consumed by guilt for having taken an innocent life? Or was Mrs. Broughton's death merely a temporary setback to his plans, which he would soon rectify? At this thought, my earlier doubts about Broughton vanished and I felt a rush of fear for the senator. Even if I was wrong about Wylde being the killer, Broughton's life was almost certainly in danger.

When the service was over, we took our place behind other mourners waiting to offer sympathy to the widower. Broughton was very pale and his grief seemed genuine, but I was sure I also detected a strong note of fear. As he received each mourner, his eyes darted about the church as if he were looking for someone. The person responsible for his wife's death, I wondered? The killer he knew would return to finish the job he'd started?

When it was our turn, the senator politely accepted our condolences, then introduced his wife's mother, Mrs. Matthia Reynold, who, he informed us, resided with him and his late wife.

"Were you close to my daughter?" Mrs. Reynold asked Mama in a loud voice, as the hard of hearing are prone to do. Despite the elderly woman's proud carriage, it was possible to see her red-rimmed eyes beneath the thin black veil. She appeared frail and unutterably sad, and my heart went out to the old lady as I imagined the extent of her sorrow.

"We worked together on several charities," Mama said with a kind smile. The old woman obviously felt Mama's sincerity, for she held onto her hands with thin, arthritic fingers. "Martha was a tireless worker," Mama went on. "She'll be sorely missed."

Tears filled the old woman's eyes. "Indeed she will. Many's the time I told her she worked too hard. More than was appreciated by some people." To my surprise, the old woman glared at Broughton. Mama looked at me, as taken aback as I by the woman's malevolence.

Broughton's face flushed red and I sensed the effort it took to keep his voice civil. "It's been a long day, Mother-in-law. I think it's time we returned home." He took her arm, but she pulled away with a strength surprising for such a tiny woman.

"I'm not in the least tired," she snapped, and turned back to Mama. "I'd be pleased if you'd call on me, Mrs. Woolson. It would be a comfort to speak to one of Martha's friends." Again she shot a meaningful look at her son-in-law.

Mama smiled warmly. "It would be my pleasure, Mrs. Reynold."

I started to follow Mama out of the church, then noticed Yvette Wylde approaching Mrs. Reynold. Looking around, I saw her father speaking to a man I didn't recognize. Telling Mama I'd join the family shortly, I waited until Yvette had paid her respects, then contrived to cross her path as she moved back toward her father.

"I'm sorry," I said, feigning embarrassment. "I fear I wasn't paying attention to where I was going."

Up close, I realized that Yvette was one of the most beautiful young woman I'd ever seen. Fleetingly, I wondered how a grim man like Wylde had managed to produce such a delightful creature.

"Please, *madame,* do not distress yourself," she said with the charming trace of a French accent. "Mrs. Broughton's death has been a shock to us all."

"Yes, it's a terrible tragedy." I proffered my hand. "Allow me to introduce myself. I'm Sarah Woolson. And you are—?"

"*Je m'excuse,* Miss Woolson. I am Yvette Wylde. I have come from Paris to visit my father, *Monsieur* Wylde. You know him perhaps?"

"As a matter of fact I do, Miss Wylde. I'm also a lawyer. Your father and I have had occasion to meet professionally."

The girl's eyes opened wide. "You are an *avocat*—a woman attorney? But is such a thing possible?" She flushed becomingly. "*Je vous demande pardon, madame.* I did not mean to offend."

"Nor did you. I assure you that your reaction is mild compared to some I've received." To my surprise, I found I liked Wylde's daughter very much. Despite her extraordinary beauty, she appeared remarkably sweet and unspoiled. I was, however, confused by her relationship with Martha Broughton. "You live in Paris,

Miss Wylde, yet you speak of Mrs. Broughton as if you knew her well."

Fresh tears appeared in the girl's eyes, "Madam Broughton was my godmother. I have seen little of *Tante* Martha since Mama and I moved to France, but we often corresponded. I shall miss her very much. Poor *Oncle* Willard. It is going to be difficult for him."

"Yes, I fear you're right," I murmured, especially if "*Oncle* Willard" suspected that he, and not his unfortunate wife, had been the target of the speeding carriage.

"*Pardon,* Miss Woolson," Yvette Wylde was saying, "but I must find Papa. It has been a pleasure to meet you."

My gaze followed the girl as she moved gracefully toward her father who, I realized with a start, had been watching us. His hostile gaze remained on me until Yvette tucked her hand through his arm. Only then did he turn and lead his daughter out of the church, leaving me with an unwelcome feeling of disquiet.

The next few days brought more frustration as Samuel, Celia and I tried to piece together a case against Benjamin Wylde. Adding to my annoyance, Frederick and Hortense were making more of a nuisance of themselves than usual as election day grew nearer. Somehow Frederick had overtaken both the Democratic and Workingmen's party candidates to take the lead in the senate race. Even more mind-boggling were those who predicted his eventual victory. To avoid the folderol, I sought refuge at the office, but even there I was too preoccupied by my client's dilemma to do any real work.

The only thing I had accomplished since Mrs. Broughton's funeral was the brief I'd promised my employer regarding the carriage driver who refused to pay damages to Rebecca Carpenter.

Although Shepard's only response to my long hours of work was an absentminded grunt, Eugene Ackroyd, the associate attorney in charge of the case, seemed delighted and felt certain Mrs. Carpenter had an excellent chance of obtaining payment.

I should have been pleased, but oddly, I was not. No matter what task I set myself, Annjenett's tortured face was never far from my thoughts. The days flew by with appalling speed as her trial date grew closer. I had Samuel, Celia and even Robert running about like amateur sleuths, yet despite our efforts, we weren't one step closer to proving the unfortunate woman's innocence.

But there was another distraction: I began to fear I was being followed. Since I had no desire to wake snakes until I was certain, I told no one of my suspicions. Instead, I took steps to learn if my fears were justified, or merely the result of an overactive imagination. I varied the time I left for the office, as well as the direction and method I took to get there. When walking, I'd cross the street, then suddenly double back, all the while checking to see if anyone was behind me.

The results of these experiments were maddeningly inconclusive. Once or twice I caught sight of a suspicious individual, only to have him seemingly disappear. I'm not nervous by nature, but I soon found myself jumping at every unexpected noise and imagining sinister scenarios for every stranger who passed me on the street. I tried to tell myself I was just overwrought by fatigue and worry over Annjenett's case, but the certainty that someone was dogging my every move grew stronger with each passing day.

Samuel, Celia and I arranged to compare notes when the rest of the family was out of the house. My brother's report was short and disappointing. Despite speaking to almost every member of the Bohemian Club, and as many Pacific Union Club members as he could reach, no one had seen Benjamin Wylde on the nights in question.

"That doesn't mean he's a murderer," Samuel insisted. "He could have been any number of places, all of them perfectly innocent."

"Perhaps," I said thoughtfully. "It's unfortunate we don't have the resources available to the police. Speaking of which, have you heard from George?" Several days earlier, I had asked Samuel to speak to George about the possibility of placing a police guard outside Wylde's house. If I were wrong in my suspicions, no harm would be done. But if I were proven right, a life might be saved.

"I saw him," my brother said without enthusiasm. "The police refuse to believe that the attacks on the Broughtons had anything to do with the murders. Which means, of course, that Fowler and Mrs. Hanaford remain their chief suspects. Sorry, little sister, but there's no way they're going to place a watch on Wylde's house."

I was frustrated, but not surprised. As usual, our newly formed police department's first concern was political expediency. It was a wonder their unfortunate new uniforms didn't come equipped with blinders.

"They can see no farther than their noses," I pronounced wryly, then turned to Celia. "Has Ina spoken to her sister yet?"

"They met in the park yesterday," she answered. "But I think it best if Ina relates the conversation herself."

Our little maid was sent for, and she entered the room looking ill at ease. After a quick curtsy, she kept her eyes downcast, her reddened hands twisting nervously in front of her spotless apron.

"Go on, dear," Celia urged. "Repeat what you told me."

Ina's gray-green eyes darted to Samuel, then back down to the floor, and I realized he was the reason for her reticence.

"It's all right, Ina," I told her reassuringly. "Whatever you have to tell us may be said in front of Mr. Woolson."

She gave me a pained look. "It's not a proper sort of thing to talk about, ma'am," she said plaintively. "Lotty was that upset to tell me. And I'm her sister!"

A small shiver of anticipation tingled down my spine. "What is it, Ina? Anything you say will be held in strict confidence."

Ina looked near tears. "I would never tell anyone, ma'am, if it wasn't for that poor woman who fancies Mr. Wylde. She deserves to know." The poor girl's wide eyes sought validation.

"If you can help our friend, Ina, it's the right thing to do," I agreed quietly, refusing to meet my brother's eyes.

"That's what I told Lotty, ma'am," Ina said, sounding a bit more confident. "And she was that happy to help. It wasn't hard to find out that Mr. Wylde hasn't left the city since Easter, but he's gone a lot all the same. I mean, he spends nights and some weekends away from home an' all." Ina's cheeks colored bright pink. "It was when Lotty tried to find out where he might have met that lady friend of yours that she found—" Her voice trailed off, and once again her eyes traveled nervously to Samuel.

"Go on, Ina, please," Celia prompted.

Ina swallowed. "Well, Lotty was dustin' Mr. Wylde's study and happened to open one or two of his desk drawers." She regarded us nervously, as if fearing our reaction to this brazen revelation, then hurried on. "Well, Lotty come across some books—and some pictures. A nasty lot, they were, too. Sure 'n not the sort of things any decent lady would want anything to do with. Nor the man who owned 'em. I thought you should know so's you could warn the poor woman who's so taken with Mr. Wylde."

"Oh, my!" I said, as I suddenly imagined the nature of Lotty's find. The fact that Celia had already heard the story did nothing to lessen her discomfort at hearing it a second time. Only Samuel seemed to find the situation amusing.

"Come, ladies," he said smiling. "It may seem shocking, but it's not unusual for a man to keep items of that nature."

"There's somethin' else," Ina said, looking miffed at Samuel's reaction. Reaching beneath her apron, she pulled out a small white rectangle of cardboard. "Lotty found some of these in Mr. Wylde's drawers. She didn't think anyone would notice if she took one." She hesitated, then rushed on. "They were buried under bits of lace and odds and ends of ladies' apparel—*intimate* apparel," she added, eyeing Samuel triumphantly.

She had our full attention; even Samuel had leaned forward in his chair. I took the object from Ina. It was a white business card depicting the head of a black masked devil over four pick axes grouped together in a circle, handles upright.

"I've seen this before," I said. "In Mr. Hanaford's desk."

Samuel rose from his seat and, looking frankly baffled, took the card from me. "I've never seen anything like it."

Celia looked over his shoulder. "What can it mean?"

I was so surprised to see the card again, I'd nearly forgotten Ina, until she said, "The worst of it is that one of the other maids came in while Lotty was pokin' about. Quick as a wink, Lotty went back to her dustin', but she's that worried the maid saw what she was doin'. Our Lotty will be sacked for sure if Mr. Wylde finds out."

"Don't worry, Ina," I reassured her. "Please assure Lotty her secret is safe with us."

"Thank you, ma'am," she said, looking relieved.

We thanked Ina, then when she'd left the room, put our heads together in an effort to make sense of Lotty's find.

"At least now we know for sure that Wylde was in town when the attacks occurred," I began.

"Yes, but we still have no idea if he left his house on those nights," protested Celia.

"Or if he did, where he went," Samuel put in.

Celia eyed Wylde's card with distaste. "Do you think this awful thing is meant to be some kind of a joke?"

"That's what Robert and I thought when we found its twin in Hanaford's study," I said. "Now I'm not so sure."

Samuel held the piece of cardboard up to the light and for the first time I noticed that it was slightly yellow. "This has probably been buried in that drawer for years. I'm sure it has nothing to do with the case."

"Possibly," I mused. "But what about the undergarments Lotty found?"

"It could be clothing his wife left behind when she moved to Paris," Celia ventured.

"And he keeps them in the desk drawer in his study?" I shook my head. "No, I can't help feeling there's more to this than meets the eye."

The following morning I paid a visit to Annjenett. As usual, her face lit with expectation when she saw me, and I felt guilty that I was unable to report any significant progress on her case. She blinked back tears of disappointment, but her determination not to hold me to blame merely exacerbated my feelings of failure.

We spoke of several personal matters she wished me to attend to on her behalf, then she begged for news of Peter. I tried to present the actor's trial in a positive light, but she saw through my feeble lies. The last thing I wanted was to cause her more pain, yet that was exactly what I had done, not only because of my awkward untruths, but because I could offer no real hope.

We talked a bit longer, but I did not mention the planned insanity plea. I saw no reason to burden her with Paulson's plan as long as there remained the slightest chance I might change his mind. When it was time to leave, I showed her the card Lotty found in Wylde's study, but could detect no sign of recognition on her pale face. Whatever Hanaford's reason for possessing such a card, I was convinced he had not shared it with his wife.

I left Annjenett with a heavy heart. The awful shackles of powerlessness hindered my movements and slowed my thoughts. There must be something I had not tried, some clue I had overlooked, some page I had left unturned. But what?

Exiting the jail, I again ran into Thomas Cooke and was forced to repeat our bleak progress on his daughter's case. Then, not expecting anything to come of it, I showed him Wylde's card. To my surprise, he regarded it as if it was a venomous serpent.

"You've seen this before?" I asked.

"N—no," he stammered, but the lie was clearly written on his drawn face. I was surprised to detect revulsion and outright fear there as well. "It—it is just rather dreadful, isn't it?"

"Actually, it was discovered at the home of—"

"Excuse me, Miss Woolson," he interrupted so suddenly that I gasped at his rudeness. His face had grown pale, and he seemed visibly agitated. "It is growing late. I must see my daughter." With that he turned and walked hurriedly into the jail.

A few days later, Robert and I shared a carriage to Paulson's office. Peter's trail was in its fifth day, and we were meeting to finalize Annjenett's defense before her trial began the following week. I readily admit that I was not happy at the thought of seeing Benjamin Wylde, who would also be in attendance. I knew, of course, that the conference was little more than a formality. Paulson and Wylde had already decided that insanity was our only recourse. Robert, of course, agreed with this strategy, and even Samuel felt there was little choice under the circumstances.

It was a silent ride, Robert and I both lost in our thoughts. I had tried for days to learn more about the mysterious cards. After Thomas Cooke's curious reaction to it at the jail, I had shown the card to Eban Potter at Hanaford's bank. If anyone was privy to the four miners' secrets, I thought it would be him.

I had been prepared for the bank manager to deny having seen the card before, or perhaps, like Mr. Cooke, to show repugnance or fear. To my surprise, he had merely seemed amused.

"My, my," he'd said when I'd handed him the card. "I haven't seen one of these in years."

"You know what it represents?" I'd asked hopefully.

"I'm not sure that is the word I would use. Unless one takes it to represent the foolish bravado of youth. The four partners had them printed when they returned from the mines. I think they wished to depict themselves as daring adventurers."

"You mean they actually gave these cards out socially?"

"More as a joke really. Once they'd settled back into the business of everyday life, I'm sure the novelty wore off, or more likely, they began to find the cards an embarrassment. As I say, I haven't seen one of them in years."

"Are you certain the cards didn't symbolize—" I had hesitated, then opted for candor. "Well, something more sinister?"

A strange look had crossed his face at this; initially I took it to be a reaction to what must have seemed the ramblings of an anxious female. In hindsight I wasn't so sure. Had I touched on something he didn't wish me to know—or pursue?

"You would know, wouldn't you?" I had pressed when he didn't answer, "if there was a more ominous meaning to the card?"

"My dealings with the partners were quite amicable," he'd reassured me. "I'm certain I would have been aware of any menacing connotation. Believe me, Miss Woolson, it is a mistake to read more into those absurd cards than youthful imprudence."

I'd left the bank manager feeling oddly deflated. Now that the repugnant little cards had been explained, I wondered how I could have thought them evil. Desperation had led me to grasp at straws, I decided. Still, as I sat next to Robert in the bouncing carriage, I could not shake the recurring feeling that I was overlooking something important. What it could be, however, perched maddeningly just beyond my reach.

When we arrived at Paulson's office, we were greeted by the jovial attorney who, as usual, exuded confidence that he had matters well in hand. I continued to like the man personally, but had long since given up hope that he had either the ability or the inclination to actually help Annjenett.

Wylde came in a few minutes later and the meeting began. It went much as I'd expected. Paulson and Wylde had decided upon Annjenett's defense before our arrival. The damaging case being presented against Peter even as we spoke served to solidify their position. There could be little doubt how the jury would decide. And when Peter's trial was over, the state would accuse Annjenett of being an accessory to her husband's murder. As feared, there was talk of charging her as an accessory in Rufus Mills's case as well. The only possible defense against such overwhelming evidence, Paulson patiently explained, was insanity.

The attorney went on to outline our roles during the trial. He, of course, would act as chief counsel. Campbell—as per his agreement with Joseph Shepard—would be second chair. I would take notes on the proceedings and, if necessary, search for legal precedents pertinent to our case. In other words, I was to act as Paulson's secretary and general errand girl—a position that under other circumstances I would have been happy to fill if it would have helped Annjenett. Since I so strongly disagreed with the strategy Paulson was determined to follow, I was not happy at all. Once again I argued my client's innocence, but it was useless. Her fate had been sealed. And we had yet to step inside a courtroom!

When the meeting was over, Paulson asked Robert to remain to go over last-minute strategies. Recognizing that as my cue to leave, I exited Paulson's office. I was about to join a group of people waiting on the corner for an approaching horsecar, when my arm was suddenly seized from behind. I spun around to see Benjamin Wylde standing over me, his raw-boned face dark with fury.

"Unhand me this instant!" I demanded, tugging to free my arm.

Ignoring my pleas, he pushed me into a doorway. His voice was tightly controlled, his eyes malevolent slits. "You try my patience, Miss Woolson. Why have you been prying into my affairs?"

My heart caught in my throat, making it difficult to breathe. His grip tightened on my arm until I winced in pain.

"You're not as clever as you think," he hissed. "I'm aware that your brother has been making inquiries at my clubs, and that you have asked about me all over town. You were foolish to persuade one of my servants to spy on me. Lotty Corks has been dismissed without references. What happens to her now is on your conscience."

"That's unfair. She—"

"The girl betrayed me!" His face drew so close I could feel his hot breath on my cheek. "What did you hope to discover, Miss Woolson? What was so important that it has cast a young girl out on the streets to beg for her survival?"

"That was cruel and unnecessary!" I protested, the injustice of his act overcoming my fear. Worst of all, I knew he was right. A dismissed servant lacking references might well be reduced to begging or, in dire cases, to selling her body. My voice shook in anger and with the knowledge that my actions had brought disaster upon Ina's sister. "Lotty acted in innocence. She thought she was facilitating an affair of the heart."

"More fool she," he said in a pitiless voice. A couple walked by and Wylde pulled me deeper into the recessed doorway. "I'll ask you one last time, Miss Woolson. Why have you been spying on me?"

"I'm interested in any person connected to Hanaford and Mills," I managed as his terrible glare filled my vision.

The dark shadows played upon his sharply angular face until, to my frightened eyes, it resembled a ghoulish specter. "And you think I may be involved in their deaths?" His tone mocked me. "Weren't you afraid I might decide to make you my next victim?"

"This is hardly a laughing matter," I said shakily. "A woman's life is at stake."

His fingers dug into my arm. "That woman may be you unless you stay out of this business."

He was gone before I could release my breath, but I was shaking so violently it was several minutes before I could move. The audacity of the attack—in broad daylight and on a crowded street—left me numb. I was willing to swear that I had glimpsed pure evil in those shadowy eyes. I shuddered, remembering the steel-like hands that had pinned me to the wall. Had those same hands slashed the life's blood out of two men, or held the reins that crushed an innocent woman? I had to answer these questions, I thought, taking my seat inside the horsecar. And soon!

Wylde had not exaggerated Lotty Cork's fate. I returned home to find Celia in her room trying to comfort a hysterical Ina. Lotty's employment had indeed been terminated, and our little maid was convinced that poverty and destitution lay ahead for her sister. Celia's kind eyes reflected my own feeling of responsibility. We had created the situation. We were morally obligated to set it right.

After a restless night, a surprisingly suitable solution came to me and I hurried to the office to place the matter before Mr. Shepard. Enduring the inevitable argument I had come to expect whenever he was presented with a new idea, I finally convinced him of the practicality of the plan. Not only would it help two women in distress, it was certain to generate goodwill for the firm.

That night I told Ina that arrangements had been made for her sister to help Rebecca Carpenter take care of her family while she recuperated from a traffic accident. Although the Carpenter family lacked the funds to pay Lotty, my employer had agreed to advance the necessary money in lieu of the settlement Mrs. Carpenter was almost certain to receive. Best of all, when it was time to seek a new position, Lotty would be provided with glowing references.

That matter settled to everyone's satisfaction, I was more determined than ever to prove Benjamin Wylde's guilt. I won't pretend that his threats hadn't unnerved me, but as the days marched inexorably toward the beginning of Annjenett's trial, I made a determined effort to stifle my fears by turning all my attention on her defense. I wracked my brains to come up with a strategy—no, let's be honest—with a *miracle* that might save my client from the gallows, or equally repellent, from a lunatic asylum. I could not allow myself to contemplate failure.

W hat have you done to aggravate Benjamin Wylde?" Mr.
Shepard demanded several days after the meeting in Paulson's office. "Whatever it is, it must stop," he went on before I could muster a suitable retort. "He is one of our most prestigious clients."

The injustice of this remark stunned me. "Did Mr. Wylde mention that he accosted me on the street and threatened my life?" I asked from between clenched teeth.

Shepard regarded me over his pince-nez, his face slightly flushed above a starched, high-winged collar. "I am not interested in excuses, Miss Woolson. From this day forward, you are to have no contact with either Mr. Wylde or Mr. Paulson. I am appalled by reports of your obstreperous behavior."

"Are you serving me with notice of termination?" I asked.

He hesitated and I knew he was thinking of my father, and the consequences of having such a powerful enemy on the bench. "Well, er, not exactly." I watched as he searched for a face-saving way out of this dilemma. "You may stay, but on a probationary basis, contingent upon your future conduct. Is that clear, Miss Woolson?"

"Perfectly clear. Rest assured I will do nothing to compromise my integrity as an attorney, or my responsibility as a human being."

Shepard nodded his head curtly, but when I turned for the door I could see he wasn't quite sure what I had just agreed to.

I was still fuming when I hailed a cab and instructed the driver to take me to Senator Broughton's home on Nob Hill. If Benjamin Wylde thought to frighten me off by complaining to my employer, he'd chosen the wrong means. I would be lying if I pretended his threats hadn't unnerved me, but I honestly believed I was Annjenett's last hope. With her life at stake, I had no choice but to carry on, regardless of the possible consequences.

I had embarked on my present errand for two reasons. First, I was convinced Senator Broughton knew more about his partners' deaths than he had admitted and, secondly, I truly feared for his life. My conscience would not leave me in peace until I had at least made an effort to warn him.

Arriving at the Broughton's residence, I paid the cabby and pulled the bell on the heavy oak door. A liveried footman wearing a black armband took my card and ushered me in, leaving me in the entry hall while he inquired if the senator was receiving visitors.

Restlessly, I paced the hall while I waited. The large, vaulted foyer was like a small museum. In addition to several sculptures, a number of paintings and an excellent tapestry decorated the walls. My eye had just fallen upon a landscape by Camille Pissaro—a French painter who was making a name for himself in the so-called Impressionist school—when I had the feeling I was being watched. Turning my head, I spied a burly man partially concealed behind a marble statue. He wore a shabby brown suit, and a heavy beard concealed the lower part of his face. His eyes were dark and piercing to the point of rudeness. Was he a tradesman, I wondered? Or a workman hired to do repairs? If so, what was he doing in this part of the house? And why did he make no move to go about his business, instead of standing there openly staring at me?

I was still pondering these questions when the footman returned to lead me up the curved staircase. As we ascended, the strange man's eyes rudely followed our progress, an act that clearly made the footman nervous. On the second floor, I was led into the senator's study. The room was gloomy; the draperies were drawn and only one or two sconce candles along the walls had been lit. It took a moment before I was able to make out the figure of Broughton sitting in a chair facing the fire. His greeting was not enthusiastic as he motioned for me to take the seat opposite his. He did not offer refreshments and, to be truthful, I would have declined them if he had. My mission was awkward, and I didn't care to be sidetracked by social niceties.

Now that my eyes were accustomed to the gloom, I was shocked to note the senator's altered appearance since his wife's funeral. His face was drawn and pale as ash, his overbright eyes rimmed by dark circles, as if he hadn't slept well in days. Normally a stylish dresser, this afternoon his clothes were rumpled and disarranged. Of course he was in mourning, but I suspected this remarkable transformation was due to something more ominous than bereavement.

After a few moments of polite, if strained, conversation, I searched for a way to introduce the real purpose of my visit.

"I'm relieved that you have recovered from the attack you sustained outside your club," I began, treading carefully.

He seemed taken aback. "It was hardly an attack," he said tersely. "The penny press blew the incident out of proportion."

Again I found myself wondering why Broughton was so determined to minimize what had clearly been a deadly assault.

"You don't think it a coincidence that you were set upon by a man wielding a knife so soon after your late partners' deaths?"

"No, of course not. Why should I think such a thing?" His eyes narrowed. "That's right. I remember—from your brother's party. All those questions about Cornelius. You fancy you know something about crime. And you take perverse pleasure prying into people's lives."

"Senator, I meant no—"

"Well, you will not meddle in mine. I won't have it!"

"The situation is too desperate to mince words," I said, ignoring his insults. "I believe Mr. Hanaford and Mr. Mills were murdered by the same man. I'm also convinced that you, not your wife, was the intended victim of that runaway phaeton."

His pale face slowly suffused with color. "How dare you!"

"Senator, your life is in danger. The killer has three souls on his conscience. I'm sure he won't hesitate to strike again."

Eyes blazing, Broughton rose, and with noticeably shaking hands, reached for the cord to summon the footman. "You will leave my house at once," he said tightly.

"Senator, you must—"

"Miss Woolson. Please go!"

I stared at him for a long moment. Behind the anger I sensed a debilitating terror. The senator did not require my warning, I realized with a little shock. He already feared for his life.

Recognizing there was nothing more to be said, I stood and wordlessly left the room. As the footman led me to the door, I again spied the strange man I had seen on my way in. His dark, probing gaze remained fixed on me as I was escorted outside, and the large oaken door had been firmly closed behind me.

The afternoon had turned dark, and heavy clouds were rolling in from the Bay. The wind was blowing so hard I had to hold on tightly to my hat, and I felt drops of rain on my face as I walked down the hill toward Powell. There I boarded a cable car to Sutter Street, where I could transfer to a second line that would deposit me at Market and Battery Streets, a short, if uphill, walk to my home. I was lucky to find an unoccupied seat inside the trailer car, and after settling myself between two men of burly proportions, I looked outside to find the drizzle had turned into a downpour.

The weather matched my mood. Straightening my damp skirts, I mulled over my visit with Broughton. Any fool could see he was frightened—but of what? If he truly believed his wife's death was an accident, why did he appear so terrified? Was it possible he knew the identity of Hanaford and Mills's murderer, or the reason why they'd been killed? Yet if he had any suspicion of the killer's identity, why hadn't he taken this information to the police?

My head ached as I struggled for answers. If Broughton suspected that Wylde was a merciless killer, why protect him? So far, my inquiries had come up with no obvious improprieties in Broughton's past. If the attorney was blackmailing his ex-partner, it was for a reason I had thus far failed to uncover.

Then there was the man I had seen lurking—for really that best described his strange behavior—in the senator's foyer. He was dressed too shabbily to be a guest, nor did he have the appearance or the demeanor of a servant. So, who was he?

The answer came to me as the car slowed for my stop: Broughton must be so afraid for his life that he had hired a professional to guard his home and his person. That would explain the man's bizarre presence. Had the senator become so mistrustful that even his female guests were subject to vulgar scrutiny?

The cable car stopped, and I held a discarded newspaper over my head as I transferred to the Sutter Street line. When I left that car a few blocks later to walk the short distance to my home, the newspaper soon became too soaked to be of any use. The afternoon had grown so dark that it was difficult to see more than a few steps ahead as I made my way up the hill.

Suddenly, the skin on the back of my neck prickled. Someone was following me! I tried to tell myself it was only my imagination, but the terror gripping my heart was too real to ignore. Bending my head against the wall of wind and blinding rain, I increased my pace and struggled up the hill toward warmth and safety.

When I felt a hand grasp my shoulder, my heart nearly stopped beating. Strong fingers dug into my arm as I tried to pull away. Spinning about, I tried to confront my attacker, but all I could make out in the pounding rain was a shapeless figure. I opened my mouth to scream, but my cries were drowned in the howling wind.

They say at times of extreme terror, your life passes before you in the blink of an eye. In my case, I felt nothing but incapacitating fear, and the certainty that I was going to die on this rain-soaked street without ever knowing why or by whose hand.

Over the sounds of the wind, I realized the man was speaking, but I was too distraught to make out his words. Then, slowly, the sense of what he was saying began to breach the storm and the panic hammering in my ears. He spoke in broken English—an accent I found strangely familiar. As I strained to see the man's face through the rain, his features slowly began to take shape. With a shock, I realized my assailant was Chinese!

"Missy, please, you take," he said, attempting to push a piece of paper into my hand.

"What is it?" I cried. "Who are you?"

Releasing my arm so abruptly that I nearly fell over, he said, "You need help, you go this place."

I stared at the note he had pressed into my palm, but it was too dark and too wet to make out the writing.

"Who told you to give this to me?" I asked, then looked up to see that the man was no longer there.

Like a shadowy specter, he had vanished soundlessly into the stormy night.

CHAPTER TWELVE

Thankfully, no one was home when I slipped, drenched and bedraggled, into the house. Never had my bedroom looked so inviting—and so safe. Angry at myself for allowing the Chinese to cause me such fright, I fumbled with buttons and hooks and pulled off my wet dress and undergarments, then slipped on a robe and rang for the maid. When Hazel appeared, I requested hot tea and a large snifter of brandy. Although the latter request resulted in a raised eyebrow, my devoted maid speedily delivered both restoratives to my room, then mercifully left without comment.

When I was alone, I swallowed the brandy in one long gulp, then sat down to sip the tea while I brought my nerves under control. As the brandy and tea spread welcome warmth through my shivering body, I drew out the note I'd been given, which was written on white, high-grade bond paper. The writing itself was precise and neat, if a bit spidery; the grammar perfect. It read:

Miss Woolson. If you require assistance, come to the Yoot Hong Low restaurant on Clay Street, between Dupont and Waverly Place. Kin Lee, the proprietor, will know how to reach me.

I stared at the message, which could only have been written by one man: Li Ying. But for what reason? Had he come across some new information regarding the case? If so, why not simply tell me in the note? Or was it of such a sensitive or dangerous nature that it could only be delivered in person?

Since there was nothing to be gained from idle speculation, I put the note aside and made it an early night. Whether because of the brandy, or sheer exhaustion, I slept soundly and was one of the first to arrive at work the following day. I planned to clear my desk before noon, then seek out the Yoot Hong Low restaurant. Circumstances, however, conspired against this endeavor.

The distraction came in the form of a request from Eugene Ackroyd. The young associate had been so impressed by my work on the Carpenter case, he sought to employ me on a project concerning a recently divorced woman in danger of losing custody of her two small children. The wife's husband, a known wife beater, was to have his case heard the following week. When I expressed my surprise that the matter had been left until the last moment, Mr. Ackroyd claimed the woman's case had become buried in paperwork. I thought it more likely that my male colleagues had thought little of the woman's chance of winning, or they secretly sided with the husband. My money was on the latter. Despite the concerns weighing so heavily on my mind, I could not bring myself to turn my back on the unfortunate mother.

As fate would have it, the fact that I worked on the brief until well after my usual departure hour caused me to happen upon a discovery pertaining to the Nob Hill murders (the name I had taken to calling the case) that I might otherwise have missed. It was, in fact, eight o'clock when Robert barged into my office and announced that it was high time I left for home. I started to protest that I would leave when I was ready, then reconsidered. Remembering Wylde's threats, as well as my fright the night before, I decided there was an advantage in having Robert escort me outside and into a taxi.

It was dark when we emerged from the building and unfortunately there wasn't a brougham in sight. Complaining that by now he had missed supper at his boardinghouse, Robert suggested we eat at a nearby hotel, then walk to Montgomery Street where we'd be more likely to find an unoccupied taxi. Realizing that I, too, was hungry, I readily agreed to this sensible plan.

As if by silent agreement, we didn't speak of the murders—or the beginning of Annjenett's trial—as we made our way toward the hotel. The evening was mild and I found myself enjoying the brisk walk. And, amazingly, Robert's company. When he wasn't going on about my imagined faults, or the folly of women in the workplace, he was not unpleasant company.

We had just settled into a lively discussion concerning recent demands by the Workingman's Party for a Chinese exclusion act, when I spied two men leaving a nearby bar. I fear I gave Robert a start when I grabbed his arm and pulled him into a nearby doorway.

"Look! Over there," I whispered. "It's Benjamin Wylde."

"So, what if it is? I see no reason to—"

"Shh. I think I know his companion."

The man I referred to was short and stocky, with unkempt hair and the unfocused look of the inebriated. In fact, Wylde didn't seem at all pleased by the man's intoxicated condition.

"I can't remember his name," I continued in a low voice, "but I know I've seen him before."

Robert gave a snort of disgust. "Of all the ridiculous—"

Ordering him to be quiet, I strained to hear what the men were saying, but we were too far away. The older man began to flail his arms about as if arguing a point, but Wylde appeared to have had enough. Taking his companion roughly by the arm, he propelled him down the street in our direction. As they passed within several feet of our hiding place, I heard the attorney snap that if the other man knew what was good for him, he would hold his tongue.

Suddenly, I knew where I'd seen the man before. His name eluded me, but I was sure he was one of my brother Charles's colleagues. What in the world, I wondered, was he doing with Benjamin Wylde?

The incident cast a pall over our dinner. Despite my protests that the confrontation we'd just witnessed might be important to Annjenett's case, Robert insisted on referring to it as my "damned female imagination working overtime again."

It was a relief when the meal was over and we were able to locate a cab on Montgomery Street. I didn't bother to look back at my fractious dinner companion as the driver clicked his horse toward Rincon Hill.

I was pleased to find Charles alone in the parlor when I returned home. During the ride I had wracked my brain to remember the mysterious doctor's name and finally decided it was either Langley or Langton. When I described him to my brother, he thought I must be referring to Howard Lawton, one of his instructors at medical school.

"I heard he was no longer teaching. A scandal of some sort, I believe. I can't imagine what he'd be doing with Mr. Wylde."

"What sort of scandal?" I urged.

Charles looked uncomfortable. "If it's all the same with you, Sarah, I'd prefer to leave it at that. The particulars aren't important. Certainly it can have nothing to do with Mrs. Hanaford."

"We can't know that until you tell me. Was it a disagreement with the school administration? Did he falsify a grade? Or perhaps he published a controversial paper?" I was struck by a sudden thought that would explain my brother's embarrassment. "Was he by any chance caught performing an abortion?"

There was no need for Charles to reply. The answer was written clearly on his face, which was flushed.

"It was the lady friend of one of his students," he admitted. "When the boy failed to abort the girl's pregnancy himself, he came to Lawton. The girl's parents found out and informed the university. Lawton was dismissed, but in an effort to avoid adverse publicity, no formal charges were filed against him."

"He's in general practice now?"

"Yes. Although I've heard rumors that he still performs the procedure. For a price."

"I see."

"That's why I find Wylde an unlikely patient. For obvious reasons, Lawton doesn't attract a prestigious clientele. I've also heard he's taken to drink, which makes him even less appealing to reputable clients."

"But what if Wylde did require Lawton's services?" I was ashamed for even thinking such a thing, but felt compelled to push on. "He has a daughter visiting him from France."

"Are you suggesting the girl came over here to terminate a pregnancy?" Charles asked, looking shocked.

"I don't want to think so, but it might explain why a prominent attorney is associating with a man like Lawton."

"That's a serious accusation, Sarah. If even a hint of what you suspect gets out, it could do irreparable damage to Miss Wylde's reputation. And to her father's, as well."

I didn't give a fig for Wylde's reputation, but I realized I did care a great deal what was said about his lovely daughter. On the other hand, time was running out and I simply could not afford to ignore any possibility, no matter how remote. I also knew I would have to share my discovery, at least with Samuel.

Once again my plans were thwarted. Samuel had already left the house when I came downstairs the following morning. As I ate a solitary breakfast, I decided it would be best to turn the divorce case I'd been working on over to Mr. Ackroyd, then spend the rest of the day following this latest lead. I was, in fact, about to board a horsecar when Samuel's brougham pulled up beside me. One look at his grim face told me this was not a chance meeting.

"I was hoping to catch you before you left for the office," he began as I settled into my seat, then said bluntly, "Senator Broughton's dead. They found his body in front of a confectioner's shop on Union Street. And yes, before you ask, he was stabbed in the genitals. I've just left George. He says Broughton was killed sometime during the night." He gave me a sheepish look. "It pains me to admit it, but it seems that—"

"I was right," I finished, without the least satisfaction. For the first time in this wretched affair, I wished with all my heart that my instincts had been wrong. "I don't understand, Samuel. I'm sure he feared for his life. I have reason to believe he even hired a body-guard. Why would he go out without him, especially at night?"

"You're right, Sarah, he did hire a man for protection, a fellow by the name of Mick Preed. According to Preed, a street urchin delivered a letter to the senator shortly before eleven last night. Broughton read the message, then sent Preed on an errand—a bogus one, he now believes. According to the butler, Broughton left soon after Preed, without saying where he was going."

"Or, presumably, why." The carriage hit a pothole in the street and Samuel and I were jostled against one another. So lost was I in this latest tragedy, I was only vaguely aware of the driver swearing loudly at someone, then taking a corner faster than was prudent. "I'd give a great deal to know what was in that letter. I don't suppose it was found on the body?"

He shook his head. "Either Broughton destroyed it before he left his house, or the killer took it from him."

"Either way, it must be incriminating. Yet assuming Wylde wrote this mysterious letter, surely the senator would never agree to meet him so late at night—and alone in the bargain."

"Not if he considered him a murderer." He paused. "But what if someone else wrote the letter? You said Li Ying was blackmailing the partners. Maybe he demanded Broughton meet him with a payment. You said he'd sent a similar message to Hanaford."

I nodded reluctantly, annoyed to realize how much I did not want the murderer to be Li. I, who took pride in my objectivity!

"I've come across several perfectly charming murderers," my brother said, reading my mind.

I grimaced, embarrassed my thoughts were so transparent. "Four murders, Samuel. When is it going to end?"

After promising to keep me apprised of any further developments he might learn from George, Samuel dropped me at the law firm. My own plans were unformed. I'd give Ackroyd the divorce paperwork, but my original plan to go to the Yoot Hong Low restaurant was now less certain. Despite my ability to judge character, I realized it would be foolish in the extreme to meet with Li Ying alone.

But what if I weren't alone?

After a short meeting with Eugene Ackroyd, I found Robert in his cubicle, head buried beneath the usual disorderly pile of books and papers. Ignoring his complaints at being disturbed, I tersely informed him of Broughton's death, as well as the call I'd paid on the senator earlier in the week.

Forestalling the predictable tide of criticism, I reached for his topcoat. "Here, put this on. For once, I'm requesting your company. Please hurry. We have little time to lose."

We rode in silence to Chinatown. Mercifully, Robert did not subject me to his usual tirade about impetuous females, nor did he question the need for immediate action. Broughton's death had obviously sobered him. The situation was desperate; we would have to accept assistance from wherever and whomever we could, even if the helping hand came from an infamous tong lord.

The Yoot Hong Low restaurant differed little from other shops crowding Waverly Place. It displayed one or two signs covered with Chinese characters, and several brightly colored lanterns. My request to speak to Kin Lee was silently received by a waiter wearing a loose, white cotton tunic and black pants. He gave a low bow, then retreated behind a screen at the back of the room.

Moments later an older man emerged from behind the screen, his quiet air of authority instantly proclaiming him to be the proprietor. He bowed, and in passably good English introduced himself as Kin Lee. He did not seem surprised when I requested an audience with Li Ying, leading me to suspect our visit was expected.

Nodding his head, he said, "Please, you come."

Without waiting for us to agree, he turned back toward the screen. When I started to follow, Robert took hold of my arm.

"I don't like this," he told me darkly.

"We have little choice," I said softly. "If Li has information about the case, we must meet with him on his own terms."

Robert grumbled, but without letting go of my arm moved behind the screen after Kin Lee into a private, and currently unoccupied, eating area. Nearby, I heard sounds of cooking utensils being slammed about and men laughing and conversing in Chinese. Kin pulled out a chair for me at one of the tables and motioned for us to be seated. Never taking his eyes off the man, my wary watchdog reluctantly took the chair opposite me.

"Mr. Li arrive soon," Kin told us. "You have tea."

The proprietor slipped away, returning a moment later with a pot of hot tea and two dainty cups.

"What is this?" Robert demanded, looking at the beverage as if he suspected it contained arsenic.

I lifted the cup to my lips, smelled its delicate, slightly flowery fragrance, then took a sip. It was delicious.

"It's some sort of Chinese tea. Try it. It's quite good."

Suspiciously, Robert took up his cup, which was nearly dwarfed in his large hand, and brought it to his mouth. Naturally, he was too stubborn to admit he liked it, but he drained the liquid in one gulp and was refilling both our cups from the daintily painted pot when I realized we were no longer alone. Like a wraith, Li Ying had noiselessly appeared at our table.

"Miss Woolson," he said with a polite bow. "It is a pleasure to meet you again."

"Mr. Li," I responded. I turned to introduce Robert, but Li was already bowing to my companion.

"Mr. Campbell," he said courteously. "We meet at last." With a brief nod, he accepted the seat and the cup of tea that Kin offered him with bowing deference.

Out of the corner of my eye, I could see Robert taking Li's measure as I thanked the tong lord for sending the note. "You suggested in your message that you might have information regarding the four recent murders."

"That is correct, Miss Woolson," Li Ying answered gravely. "I have, of course, heard of Senator Broughton's unfortunate demise. There is, however, an additional death that may have escaped your notice."

"What?" Robert said suspiciously. "Who else is dead?"

Li regarded him enigmatically, but his words were for me. "The man you saw in Mr. Wylde's company last night was Dr. Howard Lawton, a physician of somewhat dubious reputation. He was found dead this morning in his room on Bay Street."

I stared at Li, finding it difficult to digest this latest bombshell. "How did you know I had seen Dr. Lawton last—"

"How was he killed?" Robert broke in, regarding the Chinese distrustfully.

"He was stabbed, Mr. Campbell. No, not like the others. Dr. Lawton was knifed in the heart. His right hand, however, had been severed from his arm."

I grimaced involuntarily at this gruesome detail, but again Robert spoke first.

"What makes you think Lawton's death has anything to do with the other murders?"

"I do not, of course, know that with certainty," Li answered. "However, Dr. Lawton had long been associated with Cornelius Hanaford and his three associates." He held up a hand as Robert started to ask another question. "Perhaps it would clarify the situation if I related another discovery I have made in recent days. Or perhaps I should say *re*discovery."

"Yes?" I asked, leaning forward expectantly.

The tong lord looked from me to Robert. "As you know, after their time in Virginia City, the four partners returned to San Francisco wealthy men. This money gave them freedom to indulge in behaviors not uncommon to other young men in San Francisco at that time. With the passing years, however, their appetites became increasingly insatiable. One might even say, jaded."

"What are you implying, Li?" Robert demanded.

Li regarded him calmly. "Mr. Hanaford and his friends found an ingenious way to satisfy these cravings. They formed a club, for themselves and for other like-minded young men.

"What kind of club?" I asked. I sensed that Robert was about to object and kicked his shin beneath the table. He shot me an aggrieved look, but I ignored him, giving Li my complete attention. "I assume you refer to sexual predilections?"

Li did not flinch at my forthrightness. I believe I mentioned at the start of this narrative that I abhor dissimulation. At no time in my life had this virtue seemed more relevant than at that moment.

Li inclined his head slightly. "That is correct, Miss Woolson. I had heard of this club at the time of its inception, but considered it a folly of youth, one to be outgrown with the advent of marriage and a family. I was mistaken. As I say, I recently discovered that although carefully hidden, the club still exists. It has become a safe harbor where the rich and powerful may go to indulge their most aberrant sexual fantasies."

Robert could contain himself no longer. As Li spoke, I had noticed his face suffuse with color. It had now turned crimson.

"Curse it, Li!" he shouted, his voice so loud that sounds of activity abruptly ceased in the kitchen, and a startled Kin peeked apprehensively into the room. "This is hardly the time or the place to discuss such outrageous and despicable—"

"It's exactly the place," I broke in. "And it is certainly time we placed all our cards on the table. I may be a woman, but I'm not a fool. Nor am I blind or deaf. I'm aware that certain men are susceptible to perversities of a sexual nature. I agree with Mr. Li. This club obviously has a bearing on the case. It can't be ignored just because it offends your sensibilities."

"*My* sensibilities!" he yelped. "My concerns are for you, you infuriating woman."

"Don't expect me to applaud your gallantry when it is so patently misplaced." I turned back to Li, for really there was little time to lose. Already I had begun to detect a faint light at the end of the tunnel and I was anxious to pursue it. "Tell us more about this club, Mr. Li. I presume the members pay women of a certain proclivity to participate in these—er, practices."

Although Robert's face remained an unhealthy shade of red, he refrained from further objections. Li looked at him with an expression I can only describe as restrained amusement, then quietly resumed his narrative.

"Frequently that is the case. Occasionally, however, innocent young women are induced to take part, sometimes girls no older than fourteen or fifteen."

For all my brave words only moments before, I could not hold back a gasp of shock. "Good heavens! So young?"

Li nodded and said with the merest trace of censure, "Chinese girls are sold into white slavery as young as seven or eight."

I thought of the young women—little more than children—I had seen the night of Miss Culbertson's raid. "You're right," I said, regretting the naiveté of my remark. "I suppose it was to—er, administer to these young women that the four partners hired Dr. Lawton. I understand that's his specialty."

"You are, as usual, most astute, Miss Woolson," Li said. "Considering the other deaths, I find it too much to suppose that the doctor's demise is an isolated incidence. The dismembering of his right hand is also suggestive, don't you think? The hand used to abort the life of an unborn child?"

"My thoughts precisely," I said. I was about to elaborate on this point, when Robert broke in.

"I think you're both jumping to conclusions. It seems to me the gravest danger facing Wylde and those other vipers was keeping their depraved club a secret. If word got out, it would destroy their reputations—and they all had a great deal to lose. Yet if someone were threatening to expose them, surely *he* would have been the one killed, not the partners. Another possibility—assuming Mrs. Hanaford and Peter Fowler are innocent—is that the murderer is someone who was refused admission to this club and sought revenge."

I stared at Robert. What he'd just said, coupled with Li Ying's revelation, turned everything upside down. For the first time I was beginning to see the case from an entirely different perspective! True, there was a great deal I still didn't understand, but the light at the end of the tunnel seemed to glow a bit brighter.

"What's the matter with you, Sarah?" my colleague demanded. "You haven't heard a word I've said."

"Oh, but I have. Every word, I assure you." So deep was my gratitude, I had to resist the urge to throw up my arms and kiss him. Instead, I turned to Li. "Where is this club located?"

Li handed me a piece of paper upon which was written an address. "It is on the corner of Powell and Union Streets."

I stared at him. "Union Street?"

Li Ying gave a faint smile. "Interesting, is it not?"

Robert looked appalled. "Don't tell me you want to go there?"

I didn't bother to answer. Anxious to be on my way, I picked up my reticule and stood.

"Mr. Li, your information has been exceedingly helpful. What you've told us today may well save another life. I find myself increasingly in your debt."

Without waiting to see if Robert was following, I gave the tong lord a respectful bow and walked briskly from the room.

R obert entered the carriage in a foul mood, which did not improve when I refused to answer his questions about the new "bee in my bonnet," as he put it. After I had informed the driver where we wished to be taken, all I would say to satisfy Robert's curiosity was that we'd been looking at the case from the wrong perspective. After that I sank into my own thoughts, remaining largely oblivious to his caustic cataloguing of my numerous character flaws.

I looked out the window as we made our way through the mostly residential neighborhood where, we'd been told, four of San Francisco's most prominent men had established a private club for the sexual gratification of themselves and a select number of their peers. It was also—as I'm certain the readers of this narrative must realize—the street where Senator Broughton's body had been found. The fact that it was so near the club he had helped establish strained the boundaries of happenstance. It also opened a Pandora's box of questions.

The carriage stopped in front of the bakery where Broughton's body had been discovered. Leaving a still grumbling Robert to deal with the driver, I gave the exterior of the shop a thorough inspection. Robert soon joined me and we stepped inside to be greeted by delicious smells and a delightful array of freshly baked goods temptingly laid out upon a counter.

A portly man, wearing a white apron and a broad smile, stepped out to serve us. As I made a show of examining some cakes, I extended my sympathies to the man on his grisly discovery. To my disappointment, the clerk said it was the baker—who came in at three A.M.—who had stumbled on the body, looking for all the world like a heap of discarded clothing. Ascertaining that the bundle was, or had been, a human being, the man summoned the police. That appeared to be the end of the story. The baker had been questioned by the police, then finally permitted to get on with his by now belated chores.

"That was a waste of time," Robert said as we left the shop.

"On the contrary," I replied, noting the time on my lapel watch and setting off at a brisk pace. "We've accomplished two things. First, doesn't it strike you as significant that Senator Broughton's body was found in such close proximity to his club?"

"A coincidence," he grunted with a remarkable lack of acumen.

I sighed in exasperation. "If you and the authorities are to be believed, this case is riddled with coincidences. It defies reality to presume that three out of four mining partners should be murdered within a three-month period. And dispatched in the same, distinctly unusual manner. Or that the last victim was discovered only a few minutes from a secret club the four men had been operating for years. Don't you see, Robert? This explains how the murderer was able to lure Broughton out of his house, despite the senator's obvious fear for his life."

"And just how do you arrive at that——?"

"Oh, for heaven's sake, man, use your head! What was the one pretext Broughton could not ignore, no matter the risk?"

"I——" he stumbled, taken aback by my vehemence.

"Fear of exposure! You said yourself that each of the four partners had a great deal to lose if their sexual hideaway became known. The note Broughton received last night must have alluded to some problem at the club, or perhaps a threat of discovery. That was the one place he couldn't risk taking his bodyguard. It was the perfect ploy to entice him out of his house alone."

"You spoke of two things," he grumbled. I was sure my logic had led him to change the subject. "What's the second?"

"The lack of blood in the doorway, of course. The baker's boy was undoubtedly set to scrubbing the entryway after the police completed their investigation, but blood is difficult to wipe clean. Yet I was able to detect only one or two stains consistent with dried blood, hardly typical of the site of a stabbing, especially one that resulted in the victim bleeding to death."

"What are you saying? That Broughton was killed elsewhere and left to be found at that shop?"

"Exactly. If my theory is correct, the killer wouldn't have wanted the body found too close to the club. Which is why we're completing the remainder of our journey on foot." I stopped and looked at the street sign, then again at my watch. "Only see. We're there. A short five-minute walk."

"Not if you're carrying a dead body!"

"It's barely two blocks. And who's to say the murderer didn't have a carriage?"

But Robert wasn't listening. He was staring at the only building—save two small shops on opposite corners—to grace the intersection of Union and Powell. I stared as well. The structure was a church, a neat brick building with an old bell tower and a pious wooden cross. Without a word, I crossed the street and tried the church's heavy oaken doors. They were locked.

"Admit it, Sarah," Robert said from behind me. "We've been sent on a wild goose chase."

I can't deny that for a moment I shared his doubt. Had Li received faulty information? Or was he, for some reason of his own, trying to lead us astray? Then I had a thought.

"Wait, Robert! What better place to hide such a sordid establishment than a church? It would be the last place anyone would think to look."

"Don't be ridiculous. No pastor would allow that kind of club on church property."

"He might," I said slowly. "If the minister himself were a member."

Robert stared at me. "Good god, woman! Think what you're saying!"

"I'm saying that a clerical collar doesn't automatically bestow virtue upon its wearer. I'm not ready to reject Li's informants until we've conducted a thorough search of the premises."

"But the doors are locked."

"In the front, yes. We haven't tried the back. You stay here in case someone comes out while I go around the side."

"You'll do no such thing. You wait here. I'll see if there's a back door."

I wasn't pleased with this arrangement, but didn't care to attract attention by engaging in a public argument. "Very well," I agreed. "But make a good job of it. The entrance may be hidden."

Throwing a pained look over his shoulder, Robert trudged around the church. Feeling conspicuous standing in front of the building, I crossed the street and took up a position beside the shop on the opposite corner. Two women passed, small children in tow, then a man hurried by. No one paid any attention to the church.

So intent was I on my watch, that I gasped when I was suddenly grabbed around the waist and pulled into the narrow alley between the shop and the adjoining building.

"Damn it, woman! How in hell did you find this place?"

I twisted my head to find Benjamin Wylde's face looming over mine, his expression of loathing so intense it made me shudder.

"Let go of me!" I cried with a bravado I didn't feel.

His hand closed over my mouth. "I gave you fair warning, but you wouldn't listen. Now you've left me no choice but to take care of you once and for all."

The tone of his voice chilled me. I had no doubt he meant to kill me. Unless I came up with a plan—and quickly—he might succeed!

Then, without warning, I had my chance. A howling cat came flying through the alley, a dog hard on its heels, distracting Wylde just long enough for me to bite down hard on the fingers pressed against my lips. As he cursed in pain, I pushed against him and broke lose of his grasp. I wasted no time crying out, but ran as fast as I could back down the alley toward the street. I heard him take off after me, then felt his hand brush my shoulder.

This time I did cry out, praying Robert would hear me. Then I was free of the buildings. On the other side of the street a man and woman were passing the church and I ran toward them. I had gone only a few steps when I collided with a muscular man who seemed to materialize out of nowhere. Without a word, he pulled me tightly into his chest, muffling any cry I might have managed.

"Watch her teeth," Wylde told the man, wrapping a handkerchief around his bleeding fingers. "She bites like a wildcat."

Admonishing the man not to attract attention, they held me

wedged between them and walked across the street to the church. The stranger kept my head pressed against his shoulder preventing me from calling for help. Robert! I thought wildly. Where was Robert?

"What are you doing here anyway?" Wylde asked the man as we reached the church. "I told you never to come here during the day."

"Somethin's happened," the stranger said in a rough voice.

"Well, what is it, man?" Wylde demanded, pulling a key from his pocket and inserting it into the lock.

"Yer daughter's been took," the man blurted, obviously fearing Wylde's reaction. "Yer butler, Mr. Bateman, sent me t' fetch yer."

Wylde froze, then spun on the man. His voice was tight with alarm. "Yvette? What do you mean she's been taken?"

"That's all I know," the man said defensively. "Mr. Bateman says she went out this mornin' and a while later he got a note sayin' she'd been taken. "He says for you t' hurry home."

"My god, Will! Why didn't you tell me?" Wylde pushed open the church doors, seeming not to care now who saw us. "Tie this woman up in the storage room. I'll attend to her later."

Grunting his assent, the man called Will dragged me inside the darkened church. I heard Wylde's rapidly receding footsteps before the door slammed shut behind us. The only sound now was the echo of Will's shoes as he hoisted me over his shoulder and carried me, kicking and demanding to be released, down a flight of stairs.

At the bottom of the stairs he entered a room whose only illumination came from a slit of a window, high on one wall. Despite the gloom he made his way through several equally murky rooms without so much as a hesitation. For my part, I was too busy pummeling his back with my fists and trying to impale him with my boots to notice where we were going. I might have been a pesky fly for all the notice he gave me. Only once, when he shifted my weight and the tip of one boot happened to hit him in the groin, did he cry out, and I was rewarded with a hard smack on my backside.

"No more of that!" he snapped. "Or it'll go even harder on ya."

We passed through a room with a belching black furnace, then the man kicked open the door to what must have been the store-room and dumped me unceremoniously onto the floor. I cried out as my tailbone hit the hard ground, but had no time to rub the afflicted area as my hands were painfully jerked behind my back and bound with a length of rope.

"This'll keep yer yap shut," he grunted, pulling a smelly cloth across my mouth. Without another word, he turned and left the room, slamming the door shut behind him and leaving me in total and terrifying darkness.

CHAPTER THIRTEEN

I don't know how long I sat in the awful silence hoping, fool-
ishly I know, that my captor might somehow change his
mind and come back to free me. Then, when I could no
longer hear his retreating footsteps, I knew my fate lay in my own
hands. Where was Robert? I kept asking myself, aware of the awful
irony. He who for weeks had made a nuisance of himself following
me everywhere was, when I needed him most, nowhere to be
found!

I strained to see in the windowless room, but it was useless.
Now that it was too late, I bitterly regretted not paying more attention to the storeroom when I'd had a chance. About all I could
be grateful for was that my legs hadn't been bound along with my
arms. As it was I retained some movement, however slight. Gingerly, I began scooting my body across the floor—feeling before me
with my feet and behind me with my bound hands—for anything
that might loosen the ropes, or tug off the filthy gag that prevented
me from crying out. My progress was exasperatingly slow; I banged

into walls and knocked over several cans from shelves above my head. The contents of one of the cans spread along the floor and I knew by the smell and the sticky feel that it must be paint.

I have no idea how long I went on in this undignified manner, when suddenly my feet brushed against a broom hanging on the wall. Energized by this discovery, I managed to struggle to my feet, but the nail from which the broom hung was too high up to be of any use in ripping off either my gag or my bonds. Cursing mentally, I continued to feel along the wall, but succeeded only in knocking down more cans of paint, and heaven knows what else, onto the floor.

Frustrated, I stopped to collect my breath, and my wits. It was then that I heard it—the voice I had never expected to welcome with such fervor. I tried to call out—for of course the booming sound had come from Robert—but all I could manage was a muted grunt. Fearing he would never find my isolated prison, I fell back onto the floor and, heedless of the sticky paint and broken glass from toppled jars piercing my skin, began banging on the walls with my boots. I was rewarded by the sound of approaching footsteps and the familiar bellow of Robert's curses as he made his stumbling way through the darkened rooms, stopping at last at my door.

It jerked open with a bang. There before me, filling the door with his towering frame, stood the inimitable Scot, a lighted candelabra he must have pilfered from the altar in one hand, a wriggling boy of about twelve in the other.

"So, this is where you've got to," he said, squinting through the dim light. He stepped into the room, banged the candleholder down on a shelf, then, retaining his hold on the boy, used his free hand to yank off my gag. "I should have known you couldn't be left alone for five minutes without getting into trouble. How did you manage to get yourself trussed up like a Christmas goose and locked in here, anyway? And why are you bleeding?" he added before I could catch my breath to answer.

"I was trying to free myself, of course," I retorted, beginning to wonder why I'd been so pleased to see him. I nodded my head at the squirming boy. "Who's that?"

Robert looked down at the lad as if he'd forgotten he was there.

"Oh, him. He was coming out the back door. When I tried to ask him a few civil questions, he took off like a frightened hare. By the time I caught him, I discovered you'd disappeared and guessed you'd been foolish enough to enter the church on your own. I was in the process of looking for you when I heard a godawful clamor down here." He regarded the terrified boy. "This young scoundrel obviously knows something, but for the life of me I can't get him to open his mouth."

Robert fumbled in his pocket for a knife, then struggled to open it with one hand while keeping hold on the boy with the other. As he bent to cut the rope binding my hands, the villainous child kicked him in the face with his boot, causing Robert to howl and drop the knife and his captive at the same time. The boy bolted away so quickly I doubted anyone could have stopped him, much less a man holding a severely bleeding nose.

"Damn it!" Robert swore. "The little hellion broke my nose."

"I doubt that. But if you'll free my hands, I'll have a look at it."

Awkwardly, he worked to cut my ropes while trying to staunch the blood flowing from his injured appendage. When I was free, I got to my feet and rubbed my fingers to regain circulation, then examined Robert's nose by the light of the altar candelabra.

"I can't feel any broken bones," I told him, ignoring his howls of protest when I touched his rapidly swelling beak. I handed him a handkerchief. "I'll have my brother Charles look at it later. Now we must hurry. Benjamin Wylde may be back any minute."

Robert's face darkened. "Wylde did this to you?" His voice trembled with rage. "Why that cowardly bastard! When I get my hands on him, I'll—"

"I have no doubt you will," I said, cutting him short. "Come on, I want to search this place while we have the chance. I was too preoccupied on my way in to notice anything but the muscles of my abductor's back. Not Wylde's," I hastened to explain, as he sucked in breath to launch another outburst. "The man who came to tell Wylde that his daughter's been kidnapped."

"What? Stop!" Robert placed firm hands on my shoulders before I could get halfway to the door. "We're not stepping another foot until you tell me exactly what happened to you, as well as this business with Wylde's daughter."

In as few words as possible, I described the events of the past half-hour. "So you see why haste is of the essence. I don't know why the girl was taken, but I'm sure it has something to do with the murders, and probably with this place as well. Now come on. We've wasted too much time already."

With the help of the candles, I was able to make out much more of the church basement than on my way in. After we had passed through the furnace room, we came to a larger chamber whose reason for existence soon became shockingly clear. The room was windowless, and on three of the four walls were hung what could only be a variety of sexual paraphernalia that, until now, I had not known existed. Some of the more obvious implements struck me as being decidedly unpleasant, others merely silly. The purpose of one or two pieces eluded my imagination altogether.

On the fourth wall hung a mirror and dozens of assorted cos-
tumes, some extremely skimpy, some with cutouts in what seemed
very inappropriate places. I caught sight of Robert's face in the
mirror and, despite the circumstances, very nearly laughed out
loud. The eyes above the handkerchief he held pressed to his nose
were wide with mortification.

"You're the one who was in such a hurry," he said, nudging me
toward the door. "Let's finish this confounded inspection and get
out of here."

We passed through several smaller, also windowless rooms, each
containing a bed, one or two chairs, and a table laden with water
pitchers and bowls. The purpose of these rooms was also readily
apparent and required no verbal speculation on our parts.

Finally, we came to a room considerably larger than the others,
and my first impression was that it was a meeting hall of some sort.
High windows along two of the walls allowed in sufficient afternoon light so that we could clearly view the framed oil paintings
hung to either side of the chamber. Each picture featured one or
more voluptuous, mostly nude women, some of them arranged in
poses so lewd I couldn't help but gasp.

"We've seen enough," Robert said, placing his hand on my
arm. "If this really is Wylde's club, he's a very sick man."

"Wait." I said, resisting his efforts to lead me away. At the front
of the room was an oversized picture—more like an emblem—of
a masked Satan. Below the leering devil's head were four pick axes
stacked together, blades facing down.

"That's the illustration on the partners' cards," I murmured, unable to take my eyes off the image, made many times more horrible by its overblown size. Then, as I continued to stare, I suddenly
remembered a forgotten conversation. For a moment I thought I

must have misremembered, but on further reflection I knew I had not. My memory is excellent. It was, moreover, a discussion I was unlikely to forget.

"He would have known, of course," I said, more to myself than to my companion.

"Whatever you're going on about we can discuss outside," Robert said, urging me more vigorously toward the door.

I hardly heard him. My mind whirled with questions, with inconsistencies that eluded comprehension. What did it mean? Why lie about such a thing? Unless—

"Oh, my god!" I gasped as the answer came to me at last. The final, elusive pieces of the puzzle slid smoothly into place, forming a picture so monstrous that to this day I still shudder to think back upon it. It was all there, clear for anyone possessing the eye and the resolve to see it. Even Dr. Lawton's terrible role in the drama fit neatly into the deadly tapestry.

"What is it, Sarah?" Robert demanded. Then he saw my face and his impatience turned to alarm. "Good lord, you'd better sit down. You're white as a sheet."

I ignored the chair he pushed beneath me, although in view of my spinning head it wouldn't have gone amiss to his advice.

"I think I know who the murderer is," I said, my thoughts falling like hailstones, one on top of the other. "And I think I know where Wylde's daughter has been taken!"

Never did a ride seem to take so long. As our carriage made its way at a snail's pace through late afternoon traffic, I described to Robert the sequence of events I felt certain had led to Cornelius Hanaford's death, and inexorably to those of his partners. Robert stared at me as if I'd gone mad, but didn't interrupt.

We would know soon enough if I were wrong. In the meantime, one, perhaps two, lives hung in the balance. Neither of us wanted them on our conscience. It was this fear, I knew, that kept Robert from daring to dispute my logic.

When we finally arrived at our destination, there was no sign of our quarry. Yet so certain was I of finding them, that I stopped several boys who were playing baseball in the street and offered them each a coin if they could locate a policeman.

"More than one, if you can," I called out, as the boys took off at a run.

"What makes you think they're here?" Robert asked, as we followed the nearest path into the park—the place where I was gambling we would find both the murderer, as well as his next, and probably final, victim.

"This place has special meaning for him," I answered, my eyes taking in every tree, every bush and rock, alert for the smallest movement, the slightest sound. "Don't you see, Robert? This last murder will be his coup de grâce. Wylde is the only partner to have a daughter. The murderer will see it as poetic justice—the payment of one promising young life for another."

"If you're right, he must be a madman."

"What was done to him might well drive any man mad," I answered softly. "I deplore the act, but I can't bring myself to condemn the man." I stopped, straining to see between the elephantine branches of a giant sequoia tree. "Look! There's someone by the pond—in front of the grotto."

We made our way slowly forward, until a break in the bushes confirmed my worst fears. Through the foliage we could see Eban Potter standing in front of the rocks on the opposite side of the pond. One of the banker's arms encircled Yvette Wylde's narrow waist, the other held a knife to her smooth, white throat. Benjamin

Wylde, frozen with fear and helplessness, watched this tableau from the other side of the water.

My breath caught in my throat. My suspicions had been correct! I hadn't wanted it to be true, but of course the killer could be no one else. Why, I tortured myself, hadn't I seen it sooner? Lord knows there had been signs, contradictions I should have grasped. As it was, my first inkling hadn't come until Robert suggested revenge as a possible motive for the killings. Not because someone had been refused admittance to the partner's sex club, but rather the fury of a father whose daughter had been violated.

Still, the final piece of the fatal puzzle had not slipped into place until I finally comprehended the true significance of the devil's head. Potter had assured me it represented nothing more than youthful bravado. By his own admission he'd been on intimate terms with the four mining partners after their return from Virginia City; he swore he would have known if they'd had a more sinister connotation. Now, too late, I understood the peculiar look that had crossed his face when I had questioned him about the cards, as well as the mysterious evil he'd warned me of the morning of Martha Broughton's funeral. He'd understood all too well the awful meaning of the pick axes and the devil's head. The four villains who had hidden behind that terrible mask had destroyed his only child, had ripped from his arms the person—perhaps the only surviving person—who mattered to him in this world.

These thoughts flew through my mind in a heartbeat as I stood immobilized, taking in the horrifying scene before us. Then Wylde's anguished voice shook me free of my stupor.

"For god's sake, Potter, let her go. She's an innocent child."

Potter started to answer, then caught sight of Robert and me as we stepped out from behind the bushes.

"Miss Woolson," he cried out, looking confused. "What are you doing here? This business does not concern you."

Wylde whirled around at Potter's word, and it was a shock to see his controlled, arrogant face utterly devoid of color. His skin had a sickly sheen to it, and the eyes that had looked upon me with so much malevolence little more than an hour ago, were wild with desperation. For the moment at least, I thought, recognizing the irony, mutual concern for Yvette's safety had made us allies.

"But it does concern us, Mr. Potter," I said, struggling to keep my voice calm. "Yvette doesn't deserve to suffer for her father's sins."

Potter's eyes darted from Wylde to me, and the hand wielding the knife trembled so violently I feared it would inadvertently pierce the girl's skin.

"What of my Louisa?" he cried. "She was barely eighteen! What did she know of life? Or the evils of such men? Yet Hanaford and the others raped and defiled her, robbed her of her innocence. Then, when they discovered she was with child, they took her to Dr. Lawton. Those four devils are as responsible for her death as that drunken butcher."

Potter's face suffused with rage. He glared at Wylde as if the man were a messenger from hell. "You're no better than an animal," he spat. "All you and the others cared about was your own vile gratification and greed. When my wife became ill, I begged Cornelius to advance me the money necessary to provide her with proper medical care. I was one of his oldest friends—I had gladly lent him my life's savings when he went to the mines—yet he refused my pleas. Can you begin to imagine what it feels like to watch your wife die slowly and painfully before your eyes and be powerless to save her? He let her die rather than part with one dime of his miserable fortune."

Once again the knife jerked in Potter's hand and I started forward, only to be stopped by Robert's hand on my arm.

"Don't push him," he whispered urgently. "He's unstable. There's no telling what he might do."

Robert was right, we couldn't risk any rash movement. Our best hope was to keep Potter's attention on something else until help arrived.

"What of Mrs. Broughton," I said hastily. "Surely you didn't hold her responsible for harming your wife and child."

A look of pain crossed Potter's face, and his eyes filled with regret.

"That was a mistake. I meant to revenge myself on Broughton privately, but that became impossible after the coward hired a bodyguard. When my first attempt failed, I was forced to seek him out in public. Even then I would have succeeded if he hadn't pulled his wife in front of my carriage. Her soul is on my conscience and I'll carry it to my grave. But it is on theirs as well. The evil spread by those four vipers infected innocent lives like a plague. Hanaford was a cruel, malicious husband. He mistreated his poor wife with impunity. Who would dare call such a respectable man to task for his brutish behavior? Mills was a weak, sniveling coward. After Louisa's death, he appeased his conscience with an opium pipe and sought refuge with the dregs of society. As for Broughton, he was the worst kind of hypocrite. He preached abstinence and family values, while he helped run the most vile, contemptible club in San Francisco."

He turned his gaze full onto Wylde, tightening his grip on the terrified girl and pressing the gleaming knife against her fragile white throat.

"But you were worst of the lot," he spat at the lawyer, his voice a bitter indictment. "You were the leader, the evil mind from which sprung the venom the others embraced. It was your idea to go to Virginia City. Your scheme to defraud Li of his mine. Yes, yes, I've long known the source of your ill-gotten gains," he went on, at Wylde's startled look. "You preyed on your partners' greed and weakness, then rewarded their loyalty by providing young, innocent girls for their amusement—an unholy pimp, indifferent to the suffering you wrought.

"That's why I've left you until last, Wylde. I meant to dispose of you as I had the others, but that no longer seemed adequate payment for such iniquity. Night after night I thought of what you had done to Louisa, fantasizing how you would feel if you lost your only child, the daughter you held so close to your heart. Then, when Yvette arrived from France, I finally had the means to make you suffer as I have."

He allowed the knife to scrape Yvette's neck, drawing a thin line of blood. I stifled a cry and Robert instinctively moved beside me. Wylde cursed and started forward, then stopped as Potter readied the knife for another strike. None of us dared breathe; all eyes were on the incongruous little man who held a beautiful young girl's fate in his hands. His focus was completely on Wylde now. It was as if Robert and I were no longer there. He seemed to draw strength from his adversary's terror, and I watched Potter's agitation grow as he steeled himself to strike. Time was running out! Somehow I had to find a way to divert his attention until help finally arrived.

"How could you allow Mrs. Hanaford to be arrested for your crimes?" I cried without thinking. "You, who claim to be her friend."

Robert shot me an alarmed look and I belatedly realized this was too abrupt. Such an accusation was more likely to add to his agitation than to pacify it. But it had been the first thought to cross my mind. And I realized I wanted an answer. Potter had appeared genuinely grieved by Annjenett's arrest. Had his concern been a facade—a ploy to deflect guilt from himself? Did he honestly not care that he was the reason she had been incarcerated?

"I never meant for Mrs. Hanaford—or that actor—to be blamed for Cornelius's death," he cried, looking wildly from Robert to me. Against my better judgment—and after all he had done—I found myself believing the man. Either he was a talented liar, or his anguish at Annjenett's ordeal really had been sincere. "I'd no idea of their relationship, or that Fowler was even in the house that night. The possibility that the authorities might believe a woman capable of such an act never entered my mind. I was certain the police would realize their folly and release her, especially after Mills was killed. How was I to know that Peter Fowler was Rufus's son? Or that he and his mother had their own reasons for wanting to see the brute dead?"

His voice grew shrill as he pleaded for me to understand. Anguish was etched on his thin face, now completely drained of blood and expression. For a dizzying moment I had the surreal feeling that I was looking at a death mask. Then, the white lips moved and the awful image was replaced by the tragic visage of a desperate man who had become consumed by the need for revenge.

"The only thing I could see to do was finish the business as quickly as possible, then inform the police of their mistake." The man was breathing hard now from emotional strain. "I have dispatched a letter to the authorities explaining why I found it necessary to take justice into my own hands. It clearly lays blame where it belongs. I've made certain that Benjamin Wylde will be ruined; everyone will know of his vile past and the dishonorable way he and the others acquired their fortunes. I've described their repulsive club, and listed as many members as I could obtain. I've also supplied the name of the infamous doctor they employed to take care of their 'accidents.' Rest assured, Miss Woolson, I have made certain that Mrs. Hanaford and her actor friend will go free. My only regret is that I became, however unintentionally, an instrument to cause her pain."

Yvette was staring at her captor, eyes wide in disbelief. So intent was she on the banker's terrible accusations against her father, she seemed to have temporarily forgotten her own dilemma and the knife against her throat. Wylde's pale face had suffused with blood as he stared at his beloved daughter. The shock and revulsion he read on her face must have come as a terrible blow. He glared at Potter with such naked fury that, for a moment, I feared he might attack the banker regardless of the consequences to Yvette.

Then, suddenly, the anger faded and I watched all the fight drain out of him like a deflated balloon. For the first time he seemed to appreciate the complete helplessness of his situation. Potter was right, I thought, the attorney would be ruined. Far more devastating, he had lost his daughter's respect—perhaps even her love. As I watched these thoughts cross his face, the man seemed to age before my eyes.

"Potter, I beg you," he pleaded, the resignation in his voice rendering it nearly unrecognizable. "Put down the knife. I have money. You can go away—live comfortably in any country you choose. Think of it, man! You need never work again."

Potter gazed incredulously at the lawyer, his face a twisted mask of loathing and disgust.

"You think that's what I want—money? You fool! At one time money might have saved my wife's life, but it can't bring her back to me now. Nor can it return the daughter you and your depraved partners snatched from my arms. No, it's not money I'm after. I want you to know what it feels like to lose the only person you love in this life. I want you to experience the anguish, the terrible, final devastation of realizing she'll never grow to be a woman, that she'll never marry and have children, or comfort you in your old age. That's what you stole from me, Wylde. Now I mean to take it from you!"

Wylde was desperate. He looked frantically about for help, but for once in his life there was no one to do his bidding, no protection he could purchase, no courtroom in which to plead his case. Eban Potter had become his judge, jury and executioner.

"Do what you want with me," he pleaded. "Just please, I beg you, don't harm my daughter!"

Potter's smile chilled my heart. This sudden calm was far more alarming than his previous agitation. Robert was right—the man was mentally unbalanced. It was easy to see how it had happened. For a sensitive, lonely man like Potter, losing his wife and child must have been unbearable. Blame rested squarely on Benjamin Wylde's shoulders. But no amount of culpability justified the punishment Potter was about to inflict, especially when it was directed toward an innocent child!

"It's gratifying to hear you beg," the banker was saying to Wylde. "But it changes nothing. Don't you see, justice demands that you pay for your sins?" He raised the knife, holding it poised, point down, over the girl's heart.

"No, wait!" I cried, pushing Robert's restraining hand off my arm.

"Sarah!" he said, starting after me. "Don't be a fool."

"Robert, no!" I called, not taking my eyes off Potter. "Stay back."

Time seemed to hang suspended. There was no sound in the grotto; even the birds seemed to have been struck mute. Yvette's lovely blue eyes stared, as if mesmerized, at the knife that inched toward her breast. Tears coursed down her white face, but she did not move so much as a muscle.

"You don't want to do this, Eban," I said softly, carefully making my way closer to the tableau frozen before me. "You're a good person. And this would be a terrible thing to do."

"Stop where you are!" Potter pulled the girl back toward the rocks that rose up behind them. "Don't come any closer."

"If you harm Yvette, Eban," I went on in a voice that seemed to belong to another person, "you'll be no better than they are, these selfish men who have inflicted so much pain and suffering on others. Save one, the lives you've taken thus far haven't been without blame. But this child is. She's like your own Louisa—"

"No!" he cried. "She is nothing like Louisa—"

"Yes," I insisted, rounding the pond. "She, too, is an innocent. Don't spare her for Wylde's sake. He doesn't deserve mercy. Do it for *her* sake. Don't cut short the promise of a life scarcely begun."

"Stand back!" he screamed, pressing back against the rocks until he could go no further.

"I can't let you do this," I told him. "It would be an act every bit as reprehensible as the crimes those monsters committed." I'd drawn abreast of the two figures. Taking a deep breath, I reached my hand out for the knife.

I heard the two men behind me gasp, but neither spoke for fear of breaking the fragile spell that had fallen upon the grotto. For one of the longest moments of my life I stared into Eban Potter's eyes, fighting to keep my gaze off that terrible blade, praying I could somehow reach the gentle, unassuming soul I knew dwelt inside the shell of this broken human being.

Then, moving so suddenly I was taken completely unawares,

Potter thrust the girl at me. I staggered back beneath the unexpected weight, then watched in shock as, in one quick motion, he plunged the knife into his own heart. The girl had fainted and was a dead weight in my arms. Laying her aside, I rushed to the dying banker.

"Hold on, Eban," I whispered against his ear. "Help is on its way."

"There's nothing they can do for me," he gasped. His thin voice had grown husky and he formed the words with difficulty. "I go to face my own judge now. I only pray He will let me see my wife—and my Louisa—before—"

"I'm sure He will," I said, tears filling my eyes. But he was no longer listening. As quietly as he had lived his life, Eban Potter had slipped from this world into the next. Gently, I closed his eyes and lowered his head to the ground. Only then did I realize the police had arrived, and with them, George Lewis and my brother Samuel.

"They know what happened," Robert said, stooping down to where I still knelt by the dead man's side. "Potter's letter reached them by afternoon post. He must have intended from the start to do away with himself once he'd wrought his revenge."

With surprising tenderness, he helped me to my feet. "It's over, Sarah. You did everything you could. It's better that it end this way."

I looked at the man who lay crumpled at my feet. In death he appeared smaller and even more insignificant than he had in life, a victim rather than the villain who had taken the lives of five human beings. The tears that had formed in my eyes now coursed unimpeded down my face.

"They took everything from him," I said, the words catching in my throat. "Their poison infected him, too, and he answered evil with evil. It was all he knew how to do."

"I know," Robert said softly.

One powerful arm circled my waist. "Come, Sarah, it's time to go home."

EPILOGUE

My parents celebrated Frederick's senatorial victory by hosting a dinner party the weekend following the election. Frankly, I did not view my brother's success as cause for rejoicing. I was convinced that the men of California had suffered a severe lapse in judgment. I would like to think that had women been able to cast their own ballots, the populace might have been spared Frederick's potentially disastrous presence in its capital. As it was, I could only hope he would not have the opportunity to reek too much havoc on our fair state before the voters came to their senses in time for the next election.

Much to my surprise, Joseph Shepard accepted Frederick's invitation to attend the affair. I was surprised because since Eban Potter's suicide I had become persona non grata in the senior partner's eyes. Despite my successful efforts to have the charges against our client dropped, the sensational circumstances surrounding the case resulted in a barrage of unwelcome publicity for the law firm. Following the tragic events in the park, Shepard, Shepard, McNaughton and Hall had found its way into every newspaper in the city every day for two weeks, an invasion of privacy for which I was held personally responsible. I daresay if my employer could have found a way to effect my dismissal without generating even more unwanted publicity—and the loss of Annjenett's substantial fortune—I'm sure he would have gleefully shown me out the door. As it was, he had no choice but to publicly applaud my achievement while privately lamenting my continued presence at his firm.

Catching Shepard's eye as he spoke to a group of attorneys, I smiled sweetly and was rewarded by a look that could have curdled milk. My father noted this exchange and shook his head at me in mock reproach. Truth to tell, Papa was enjoying the situation immensely. As he put it, the worm had already begun to turn. Although I had yet to win Joseph Shepard's respect, I had attracted the attention of one or two associate attorneys who, much to the senior partner's chagrin, had started sending minor cases my way. Considering the circumstances, Papa considered this high triumph indeed.

Perhaps the happiest ending to the Nob Hill murders was the news that Annjenett and Peter Fowler were to be married in the spring. To my astonishment, the dear woman requested that I act as her Maid of Honor. I tried to decline, protesting that she must know someone more suitable, but she would hear none of it. So, it appears I shall be present when my client's awful ordeal comes full circle. Although I'm not an ardent supporter of the married state, I must admit I have rarely seen a happier couple. Annjenett is absolutely radiant, and San Francisco Society—after learning of Mills's shabby treatment of Peter and his mother those long years ago—has taken the actor under its generous wing. When last I heard, he had accepted the lead role in a new play opening at the California Theater.

That evening brought even more good news. Samuel—whose Ian Fearless had been the first to break the story of the sex club and Eban Potter's dreadful revenge—informed me that Benjamin Wylde had been spotted slinking out of town. This hardly came as a surprise. Once word of his vile club became public, his clientele all but vanished overnight. Rumors of the questionable way he had come by his mining fortune also circulated, but I'm sorry to say that when it became known that it was a Chinaman's word against his, the stories quickly faded. So much for our modern day era of justice for all! As the last surviving member of the tontine he and his three mining partners established upon their return from Virginia city, Benjamin Wylde became the beneficiary of just over two hundred thousand dollars. Despite making a great show of donating this money to charity, however, his spiraling fall from grace was swift and unforgiving. For years a sought-after guest in the finest Nob Hill mansions, he was now shunned by San Francisco Society. What must have been even more painful, his beloved daughter Yvette sailed back to Paris soon after Potter's suicide. I've since heard that she has severed all contact with her father. Wylde's present whereabouts are unknown, and I think few care. For myself, I am relieved I will no longer have to gaze upon that arrogant face and those hard, cold eyes. Eban Potter may have wielded the murder knife, but the victims' blood stained Wylde's hand as well. On his conscience, too, are the lives of all those unfortunate young women who fell into the clutches of the malevolent Devil's Club. No, I could find no pity in my heart for Benjamin Wylde. In my opinion he had received far better than he deserved.

I felt a hand on my arm and turned to find Robert standing behind me, dressed in the same ill-fitting tuxedo he had worn the night of the opera. The fabric was shiny and stretched so tightly across his broad chest that I feared the buttons might pop at any moment. At the first opportunity I would have to prod him into buying some new clothes.

"What's going on in that overactive brain of yours?" he asked. "I could see the wheels turning from across the room."

"Actually, I was thinking that you should consider a new wardrobe. You need suitable evening attire, of course, and an appropriate suit or two to wear in court. We'll want to form a favorable impression on the jury."

"*We!*" He gave a loud guffaw. "So now you fancy yourself arguing cases in a court of law. Trust me, Sarah, it'll be a cold day in hell before Joseph Shepard allows a woman attorney in the courtroom. Especially if that woman is you."

"We'll see about that," I answered primly. I was disappointed by his reaction, but not wholly surprised. I've noticed that most men have a difficult time dealing with change, especially when that change involves allowing women into positions of power. I daresay Robert was no exception. In time—and with dedicated and persistent effort on our parts—that attitude is bound to change. In the meantime, women will have to make do with conquering one small mountain at a time.

"I don't like that look in your eye," he went on. "It invariably spells trouble. Have you learned nothing over these past months? You can't mean to become involved in that sort of thing again. Damn it all, woman, it's too dangerous!"

His Scottish r's were rolling nicely as he warmed to the subject of what he termed my "incessant meddling in other people's affairs." I waited patiently until he had wound down, then remarked calmly, "You really must learn to control your temper, Robert. It can't be good for your health and will certainly prove a liability in your work. You'll have to remain composed and focused if we're to be successful in the courtroom."

"There you go again!" he exploded. "Of all the thickheaded, opinionated females—"

I refused to allow this outburst to spoil my good temper.

"Let's find some lemonade," I said, taking his arm. "It's just the thing to cool you off. After that, I'd like to discuss an interesting case that has come to my attention—"

HISTORICAL NOTE

It has come to my attention that some readers of this narrative have expressed doubts concerning my legal credentials. Considering the widespread bias against professional women during the years I have recounted, this skepticism is not wholly unjustified. I hasten to assure you, however, that not only was I a bonafide attorney in the year 1880, I was not the first female to attain this distinction. I was, in fact, the third.

The first woman to browbeat her way "through the marshes of ignorance and prejudice" was Clara Shortridge Foltz, who was admitted to the California bar in September of 1878. She achieved this triumph by drafting what became known as "The Woman Lawyer's Bill," then lobbying the state legislature until it was ratified and women were at long last allowed to become working attorneys.

Following closely upon Mrs. Foltz's victory was Laura De Force Gordon who, shortly after opening her law practice in 1879, became the first woman to argue a murder case in a San Francisco courtroom—and argue it successfully, I might add.

These two women were my inspiration. It was they who blazed the ar-

duous, frustrating trail I was to follow. Because of them, I was able to realize my dream. Whatever success I have achieved over the course of my legal career, I owe to the pioneering efforts of these dedicated and courageous women.

Yours sincerely,
Sarah Woolson